Murder at the
Palace

Murder at the Palace

A Mrs. Kelly Mystery

Jolie Tunnell

TULE
PUBLISHING

Chapter One

ELEGANT BONE CHINA held heat for a surprisingly long time. I counted on it.

Navigating stairwells, dodging oncoming staff, crossing a dimly lit basement, ducking between incoming horses and carriages, unlocking the back door and making it all the way into the shop without spilling a single drop of hot coffee deserved a medal of some sort, but setting the cup and saucer onto the counter with a soft clink of victory garnered a full round of applause.

"Nicely done, Mrs. Kelly," the young woman said, reaching for the gilt-edged white cup. "You are my hero."

"I don't imagine your Mr. Darcy has ever accomplished it," I said with a curtsy.

Not from a bustling hotel kitchen, down through a labyrinth basement, and into a glove shop, he hadn't.

Miss Rebecca Smith plopped an elbow onto her closed book and took a long sip. "No," she agreed. "But he would have thought of it, eventually. He would have brought tea." The rich brown velvet jacket she wore made the freckles on her nose visible and gave a hint of color to her otherwise washed-out Irish face.

Other than the single nod to fashion, her plain beige skirt and her plain beige chignon were the picture of appropriate for a shopgirl's ensemble. My apron, over a crisp white shirtwaist, wilted from hours in the kitchen, and black skirt felt even plainer.

I prepared myself for a full defense of her literary and beverage favorites, but she smiled gratefully and sipped again, giving me a moment to work the stiffness from my back and shoulders.

Becky's glove shop was a little oasis of warm luxury on the ruffled hem of the opulent Palace Hotel. Other San Francisco shops sold ladies' frippery, but Becky had elevated it to an experience found nowhere else. Plush carpeting and cream-striped wallpaper lent a rich background to the merchandise while tiny overhead chandeliers cast dancing light over customer's beribboned hats and swirling satins as they shopped.

The narrow glass-case displays flanking the doors held ladies' lined winter gloves and fur muffs. Men's cravats in deep, rich silks and brightly colored children's mittens. Two curving white iron chairs with velvet cushions were placed before the long curtains that hid floor to ceiling boxes of inventory against the back wall.

Thanks to an anonymous and generous donor, Becky owned the shop outright, and together, she and I rented the tiny apartment above it.

A moan came from the front glass doors as the wind whipped past. Two ladies quickly followed, skirts swirling and coats snapping, clutching feathered hats that threatened to fly off without them. Thick purple clouds held the city in ominous, drifting tendrils.

Utterly dismal for going on noon.

"Storm's coming," Becky said. "I'm that glad to be safe out of it, Sunday or no."

"You braved it last Sunday," I pointed out.

"Christmas Eve is different." She set her empty cup down with a satisfied sigh. "I still wish you had come with me. The choir brought me to tears."

For a wisp of a woman, Becky could wield her opinions with force. She knew how much I loved music.

"I'll hear plenty tonight. My shift is done, but I'm due back at ten for the party." I reached for her cup. "Seems the world might end if they run out of *krumkake*."

"It's your own fault for being fabulous." Becky slid her book aside and gave me her full attention. "Besides, it's New Year's Eve. 1883, Mrs. Kelly. You deserve to celebrate your new life. A cozy home with a good friend—that's me." She wrinkled her nose at me as she ticked the list off her fingers. "An incredible job upstairs in the Palace Hotel kitchen creating heavenly desserts. A glorious new hat waiting for you in the apartment." She paused. "Which makes your blue eyes dance, by the way. When are you going to wear it?"

"Not tonight. I'm working."

"Piffle. When the bells start ringing, I expect you to throw caution to the wind and kiss somebody. Anyone will do."

I ignored her tease. "I'm earning two days off in a row for this shift. I won't be kissing anything but my pillow the minute it's over." At thirty respectable years of age and quite beyond the impulsive youth that animated Becky, parties meant color and music and flavors to be savored slowly and from a distance that allowed for digestion.

I turned a speculative eye on Miss Smith.

"Spoon and I have a standing date tonight," she said.

Our orphaned kitten was growing fast, and we'd named him Spoon because he was always stirring up trouble.

"Assuming he hasn't destroyed the curtains again, we're going to cuddle and finish this book." She thumped the cover. "For the third time."

"How very bourgeoise of you."

"You did it for Christmas."

"I did." It felt like a windup and, again, I tensed.

"At least I have an excuse," she said, her voice prying. "I've got absolutely no one to care how I fritter away my time, but you have a teeming family in Minnesota. Don't you miss them?" She caught my look and added, "Miss church? Holidays?"

"I have a home here if my ears did not deceive me a minute ago. And I have family in you and Pearl and Spoon. I don't miss rising in the dark to milk cows, and I don't miss driving miles of road making deliveries, and I certainly don't miss cooking for eight brothers, their families, or the crowds at barn-raisings."

After a beat, she asked, "You didn't write them, did you?"

Becky grew wistful every time she thought about the family I'd left behind. But I'd come out to marry a stranger who'd promptly gone toes-up on me. I grew wistful thinking about the family I'd expected.

"There's not much to say," I countered.

"Tell them you created a pastry so decadent that people come for miles to taste it. You'll bring some back with you after tonight's over, won't you?"

"Of course." The Italian chocolate I'd scoured the city for had turned my old family recipe into gold, and I was justifiably proud of it. Mr. Ghirardelli himself had visited the hotel dining rooms and proclaimed it a triumph. My wide, rough farmer's hands were now smooth, polished, and building pastries lighter than air.

My stout Norwegian frame, however much prinked and fashioned into a lady, remained a bit heavier.

"Do you think she'll try some?" She stepped around from behind the counter. "The opera singer?"

"Madame Fabbri? Perhaps."

The exclusive parties being thrown in the Palace Hotel tonight would rival anything I'd seen yet. Swags of holly draped along seven stories of interior balconies had been replaced with white and gold bunting. Christmas reds and greens in the dining rooms swapped out for cream linens, crystal, silver vases, and gold stars. A glittering canopy billowed above the central courtyard, suspended from the third-floor pillars, and had been filled with silk flower petals to be released onto the dancing crowd at midnight.

The guest list and the menu would add layers of personalities, sparkling jewels, and culinary art to create one magnificent event.

"It's a shame you can't make it down to the California Theater for the performance," Becky said. "But the after-party should be equally entertaining. You can see them eat like regular people."

"Actors and singers are not regular people. They're artists and I admire their craft."

Her nod was eager. "Exactly. And they will admire yours before the night is over."

It was the opening I was waiting for.

"Speaking of admiration." My calculated words had the desired effect.

She took a stack of boxes from the counter and stepped behind the curtain to put them away.

"Have you heard from Mr. Merrill of late?" The question was innocent enough. "Perhaps you could fritter away some time with him on your day off tomorrow."

She took a moment before she replied. I traced the cup's golden rim with a fingertip.

"The district attorney has his hands full with fighting crime," she said pertly from behind her refuge. "I certainly wouldn't expect him to fritter anything, time in particular."

She shook the curtain back into place on her way out.

"Sam pushes paper," I said. "He could fritter if he wanted to."

If she'd blushed on my account, it faded immediately when she looked over my shoulder. Her eyes grew wide as she walked to the door. "Mrs. Kelly. Look."

I turned to follow her and gazed out onto Market Street. The busiest thoroughfare in San Francisco, it ran from the

Ferry House straight up into the hills. Wide enough for several lanes of traffic, from cable cars to carriages, it normally buzzed with people coming home from church and lately had been teeming with holiday shoppers. But now it stretched empty in both directions.

Small white bits of fluff drifted in the wind.

"Snow." Becky's mouth hung open.

There was no doubt about it.

My stomach contracted from the blow. It wasn't supposed to snow in San Francisco. Everyone knew that. How? How had I not seen it coming? Had I been outside, I would have smelled it in the wind. But I'd remained smugly in the hotel's interior for the past week, ignoring the weather.

Safe.

The pit in my stomach threatened to rise into my throat and I clutched at my shirtwaist, pushing hard against it through my corset. Becky didn't know. She didn't understand. Snow built up in thirty-foot drifts and made roads impassable. It could trick you and trap you and play with you until it decided to kill you.

It could cover you with a sparkling white blanket and you'd sleep until the spring thaw.

Betrayal thickened my voice. "I thought it never snowed in San Francisco," I stammered. "I was informed you never even had proper thunderstorms. Gray and drizzly unless bright and sunny. Those are the two options for weather here."

A smile of childlike wonder grew on her face as she watched the snow fall. "It never does. It never has. I've never seen snow." Oblivious to my complaint, she pulled the door open. The temperature in the shop dropped immediately as she stepped onto the walkway and held a hand to the heavens.

"Come back inside! You'll catch your death without a coat." My voice rose an octave. "You don't even have a hat on!" I pushed the door half-closed, putting it between me and the street to keep myself from pulling her in forcibly.

I gulped air in an attempt to slow my breathing. Where had my hasty words come from? We were not in Minnesota. This was California. The ocean protected us.

Becky squealed and wrapped her arms around herself as she opened her mouth to catch a snowflake.

My eyes darted around the empty shop. The brightly lit, fashionable, and full-of-color shop. Warm. Safe.

"Mrs. Kelly! Come out here!"

I closed my eyes, and a hand went involuntarily to one of my dangling earrings.

"It's so beautiful!"

Forcing myself to observe Becky's joy did not stop the rising bile. I blinked hard. The ground grew whiter by the minute. It was sticking. Was I the only one who understood the implications?

"Becky." Keeping a firm hand on the door, I reached for her arm and tugged her inside.

She resisted enough to point. "They're running in it," she said with excitement. "Everyone is coming out to play!"

"Not without proper coats and galoshes, they aren't." I shut the door firmly and led her toward the counter.

Gently reclaiming her arm, she stared into my eyes, and her smile faltered. Before she could speak, the door popped back open behind me.

"Miss Smith," cried a woman, shaking out her shawl with a rueful laugh, "I must purchase five pairs of children's mittens. Immediately." Her eager smile made up for the damp she dripped on the carpet.

"And you shall have them." Becky blinked, instantly distracted. She reached for a drawer. "Help me with sizes and colors." Festive mood reclaimed, the two women bent over the open drawer.

I left them to it. I'd been at work since four in the morning and my feet were aching. Letting myself out through the back door, I climbed the circular stairway up to our apartment and dropped into my chair by the window.

The snow came thicker, and I could make out grown men in the street gathering enough to make snowballs. A street car came their way, providing a perfect, if bewildered, target.

My hands twisted together in my lap.

I'd been warned about earthquakes in this city of steeply rolling hills. Fires, it seemed, were a regular and devastating occurrence in neighborhoods packed cheek-to-jowl with connected three-story wooden buildings. Dense communities had bouts of diphtheria or cholera run like a scourge through them.

But snow? What did they know of three-foot long icicles or digging out of your own house after a blizzard or losing your way in an impenetrable white swirl?

A ragged group of boys ran along the walkway across the street, arms waving, pushing each other into the gutter, scooping up wet, white missiles in bare, blue hands.

"No trees," I reminded myself aloud. "They can't get lost."

"Don't think about it," Aunt Mary said. *"I never wanted to hurt you."*

Aunt Mary was safely buried in the little family plot in Waterford Township, Minnesota. I kept her memory close. Closer than was comfortable. When I heard her voice, it filtered through a lifetime of loving memories of a woman who'd been mother, sister, and friend to me. It was the only thing I'd kept when I'd decided to make a life for myself here.

As far away from snow as it was possible to get.

"You could never hurt me," I said.

The good God would have to forgive the lie. Grief washed through me, and I touched the earrings she'd left wrapped beneath last year's Christmas tree. She'd known about my secret letters to San Francisco with a stranger who'd advertised for a mail-order bride and, hard as she'd argued against it, had, in the end, given me a wedding gift. No one else would have known the sparkling blue drops as such, but I did.

She'd loved me fierce.

Before she died.

Before she'd been murdered.

"There is a time for everything under the sun," Aunt Mary whispered.

"It was not your time to die," I reminded her.

A small bundle of fur launched itself into my lap, and I turned my startle into a stern shake. The kitten rubbed his face against my palm and purred.

It was time to rest.

Chapter Two

M<small>Y HANDS WERE</small> steady as a rock as I crowned the pavlova with small lingonberry-poached pears. A meringue was tricky in more ways than one. If the oven or the humidity or the touch wavered, the puffed perfection fell at the very end of a long, laborious process. Sometimes a chef in a hurry might overload its crack-marbled top.

I had perfected the recipe. My meringue never fell.

Luminous red glaze from the poaching pan drizzled over the creation and I accented it with bright green mint leaves to form a show-stopping dessert during Christmas. The season had turned, but the Palace Hotel refused to take it off the menu.

"It stops conversations," Pearl had confided. "People are almost too awed to eat it."

The hotel had, however, allowed me to trade out their usual tiramisu offering with my Norwegian family recipe for *krumkake*, a thin waffle cookie rolled into a cone and filled with decadent chocolate cream. The chocolate cream was my own secret recipe, and not even Pearl knew it.

The lingonberry sauce also decorated our offering of rice pudding. *Riskrem*, if I were writing out the menu. It rounded out the dessert list of nuts, fruit, coffee, and platters of cookies. Chocolate *chokladsnittar*, gingerbread *brune pinner*, and an almond shortbread, *serinakaker*.

Scents rolled through the kitchen as dessert was served. Out in the dining room, guests devoured local fish, oysters, veal, and quail. I steadfastly avoided the cinnamon and cardamom scents that attacked me with every passing waiter. Scents that tugged at my heart and threatened to release thoughts of home.

Scents that brought my brothers, one by one, to mind. They would be holding the same platters of cookies in Minnesota.

I huffed and tilted my head to inspect my creation.

Wasn't it possible to honor my ancestral recipes without dragging ancestors along on the journey?

A new year. A fresh start. I was so close.

"It's nearly midnight!" Pearl's voice carried across the kitchen and an undercurrent of relief fizzed through the staff. Most of us weren't used to working such long hours and as orders dwindled, diners were slowly moved into the south dining room so revelers would drift toward the ballroom and the grand central court.

"That may be your last one," Pearl said, stepping to my elbow. She knew better than to bump it. "The north dining room is empty, and we only have the large private parties left." She gave her caramel-colored face a pat with the under-corner of her apron and admired my progress with clear hazel eyes.

I nodded and set the last mint leaf into place. "Good."

The Palace Hotel had the honor of being the grandest on the West Coast. With 755 guest rooms, multiple street-front shops like Becky's, amenities from a billiard room and bar for gentlemen to a dedicated children's dining room, drawing room, and parlors for the ladies, it attracted visiting officials, international dignitaries, and front-page celebrities. Rooms were furnished in style, with dark mahogany furnishings, gilt-framed fireplaces, and silk wallpaper.

A porte cochère formed a massive arched main entrance, allowing horse-drawn carriages to enter the building proper directly from Montgomery Street. Coachmen stopped in the circular drive to deposit guests and luggage before driving out again to drop behind the building into the basement and underground stables. Smartly uniformed valets lined the Grand Court, eager to whisk away any open buggies for a tip. A spacious lobby opened on one side, our ballroom on the other, and the evening orchestra usually sat directly ahead, filling the court with music.

Guests seldom moved for several minutes upon arrival, however much their trip had been harried or rushed. Their gaze swept around them, taking in the columns and potted palms, the sparkling crystal and warm lamplight. Then they looked up.

Soaring seven stories above the Grand Court, curving atop row upon row of elegant balconied corridors, a glass ceiling capped the white and gold fairy wonderland. By day, it filled the heart of the building with sunshine. By night, it shimmered with stars.

Tonight, a veil full of flower petals blocked the view.

"Just as well," I muttered, stepping back from the counter.

A glass ceiling was a folly in a place that snowed. A brief glance through a window had shown white streets with little snowmen on every corner.

Such nonsense.

"It looks perfect." Pearl nodded to a uniformed boy who took the pavlova away. "Your presence is requested," she continued. "It seems one of our diners is enamored with your creations and wants to thank the chef personally." Her eyes teased, but her words held pride.

Officially, Pearl oversaw the service, from kitchen to wait staff. Unofficially, she knew every single person who worked in the Palace and nothing escaped her notice. The guest rooms had call buttons for the concierge, but nothing was faster than the backroom grapevine and she kept her ear to it. Pearl had been delighted when I'd been hired on and I considered her one of my first good friends in the city. I doubted she knew about being included in my small circle of those I now called family.

"By all means, go and take the bow," I said, wiping my hands on a towel. "If it weren't for you, I wouldn't have this job. Please take the credit."

She was already shaking her head. "Straighten your apron and get out there." She squinted over the shoulder of a passing busboy. "Plate *krumkake* on a crystal dish and tell him it's on the house. Private dining room on the left."

"Who's in that one?" I smoothed at thick, blonde strands that had escaped the twist at the nape of my neck.

"The California Theater." Without a backward glance, she moved on to scold an errant dishwasher.

Frozen in place, I reminded myself to breathe. A theater troupe! As soon as I had time enough, I promised myself as I rushed to plate the chocolate triumph, I was going to buy tickets to every show in the city. Plays and operas and ballets and traveling vaudeville shows. Anything with music and costumes and dance.

"Do you know what day it is?" Her voice brought me up short.

"It's Sunday," I told Aunt Mary. "I didn't mean today."

"Ma'am?" A passing waiter glanced at me.

"Nothing."

Briskly, I went into the giant pantry and opened a glass jar. Careful that it didn't touch the crisp cookie, I added a few decorative drops of cherry syrup to the plate. I understood presentation. And I wanted them to remember me.

I nestled one plump candied cherry against the chocolate cream, straightened my apron, then stepped into the dining room with the gift.

Several tables remained laden with half-finished plates and abandoned wine bottles, but in large, the room had emptied in favor of the Grand Court and ballroom. The orchestra played a rousing waltz, and I stepped in time to it as I cut down the center of the room toward the two private dining rooms. The corridor running between them ended in the cavernous hotel lobby on the far side.

Despite the weather, high society guests packed into the Palace regularly. While most of them, admittedly, were staying here, it was flattering to know prestigious locals like the California Theater Company considered us a destination. Private parties brought in twice as much revenue as regular diners and lasted twice as long, too.

They must have reserved the room months in advance, I thought as I approached the doorway. I'd lingered over the playbill last week. Tonight, they'd held their one hundredth performance with a gala night. All proceeds from the testimonial benefit were going to Miss Eme Roseau, a prima donna on her way east for a medical treatment. And the famous Miss Kate Everleigh, a celebrated voice and stage aficionada, had been in the headlines for weeks.

My smile grew. I couldn't wait to tell Becky about our guests of honor.

A raised voice stopped me in the corridor. "It isn't enough, Olsen. The dagger has to run through his heart."

"I won't do it," barked a man's voice that sent shivers down my back. "Improvise!"

"No matter how you spin it, this will cost you double."

"We aren't made of money," came a third voice. Female. Nasal. Subtle wisps of cigar smoke rolled out with the petulant words. The crystal plate trembled in my hand and the cherry rolled sideways.

"That's up for debate," another woman said wryly.

I beckoned a waiter over and thrust the dish into his hands. "Serve it," I whispered, taking a step back against the corridor wall.

With a puzzled look, he obeyed.

"What's this?" Yet another voice, and I gripped my skirt

in my fists, unable to move.

"Compliments of the chef, sir," the waiter said.

"I am absolutely certain that you did not make that." A woman's soft scorn. "You're black as pitch. This is Scandinavian."

"Where is the chef, man?" The voice was belligerent. Familiar.

The waiter had no chance to respond as several people spoke at once.

"It's exactly the same. Exactly."

"Anyone could make it, dear."

"I'm telling you; it must be someone local. You recognized the sugar."

"We hardly corner the market on sugar crystals."

A chair scraped across the floor.

"Why should it bother you? Eat and enjoy."

The waiter appeared at my side, lips pursed, as the voices in the room mingled and rose, unintelligible.

"Thank you," I whispered.

"You cannot make a silk purse out of a sow's ear!"

The voices rose again as if on cue, but at least one chuckle bubbled among them.

"I'm done with this." More chair legs scraped over the carpet.

A fresh voice, rich and female and dripping with scorn, said, "I have people waiting. You'll excuse me."

The waiter and I froze as figures rushed from the dining room. The first was a woman with a frame as sturdy as my own but encased in an aubergine ball gown that filled the corridor with layers of skirts and a ruffled train that dragged the floor behind her. Dark ringlets framed her face and bounced along with her earrings as she moved regally into the lobby.

"Inez, wait." An even stouter gentleman in coattails hurried after her, carrying a silk top hat. "Prima donna!"

Pausing in the lobby, she threw him a scowl over her bare shoulder and flicked open a fan in her hand. She turned toward the Grand Court, fanning herself, and they both disappeared from sight.

I took a tentative step backward.

"Don't go," a woman pleaded. "It's near midnight. Let's all head upstairs instead."

But a tall young gentleman exited, and had he not directed a fierce glare at the party speaking to him, he surely would have seen me standing like a ninny in the passageway.

"We aren't here to sleep!" His sneer was practiced. I knew it well. "I think you all must have aged twenty years since we arrived. I'll see you in the morning."

"Let him go. He's had too much to drink."

"I should have thrashed him years ago and whipped the devil out of him!"

He was hushed and voices lowered as I spun on my heel. Rushing blindly back through the dining room, my only thought was to reach the pantry. The kitchen stairs. The safety of the basement.

"Mrs. Kelly?"

It was too late. I ran headlong into Pearl, where she stood in the pantry with an armful of folded linen napkins. "Jumping Jehoshaphat! You nearly knocked me over!" she cried, staggering in my arms.

Untangling myself, I said, "Pardon me. I'm so sorry. Let me help you."

She turned her bundle away from my frantic hands. "What's going on? Where's the fire?"

"It's nothing." I moved into the corner, avoiding her eyes and putting myself to rights. "I'm sorry. I'll just put those away for you, shall I?"

A scream pierced the air, cutting through the hotel over the orchestra music, and wide-eyed, Pearl dropped her napkins.

"That came from the dining room," she said, rushing out.

I peered around the corner, watching as others of our staff joined her. No. Please, God, no. Not there.

Other diners had risen from their seats, and they stared toward the lobby corridor. And the private dining rooms.

"What is it?" Three cooks stood in the kitchen, utensils raised. Another scream.

Hiding my shaky hands behind my apron, I forced myself to follow Pearl. Each step more sluggish. Each breath harsher.

"He's choking!"

"Send for a surgeon!"

"What's happening?"

"His heart must've given out!"

"He hit his head, that's all. He'll come around in a moment or two."

"No, he's dead! All is lost!"

The orchestra no longer played, and the rising murmur of a thousand questions rolled in from the court. From the lobby.

From the past.

Waitstaff crowded the corridor, but I found myself walking directly to the doorway. Pearl and two men in uniforms from the lobby bent over a man lying on the floor. A woman knelt on either side of him, one holding his hand and frantically patting it, the other waving a tiny bottle beneath his nose.

Two men in tuxedos remained seated at the table, looking anxiously on, deep lines etched in their faces.

"For heaven's sake," cried a man with oiled hair and a thin, dark mustache, "tell the orchestra to play! Clear the hall, gentlemen! Seat the diners again!" Mr. Sedgwick, the hotel manager, was almost never seen by the staff but feared by every one of us. Bodies crushed through the passage and pushed me into the room.

Mr. Sedgwick raised his voice again. "Nothing to see here, ladies and gentlemen! On with the party!"

As if on cue, a great gong in the courtyard struck a deep, resonating tone. Receding voices rose in merriment.

A man brushed past me, loosening his tie. "You called for a physician?" he asked.

With a glance at the prostrate man, he knelt beside the ladies. Pearl motioned the lobby staff away.

The gong rang again.

"Eli! Eli, speak to me!" the younger woman pleaded with

the man on the ground.

Her lovely face pinched in trauma; she held his hand to her wet cheek and moaned.

The gong struck three.

"He excited himself! I told him to rest!" The older woman laid her hands in her lap and drooped. "This was all too much! We should never have left." Her words ended on a sob.

"Come to the table, Mrs. Berg." I knew the deep, methodical voice all too well.

I'd forgotten how tall Mr. Nilsen was. Over the course of the next few gongs, the widow Berg allowed him to help her up and into a chair. He did not offer assistance to the younger woman, nor did his companion do anything other than soberly watch.

The physician worked over the silent man. Pearl stood at my side.

Gong.

The physician sat back on his heels and looked over a shoulder at Pearl and I. "Send for the police."

Gong.

The young woman's desperate sobs turned into violent coughing, and she sat in a heap with her face buried in her handkerchief.

Gong.

Pearl vanished.

Gong.

The Palace Hotel erupted into shouts. Bright strains of "Auld Lang Syne" came from the orchestra.

Slowly, the physician rose and looked at the men. "He's gone. I'm sorry."

"Oh, my." Aunt Mary was as shocked as I was. *"It's Reverend Olsen."*

Chapter Three

CONTRASTING WITH THE music and song and cheering that roared through the building, the women's sobs created a surreal atmosphere in the congested space. Wall sconces and a small chandelier cast a warm glow over the room but couldn't completely illuminate the dead man's features.

Yes. It was him.

It was a face I could never forget. Reverend Olsen's white shirt gaped open where the physician had removed the tie, loosened the collar, and unbuttoned it, but any inappropriate hint of a chest was thoroughly mitigated by a sprawling square beard and thick mustache gone to gray. His thinning hair, though combed carefully to conceal the fact, was mussed. Dark, tufted brows formed prominent points on an angular face with a strong Roman nose.

His eyes were open in a face frozen in anguish.

And the woman beside him fought to bring herself under control.

Though most of her face remained covered, I'd seen plain enough that she was young and fair. Blonde braids, pinned up in a crown on her head and topped with a small dark hat, marked her as one of us, yet I'd never met her before. My braids had transformed into a fashionable chignon months ago. As it was highly unlikely that Reverend Olsen had discovered a long-lost daughter, it was even more absurd to think he'd remarried a girl who could have been.

Reverend Olsen's first wife had passed away when I was twelve, leaving him with a toddler and a congregation that had flocked around him, lifted him up in prayer, and taken care of him ever after with frightening solidarity.

What in the name of all that was holy, was this man doing in my hotel in the middle of San Francisco?

The physician tugged at his cuff and asked, "Who else is in your party? Where are they?" He eyed the table, set for eight.

Mr. Nilsen stood behind the chair he'd helped Mrs. Berg into. His long, bony hands clutched the curved chair back, forming white knuckles. Small, wire-rimmed spectacles reflected the gaslight. Like most of the men in Minnesota, Mr. Nilsen wore his shoulder-length hair tidy and his whiskers unrestrained. I doubted he'd bothered with a tie beneath it. Where the reverend's face was deeply lined with a lifetime of carrying congregational burdens, Mr. Nilsen's face carried the everyday weathered tan of a handyman who'd spent his considerable years doing maintenance on a flourishing Lutheran church.

He stared morosely at nothing in particular on the table, and it was my opinion that he looked downright silly in his tuxedo.

Mrs. Berg hadn't changed a whit. She sat uneasy in her

chair, alternately putting a hand over her mouth to stifle a squeak and gripping the table corner as she leaned forward to peer into Reverend Olsen's face. Her dark hair, streaked with gray, severely parted down the middle, flat to her scalp, and pulled into a tight bun at the nape of her neck, lent nothing to a plain and sagging face.

She wore black. She always wore black. A white cameo at her throat was her only adornment. She had been a childless widow longer than recollection, but no one would dare call her lonesome. Her wealth and piety marked her as one of the church's main benefactors and her constant hovering at the dear reverend's elbow marked her as the biggest nosy-body in three counties.

The fourth party at the table had not risen from his seat, but his countenance was grim as he observed the spectacle. Though the stranger's eyes followed the physician's every movement, his chin—sporting a short and wiry beard confined to that singular point—remained high. His hair, flattened on top by a hat at some point, puffed above his ears in defiance of pomade.

The physician's question was a logical one. The screams had not caused the three diners who had exited previously, to come running. It left me with a deeply uncomfortable awareness that I was alone in the room with haunts.

"Temper," Aunt Mary warned.

Surprised at myself, I took in a deep breath and forced my fists to relax and open. When had my fear turned into fury? I slipped along the wall and ducked out of the room, only to come face-to-face with Officer Wilson.

Without missing a beat, he gave me a nod, saying, "This one, boys." He motioned me in with him.

Willing myself to become one with the wallpaper, I pushed against the doorframe as men streamed into the room. Three officers entered, two in uniform and the third in a tailored suit that did not stop me from recognizing him as Officer Heyes. They blocked my view of Reverend Olsen, and I caught a glimpse of Police Captain O'Meara's red curls, and the splendidly wide paunch of Mayor Blake go by. Detective Maximillian P. Fisher entered the room slowly, at full and careful attention, taking in every part of the private room, from the ceiling to the floor to the occupants.

If his gaze flickered in recognition when it skimmed over me, no one would have noticed. He never broke stride as he pushed through the spectators and vanished from sight.

"I'll thank you all to give me room to work," he said over the hubbub. "Someone tell Ross."

My opportunity to flee closed as swiftly as it had opened. Heyes came and stood beside me, looking rather dashing for the evening. I doubted he was on duty tonight. Captain O'Meara acknowledged my presence with a thoughtful frown as he passed out of the room and the good mayor paused only to say, "Well done, that. Wouldn't want a scandal in the Palace, would we now?"

His remark brought an undignified snort from me. San Francisco was built on scandal. The mayor contributed to it regularly.

All eyes followed Detective Fisher as he bent to get a look at the body.

"Sir," the woman on the floor begged, "there must be something you can do!"

He held out a hand. The gesture sent her back into a paroxysm of grief, and she laid her head on Reverend Olsen's chest. He glanced at the physician, who looked meaningfully toward the door.

"Heyes," he said, straightening, "bring in the rest of this party. That would be…" He gave the men at the table an expectant look.

"Madame Fabbri," the man with the goatee said.

"Theater?" Detective Fisher asked.

"The same. And her husband, Mr. Jacob Muller. They should be in the Grand Court somewhere."

"Who else?"

Mr. Nilsen roused himself. "And Josiah Olsen." He cleared his throat and swallowed. "His son."

"How will we know him?" Detective Fisher jabbed a thumb at Heyes. "Go with him. Quickly. And bring them all back here." He pulled a chair away from the table, ran a hand over the seat, and set it against the wall next to me.

"If you would kindly sit over here, please, ma'am. And both gentlemen, if you would please stand aside as well?"

When he set a second chair next to it, I backed into the open doorway next to the physician. The bleak look on his face said he'd come for a party, and this had not been in his evening plans. No doubt he was in a hurry to go, but he waited patiently for the detective.

As the group came away from the table, Mrs. Berg's narrowed eyes met mine. "Who are you?" Her voice was raspy with weeping, but tears had now been replaced with a keen sense of suspicion.

Mr. Nilsen looked up and noticed me for the first time. A single raised brow told me he knew.

"Miss," Detective Fisher said, "I insist you rise and sit with your friends where they can minister to you." Bending behind her, he lifted the young woman. She drooped in his arms and Mr. Nilsen rushed to assist him in getting her into the second chair where Mrs. Berg immediately began patting and fawning over her.

The second man held himself aloof from the revival efforts and, turning to the physician, asked, "What is it, doctor? What's come over him? Bad heart?"

"I'm afraid I cannot say with any certainty, sir," the man replied. "I will assist the police if I can and return to my family." He glanced nervously over his shoulder into the corridor.

"It's awful!" the young woman cried. "It's too awful! Where is Josiah? Oh, must we break his heart, too?"

"Doctor," Mrs. Berg said, chafing the young girl's hand, "I insist you tell us immediately."

"Silence, please." Detective Fisher perused the table.

Walking around it, hands behind his back, he glared at the dirty service ware, bunched napkins, empty pitchers, and discarded oyster shells. The butt of a cigar had been snuffed in a saucer. My crystal dish was empty, save a drop or two of cherry cordial.

He knelt to peer beneath the table and then turned again to examine the reverend. Voices grew louder in the corridor, and he rose, brushing the knees of his trousers. He was impeccably turned out for the evening, though not in a tuxedo. Detective Fisher was a lean man, a direct result, I'd always thought, of a job that made regular meals a luxury. He nevertheless wore his dark suit well, kept his shoes at a high polish, and his short bristling mustache as tidy as his sandy-brown hair. A strong, clean-shaven chin and piercing metal-gray eyes lent an air of authority to a man who took his job a bit more seriously than I considered healthy.

I wondered who waited for him in the ballroom.

"Mrs. Kelly," he said, "please have the room across the corridor cleared immediately so your guests have somewhere to sit in privacy. I need to work this room before I can formulate my questions."

Relishing the discombobulation on the Minnesota faces, I dropped my eyes and curtsied before making a hasty exit. It didn't do to think what Detective Fisher made of such a display of submission, but if I could keep them guessing, so much the better.

A perfect blizzard of emotions swirled through me as I checked the other private dining room. Other than a vase full of flowers, it was already vacant and cleaned, but I circled the gleaming table anyway, trying to calm myself.

The corridor grew loud again in several octaves, and the couple who had first left the room rejoined the party. Now that I could place a name to the close-up image of the legendary Madame Fabbri, I was dismayed to find she was well past the days of her youth, and not only plain beneath her powder, but no amount of flounces would make up for her unfortunate nose.

I couldn't recall the name of her husband. All of his hair had shifted over time and ran directly into a huge set of mutton-chop side whiskers, leaving the rest of his face as bare as the top of his perspiring head.

It was difficult to imagine either of them on a stage. For that matter, where was the theater troupe?

He clutched his wife's arm and stared wildly into the room.

"Impossible!" Madame Fabbri cried, accenting each syllable on a different note. "It cannot be! Jacob, how is this possible?" While I did not detect tears, every inch of the lady quivered in animation.

I stood behind Heyes as Mrs. Berg hauled herself up from her chair, nearly dragging the hysterical woman with her, and all further words were lost as the party, one by one, crossed the corridor into the empty room. Curious guests had gathered in the lobby, peering into the corridor over their cocktails, and distressed staff paced in the dining room, as if anxious to scrub the stain of tragedy from their domain.

Detective Fisher walked up to Heyes. "Where is the other one? The son?"

Heyes shrugged. "We couldn't find him. The court is packed, Fisher. He might come to us if we wait a bit."

"Did you send for Wilson?"

"Yes, sir."

"Good man. Keep an eye on this group until I'm ready for them. You have a notebook somewhere?"

Heyes grinned and pulled one out of his back pocket.

Detective Fisher turned to the physician and held out his hand. "Thank you for your assistance. What can you tell me?"

"My family and I were dining in the main room," he said, giving a single hard shake. "I heard two screams and came running along with everyone else. I'm afraid there was nothing to do when I got here. He was already dead."

"That fast?"

The physician looked around and lowered his voice. "Poison, sir. I'd stake my reputation on it. Anything that fast is likely cyanide. Slight foaming around the mouth. Possibly strychnine. Your men should make a definite identification."

Detective Fisher's face hardened. "Someone in the room, then?"

"Or the food."

They both glanced at me.

"They were served the same things as everyone in the hotel," Pearl said from behind me. Her arms were crossed and her face dared them to continue. "Everybody ate. Nobody is sick."

The detective tipped his head in thought. "Thank you, doctor. Give your information to Heyes, here, in case I need to contact you later. Pearl, have a look at this table, please."

I leaned heavily on the doorjamb, and Heyes gave me a concerned look. "You must be tired. When is your shift over?" he asked.

Mute, I watched Pearl assess the table. She studiously avoided looking down at the body. Detective Fisher asked questions under his breath, and she nodded or answered with terse, brief words.

Would this day never end?

When they returned to the corridor, Detective Fisher said, "I need to speak with the vintner, the baker, the chefs, and the staff who waited on this room all night."

Pearl hung her head and nodded.

"Mrs. Kelly," he began. He ran a hand over his face. "Mrs. Kelly, you delivered a dish right before he died?"

I blinked. "Yes."

Heyes shifted uncomfortably.

"Did you see who ate it?"

"No. I wasn't in the room."

His voice was thick with irritation. "Pearl admits she ordered you to do it. You work in the kitchen. You don't normally serve the food." I nodded. "But she didn't watch you plate the ... what did you call it?"

"*Krumkake.*" Pearl kept her eyes on the carpet.

He paused. "Until I can find out who ate what, you stay."

"I won't go in there," I said, straightening. My heart raced. "I won't."

He looked at me in surprise. "I wasn't asking you to stay where the dead man is."

"The dead don't worry me," I said, pointing to the other room. "But I won't be held responsible for what might happen if I join that group."

He waited.

"I know them," I said quietly. "Three of them, at any rate. Mrs. Berg, Mr. Nilsen, and Reverend Olsen. It's the reverend who's dead."

The information seemed too much for him to absorb. It was still impossible for me to do so. No one spoke.

"They're from Minnesota," I said bitterly. "From my own home town."

And they'd killed Aunt Mary.

He did not need to know everything. The scandal on Aunt Mary was going to stay in Minnesota with the people who painted her with it and die with them.

It was going to follow her here over my dead body.

Chapter Four

THE CONFLICTED LOOKS on Detective Fisher's face eventually fell into grim resignation.

"Heyes has to stay with me," he said. "Ross is on his way, if they can find him. We still have a guest missing from the table." He ran a hand through his hair. "Pearl, gather the staff I need to speak with and seat them at this end of the hall." He turned to the two uniformed officers. "Close the dining room and block off the lobby end. Keep everyone away from the area."

The officers left and Pearl nodded quickly and spun on her heel.

"And take Mrs. Kelly's apron. Her shift is over." He eyed me. "She needs a cup of coffee."

I opened my mouth to protest, but he interrupted with, "I'm holding your interview last. I don't want to hear one more thing about these people. I need to keep a clear mind. And don't talk to anyone else, either. Bring a chair from the dining room and stay in the corridor." He frowned. "And be right here when I'm ready."

Seething, I turned away from his gaze as I reached behind me to untie my apron. I would tolerate his demands so long as no one discussed me with him in the interim. This was not the first body the good detective and I had crossed paths over, but our relationship had evolved to a place of mutual respect and trust in the process.

But I was no fool. I'd never seen Detective Fisher accused of murder, regardless of circumstantial evidence, which gave him a decided advantage. It would never do to lose my composure at a time when there was so much at stake.

I handed Pearl my apron and she left me to haul a heavy chair from the dining room into the corridor myself. Her back was stiff as she walked away. She couldn't possibly think ... what else had she told Detective Fisher? As much as I admired her work ethic and scrupulous respect for the authorities, I had to believe she would defend me.

I shoved the chair as close to the doorway as I could without being seen from within and sank gratefully onto the plush seat. The officer at the end of the hall watched in silence.

My hands shook as I straightened my skirt and smoothed my hair. A wave of vertigo hit, and I closed my eyes.

What were they doing here?

"We have rooms in this hotel," Mrs. Berg said in a tremulous voice, and I leaned toward the door to catch the rest. "On the fourth floor."

"I, however, do not," Madame Fabbri said. "We would like to leave as soon as possible. The weather is frightful."

"So cold-hearted, my dear."

"Jacob, we can do nothing. It is all for naught. We merely delay this poor family's grief. It is the height of rudeness to stay."

"Send them away! I lay the blame entirely on their wicked ways!" Mrs. Berg's sharp tongue was all too familiar.

"Quiet, please." Detective Fisher's voice cut through the rising tension. "Names first."

"Madame Fabbri. I hardly need introduce myself. *Impresaria* for the California Theater on Bush Street. My husband, Mr. Muller, and my stage manager, Mr. Sims."

I could picture Heyes scribbling in his notebook.

"Matthew Nilsen. I'm ... secretary to the Reverend—Doctor—Elias Olsen. The gentlemen in the other room."

Sobs interrupted his stammers, but he rallied and continued.

"This is Mrs. Berg. She's here as companion to Mrs. Olsen, who truly must be allowed some privacy for her grief, sir. Have pity."

"And what of the missing person?" Detective Fisher asked. "The last of your party?"

Mr. Nilsen sighed. "Young Josiah Olsen. The reverend's son. He left just before..."

"Oh dear! Edith!"

I nearly rose from my chair but caught myself in time.

"Stop! What's that?" Detective Fisher's question brought me to the doorway. The wife had fainted to the floor and her companion waved the little bottle in her face that I'd seen earlier. He lunged for it. Officer Heyes put a hand to his waist, feeling for a gun and registered dismay at finding nothing.

"Smelling salts," Mrs. Berg said. "You use them to revive

a swoon, you fool!"

"Mrs. Berg." Mr. Nilsen's rebuke landed on deaf ears, as well he should have known.

Mr. Sims, of all people, knelt to take her wrist in his hand. "A strong pulse," he said curtly.

Mrs. Berg smoothed back Mrs. Olsen's hair, saying, "This would never have happened if we'd stayed home. She's too delicate for travel, poor lamb."

Madame Fabbri caught my eye, and her face said otherwise.

The officer who'd rushed to my side said, "Need help, Fisher?"

A quick sniff had Detective Fisher's eyes watering, but he handed the vial to the officer. "Hold onto this. Ma'am, I need to see your reticule. And everyone, resume your seat." He squinted at me, and I disappeared around the corner again.

"But the lady—"

"Will enjoy the only rest any of us are going to get. I will go through everyone's pockets as quickly as possible and be advised that an armed officer is standing by. I would appreciate your cooperation."

"But why?" Madame Fabbri asked. "The man succumbed to heart failure. What have we to do with it?"

There was a quiet rustle before he replied. "What was your business here tonight, madame?"

"We were celebrating. Although it may have been premature, all things considered. Dr. Olsen was to be our new patron of the arts."

My jaw fell.

"You'll never see a penny of it," Mrs. Berg hissed.

"Thank you, Mr. Sims," Detective Fisher said. "And tell me, Mr. Nilsen. Are you all traveling together? Where from? And when did you arrive in San Francisco? Turn, please."

More rustles as Mr. Nilsen said, "We arrived together on the train two days ago from Minnesota and checked in here immediately. Madame Fabbri advised us that this was the proper place to stay for conducting our business."

"Can you believe her audacity?" Mrs. Berg couldn't bear to be left out of any conversation. "Yes, proud woman, I've only said what everyone in the room is thinking. Such wanton excess and waste. Palace, indeed. It's a far cry from the simple wholesome fields of Gott."

"It was perfectly acceptable to both Dr. and Mrs. Olsen," Mr. Muller boomed.

"I beg your pardon!" Madame Fabbri's abrupt tone was icy.

"If you can direct me to your pockets, madame," Detective Fisher said, "this will be faster."

"This is a silk gown that cost more than you make in a year, detective. It does not have pockets!"

"Then you will be kind enough to indulge me another question or two. Where were you when the reverend died?"

"My husband and I went out to the courtyard. It became altogether uncouth in the room, and I wanted air."

"Uncouth?"

"The conversation turned to practical matters," Mr. Sims offered. "It was nothing they needed to dirty their hands with."

"I owe it to my loyal subscribers to circulate," Madame

Fabbri said. "We went out to greet them and take a turn on the dance floor before the midnight gong. We knew nothing was amiss until Mr. Nilsen sought us out with an officer at his side."

There was a pause before Detective Fisher asked, "Which one of you smoked a cigar?"

"I did," Mr. Sims said.

"Is it customary to smoke in front of the ladies?"

"It is where I come from."

"Filthy habit," Madame Fabbri muttered.

"And which of you drank the wine?"

"Every gentleman at the table," Mr. Muller said.

Mrs. Berg hissed, and Mr. Nilsen said, "When in Rome."

"Detective, it's late."

"Thank you, Mr. Sims. I am looking for something and I cannot find it." Detective Fisher paused. "The gentleman in the next room did not succumb to a bad heart."

That was up to interpretation, I thought.

"He was poisoned."

There was a general gasp in the room.

"Where is the poison, ladies and gentlemen?"

While they had been speaking, Police Sergeant Ross, Detective Fisher's boss, had arrived with a small entourage to collect Reverend Olsen. He'd made brief eye contact with me, nodded once, looked in on the room full of chaos, and quietly gone about his business. I recoiled in my chair when they passed by with the body.

The hotel had gone blessedly quiet, and Officer Wilson watched the men leave with their burden before his steady voice continued questioning the two officers standing guard.

Pearl and several of her staff sat in the dining area. Some were nodding and one was outright asleep. Apparently, I was not getting a cup of coffee.

"You have no proof," Mr. Sims said. "There is no poison in the room or on our persons. You cannot hold us against our will. For all you know, the man choked on an oyster."

A moan came next, but there were no accompanying scurries. I imagined the stern look that Detective Fisher used to pin them all in place. Mrs. Olsen was on her own for the moment.

"Did the reverend eat or drink anything that no one else did?" His voice was strained.

I leaned forward in my chair, feeling rather desperate about the question myself.

"Unhand me!"

The command from the lobby startled me so badly, I nearly fell to the floor.

"Sir, this area is closed to guests," Officer Wilson said.

"Let me pass, I say!"

The young man's dimple was centered on a prominent chin. Even with a neatly cropped mustache, it was startling to see the reverend's son had grown to manhood. He'd not been around in the last few years, but the family resemblance was too strong for any confusion on the matter. Dark curls wrapped behind his ears, and he looked down his nose with a righteous indignation, every inch the handsome rake.

It seemed Master Josiah Olsen had also inherited his father's way with words.

The uniforms blocked his progress, and I was about to intercede when Detective Fisher stepped into the hall.

"Where is my party, if you please?" he called to Detective Fisher.

"Are you Mr. Olsen?"

"The very one."

"Let him through, Wilson."

Mr. Olsen was thoroughly rumpled. Perhaps he'd been napping in a lounge or fist fighting in the Annie Street alley or gone horseback riding in his tuxedo. He swayed as he approached, and the scent of liquor preceded him.

"Nobody in their rooms yet." His words slurred. "They must be counting out the last pennies, poor souls."

"Mr. Olsen," Detective Fisher began, "we've been waiting for you. I'm afraid—" He placed a steadying hand on Mr. Olsen's arm. "You should sit down."

"What? I'm fine." He leaned toward the doorway and cried, "Fit as a fiddle!"

"Josiah." Mr. Nilsen called from the room. "Your father. He's … he's dead."

"What?" Mr. Olsen grinned. "Always the funny one, Nilsen. It's past the old man's bedtime by hours. Why haven't you tucked him in yet?"

Detective Fisher glared into the room. "Was he gone before it happened?"

"Yes. I'm afraid so."

"Hey!" Mr. Olsen scowled as Detective Fisher patted down his pockets but made no move to stop him.

Voices and crying grew louder in the room and Detective

Fisher said, "Everyone, stay where you are." He finished and straightened. "Mr. Olsen, I regret to tell you that your father, Reverend Olsen, died this evening. I'm Detective Fisher. I'm going to do everything in my power to find justice for him."

Mr. Olsen blinked several times, his smile faltering. "Where is everyone?" he finally asked.

"Oh, Josiah!" It was Mrs. Olsen, and he shook off Detective Fisher and ran into the room. "Where were you?" she cried. "Why did you leave? Your father!"

"It's true?"

"I'm sorry, son," Mr. Muller said.

"He went quickly," Mr. Sims added.

"Father!" His cry echoed down the corridor. "But where is he?"

Condolences ran together like taffy, thickening the air and sticking to the roof of my mouth. Detective Fisher stood aloof, watching. Waiting.

"The chef!" Mrs. Berg cried. "Remember the pastries?"

Detective Fisher refused to look at me, but stepped into the doorway, facing the group.

"The *brune pinner*?" Mrs. Olsen said brokenly over a man's sobs.

"He asked about them," Mrs. Berg said. "And the kitchen sent down a specialty. Just for him."

"They did," Mr. Nilsen said. "Is that what you wanted to know?"

"*Krumkake.*"

Once the word was out, the room grew quieter.

"He ate it," Mr. Sims said. "Right before…"

"He was delighted," Mrs. Olsen said, her bitter voice small but clear. "Just like home, he said."

"Could he have choked on the cherry?" Mr. Sims asked.

"If there is poison involved," Mr. Muller said, "you will only have to look as far as the hotel kitchen to find it."

"It was set on the table?" Detective Fisher asked. "No one else touched it?"

The silence was unsettling.

"Did Mrs. Kelly do anything other than deliver the pastry to the table?"

I held my breath.

"Who?" Mr. Sims asked.

"The woman who brought the dessert. The crumb cake thing. Did she say or do anything other than set it down and leave?"

"A waiter delivered it," Mrs. Olsen said. "A black man."

Mr. Olsen gulped around his tears in the background.

I wished for the floor to open up and swallow me.

"Wait. I know the woman you mean," Mrs. Berg said. "I saw her in the shadows in the other room."

"I saw her too!" Mr. Nilsen said. "But how can she be here?"

An unholy wail rose out of Mrs. Berg that sent shivers down my spine. "It's a haunt! Sent from the fiery depths of hell to destroy our beloved reverend! Gott help us!"

"It's impossible!" Mr. Nilsen said. "She's been gone for months!"

"Who?" Mrs. Olsen asked.

"She's reaped her earthly rewards and become an angel of death!"

Mrs. Berg always did have a flair for the dramatic.

"Karine Halvorsdatter Torkelson Langland," she cried, "I demand you show yourself! Release the reverend's soul and go back into the blackness from which you've sprung!"

"Who?" Mr. Sims asked.

"Your aunt was nothing but a senile, meddling hypocrite who got caught in her own foolishness!"

I flew from my seat and shoved past Detective Fisher. Heyes fumbled his notebook and dropped it.

"I'll not hear another word from you, you miserable woman!" I put my face an inch from hers and she fell back into her chair, a hand to her mouth, eyes wide.

"Here now!" Mr. Nilsen took a step toward me, and I turned, freezing him in place.

"Thought you'd never see me again, did you?" I asked. "Thought you could come out here and ruin more lives? They should thank me." I spared Madame Fabbri a flaming glance.

I didn't feel the grip Heyes had on my arm. I didn't hear the babbling voices we left behind. I didn't care where I was, so long as the Reverend Olsen wasn't there. I found myself, shaking from head to toe, in the north dining room, surrounded by the wait staff and four police officers.

"Steady, girl," Aunt Mary whispered.

"Appalling night," Madame Fabbri said with a huff as she stalked away, with Mr. Sims on one side and Mr. Muller on the other. Her husband mumbled a reply as their backs disappeared into the lobby.

Chapter Five

"AN ANGEL OF death?"

Was that the trace of a smile? Either I was seeing things or Detective Fisher was exhausted.

I restrained a yawn. "I've been called worse. By you, I believe."

"Mrs. Kelly…"

"Happy New Year to you too."

The Palace Hotel had small parlors on either side of the main entrance, facing the sunrise. The intimate areas offered respite with leather Chesterfields and plush ottomans for those waiting for either carriages or companions. With the porte cochère secured overnight and the closed doors monitored by crisply uniformed doormen, the large parlor window offered a generous view of Montgomery Street at dawn. Last night's snow had vanished along with my sanity and left only the gray sludge and slick muck of what could have been. Wind blew the clouds into tattered ribbons in a pewter-gray sky.

I buried my shoulders deeper into my thick wool shawl, but I could not hide from his gaze.

"I'll not apologize," I said.

"It wasn't me you went after." He let the words sit as Pearl put a full coffee service on the short table next to us. "Thank God," he added under his breath.

Pearl handed him a steaming cup. "I brewed this myself," she said quietly.

The shawl fell back as I sat up to pour my own and I asked, "How long will it take Heyes to question the staff?"

Detective Fisher swallowed and said, "As long as it takes."

Pearl shifted on her feet and looked anywhere but at me.

"I doubt he'll find anything amiss," he continued. "The staff is professional and loyal to a man."

"Thank you, sir," Pearl murmured.

"But we have to do our job," he said. "And though I do not suspect you, Mrs. Kelly, you are barred from working in the hotel under any guise until this murder is cleared up and someone else is in jail for it."

I faced Pearl. "Your doing?"

Pearl's red-rimmed eyes begged my forgiveness. "You can't blame me," she whispered fiercely. "We're all about to lose our jobs. The kitchen staff are terrified. When word gets out a diner was poisoned, the hotel is finished unless they get rid of us all. No one will so much as buy a cup of tea here." She bit her lip.

"Surely your reputation is beyond reproach," I stammered.

"If I had told anyone but you to deliver that pastry," she said, "we'd have that person in jail right now. And none of this would matter."

I swallowed her bitter pill. She was right. For better or worse, only my good reputation stood between a swift and closed case or ruin for the Palace Hotel. Between me and a prison cell.

And it was eroding swiftly.

"What is the hotel going to do?" Detective Fisher asked.

"The dining rooms are closed today," she said. "Except for a few of us running room service, the staff had New Year's Day off either way. Guests will have to make up their mind about it after the papers come out…"

I turned away from her and drank my coffee.

The guests from Minnesota were upstairs in their rooms under orders to remain so until called forth for more questioning. I had spent some fitful hours dozing on the lumpy Chesterfield in the front parlor with officers standing in the doorway. I woke alone, hairpins askew and full of aches and regret.

Detective Fisher had eventually appeared with my shawl. And though he'd given Becky the briefest information in exchange for it, she had been ordered to stay away.

Pearl fidgeted with the cuff of her white glove. "What will you do, sir? If I may ask? I need something to offer the staff. Any small amount of hope will do."

He shook his head and looked out the window.

"You'll never find the poison," I said. "Or the one who used it. Not with this many people, all of whom will deny everything. Did you check the lady's bustles? Their decolletage?"

Detective Fisher's face grew red.

"You did not. I always have a secret pocket in my skirt swag. Assuming the poison was carried in a vial or something equally small, there was ample time to toss the evidence afterward, and Reverend Olsen ate the rest."

They turned to me with morbid interest.

"Even if I had done it," I said, "which I did not, you need a witness. There were simply too many people around that *krumkake*. Someone must have noticed something."

"You were alone in the pantry with it." Pearl's tone was not comforting.

I felt a headache coming on.

"And you came running in after," she said, "and nearly fell on me. You were hysterical, Mrs. Kelly."

"That rather points to my innocence."

She glanced at the detective. "The screams didn't happen until after."

"What's in your secret pocket?" he asked wearily.

"I cannot believe this." I set my cup down. "I'm wearing my work clothing, detective. The only pockets allowed are in my apron, and I gave that to Pearl."

Pearl shook her head at his quick glance.

"Do you keep a bag or locker while you work?"

I gave a short, incredulous laugh. "I live here, remember? I don't carry anything but the key to our apartment." Extending an arm, I unbuttoned the shirtwaist sleeve at the cuff, and let the key slip out into my palm.

Detective Fisher was suitably impressed.

"You see?" I asked, replacing the key. "There are ways."

"Thank you," Detective Fisher said to Pearl. "I'm afraid I

don't have anything for you yet."

Pearl left, nearly vibrating with repressed emotion.

"She doesn't believe me," I said, dejected by the thought.

"She needs her job."

Detective Fisher poured himself another cup of coffee, then picked up a notebook and pencil. There were dark smudges beneath his eyes and stubble across his cheeks. His hair was as messy as my own. I wrapped my hands around the hot cup and leaned back in the seat, wondering how much time I had before being offered as scapegoat.

"I would like you to tell me what you did today," he began, the pencil moving over the paper. "Every detail. I need to understand what Pearl witnessed. And what the diners said."

"And in exchange, you can help me understand what they said." I adjusted my shawl. "For example, why did someone talk about a dagger?"

"A what?"

"I heard him. He said something about a dagger. And improvising. I can't tell you who it was because it stopped me in my tracks. I didn't go in with the *krumkake*."

"They said a black waiter delivered it."

"I asked him to."

"Because you were afraid of a dagger?"

"No. Because I recognized one of the voices."

He sighed. "You just said you didn't know who said what."

"I don't. But hearing Reverend Olsen's voice … well. Wild horses couldn't have dragged me in there."

"That's something else I don't understand," he said. "Why you? They had the same meals served all over the hotel last night, including the desserts. But he asked for the pastry chef. What was so special about your cookies?"

"Aunt Mary."

"Beg your pardon?"

"It's one of her recipes. The *brune pinner*. He would have known it."

"Explain."

"The gingerbread is a specialty. She made it with ... well, it is unique. And the sugar crystals on top are handmade."

"Your aunt is deceased. You told me so. Did he think she made them?"

"He couldn't have. They must have reminded him of her, though. Of home at the very least."

"Did these people have any idea that you worked in the kitchen?"

"I sincerely doubt it. I left in June and no one, not even my brother Peter, who drove me to the train station, knew where I was going."

"Your family doesn't know where you are? You weren't in contact over the holidays?"

I hadn't written home. Absolutely not at Christmas. They did not even have my current address. I shook my head and drank my coffee.

He pondered that for a moment, then asked, "And did you know they'd arrived here two days ago? See them in the lobby or know they were in the private dining room?"

I shook my head again. "Unbelievable. What are they

doing here? And I don't believe for a moment that they have anything to do with the theater. The reverend's dearest lecture was against the sins of the flesh and the vanities of youth. No drinking, dancing, or trimming of the beard. And certainly, no painted ladies."

"According to Madame Fabbri, Reverend Olsen was about to become a patron of her theater."

"Not in a million years."

"It seems he has—had—quite a large sum at his disposal."

I closed my eyes. Aunt Mary standing on the porch in her coat and mitts.

"It's the ledger," she'd said. *"It doesn't make sense."*

"None of this makes sense," I said. "Mr. Nilsen is in a tuxedo. Who is he to put on airs? He was the church handyman. How can they afford to stay in the most expensive hotel in San Francisco?"

"Obviously, there's been some changes since you left."

"Six months? I can't think them capable."

"Let me tell you what I do know, and then you might think so. The newly widowed Mrs. Olsen—"

"She's his wife?" I interrupted. "I knew it! Half his age if a day. That alone is a scandal he'd never live down." I inhaled sharply. "That must be why they left. What if no one at home knows about the marriage? What if he ran off in shame?"

"But—"

"And then, after taking advantage of the reverend and forcing him to wander the earth in exile, the woman decided to murder him and take the money for herself."

"Mrs. Kelly, I must stop you there. Do you know her? Have you met before?"

"No. It must have happened after I left."

"So it seems. Mrs. Olsen has offered a large sum for the capture of the person responsible for the death of her husband."

"The money?"

He nodded slowly. "It could be the money set aside for Madame Fabbri."

"But where did it come from?"

"I'm afraid the bigger question on the fourth floor is where it will go." He consulted his notebook. "Mrs. Berg is demanding both they and the money return to Minnesota forthwith. Apparently, she is homesick."

"She can't stand not being the center of attention," I muttered.

"And the son, Mr. Olsen, who should by rights inherit everything, including any funds, has declared freedom from the clergy, his family, and his hometown and intends to lead a merry life as far away as he can possibly get from Minnesota." He gave me a speculative look. "Not the first person to do so, it seems."

"He's been gone for the last few years. Away to school and then learning a vocation, we were told. They weren't close." My coffee was cold. "I wonder when he came home? I wonder why?"

"He said—"

"Oh!" He jumped as I put down my cup. "What's to say

he didn't do in his own father?"

"Mrs. Kelly, I really am too weary for wild speculation. Please stick with the facts. I'm not certain we've exchanged any so far."

"And Mr. Nilsen. Has he come to covet things beyond his reach? What would he do to get rich?"

Detective Fisher stood up and I wrapped the shawl up under my chin.

"The police department could use the funds," he said. "You've seen the inside of our jail cells. We have convicts escape three or four times a year. The whole place is falling apart. A sum of money the size Mrs. Olsen offered would put some respect back into the place."

I blinked up at him. "You wouldn't."

"Give me someone better than you to arrest."

My headache intensified and my heart grew heavy with emotions with no names. "It's not the waiter," I said. "He had no way of knowing ahead of time that I would ask him to deliver the dish. I chose him randomly. So that's one person off your list."

"Thank you." His sarcasm was unbecoming.

I was irrationally annoyed that Pearl had been able to find the detective like a needle in a haystack last night.

"You arrived quickly," I said. "What were you doing here?"

"Enjoying the party like everyone else." He glanced at the officer in the doorway. "It hasn't stopped yet."

"With Heyes?"

"What? No."

I waited, but no further details presented. "Did you notice his shoes?"

"Heyes wasn't in uniform, Mrs. Kelly. He wasn't on duty."

"Not Heyes. The son. The new Mr. Olsen. Where was he all that time when his father died? He'd been drinking, that much was obvious. His clothes were a mess. Any number of reasons for that. But his shoes…"

"Yes?"

"Were untied."

"And?"

"The man had recently disrobed. I think you should inquire on the top floor."

His face reddened and he searched for the right words. "Lina?"

The top floor suites were, of course, some of the hotel's finest and home to more than one elite *paramour*. If Josiah Olsen had sniffed one out within two days of arriving and had the pocket money to knock on the door, then we had some questions.

Detective Fisher cleared his throat and sat down again. "I pulled this from his breast pocket." He opened his hand and showed me an earring. A gleaming blue pendant hung from a small diamond and glowed in his palm.

"I don't understand." I looked closer. "Lina's?"

"Maybe." He clearly expected something more from me. "You don't recognize it?"

A suffocating fog descended and chilled me despite the shawl as he reached out with his other hand and touched the earring dangling in my ear. I froze as it swayed.

"I wondered at first if it might be yours," he said. "But I see you have both. It's almost an identical match. Your theory stands up, then, if the man is carrying around personal female property." He leaned back again and slipped it into his pocket. "Did he take it from her room?" he mused. "Or was it a gift meant for her?"

I still didn't understand.

"I'm glad it isn't yours." This time when he ran his hand through his hair, it stood on end. "It would have tied you to this group in ways I didn't want to think about."

"You weren't going to show it to me, were you?" With every passing minute, the distance between us grew.

"No. But I'm going to do something different this time."

"This time?"

"We don't have the luxury of time, Mrs. Kelly. I might regret it later. But I've decided you're innocent. If only to narrow down my list. I've decided to believe you. This time, we work together."

I should have been ecstatic. But all I felt was dread.

That earring tied me to the group in ways I never wanted to think about ever again.

What had Aunt Mary gotten herself into?

Chapter Six

M Y STOMACH REJECTED the idea of more coffee, but I didn't know what to do with my hands. It was inconceivable that an earring exactly matching mine had been found in the pocket of Reverend Olsen's long-lost son. The same Reverend Olsen that Aunt Mary volunteered with for years. Even with sizeable gaps of time and space between these three people, together they formed a bridge.

I dismissed the idea that it had come from Lina's opulent upstairs suite. Folding my hands in my lap, I asked, "There's only one?"

"Yes." Detective Fisher's sharp mind was obviously turning over ideas, but the way he looked at me said I played a large role in them. "I didn't find a second one. It may have accidentally fallen in there. Or he dropped the other one."

"From the inside pocket of a dinner jacket?"

"What are you getting at, Mrs. Kelly?"

"He has been gone a long while. No one, not even his family, could truly know him. You say he intends to take his inheritance and be gone."

His pencil tapped on the notebook as he sat in thought.

"When he is sober," I said, "ask him where the other earring went."

"I have a long list of questions." Abruptly, Detective Fisher put the notebook into his pocket and faced me, his knee coming perilously close to mine. "Let's try this," he said. "For a moment, we are simply colleagues discussing a murder case."

"Colleagues?"

"You are currently out of a job," he said with no remorse whatsoever.

"When we first met, you told me one of your mottos. Do you recall?"

One eye narrowed at me.

"Keep your friends close and your enemies closer," I quoted. "How do I know you aren't planning to use me and then walk away once someone is in prison, or you've lost interest in an unsolvable case?"

"You don't."

"What if I don't get my job back?"

"I thought your aunt left you a sizable inheritance?"

The punch to my gut was so hard, I wondered that I hadn't cried out.

Oh, dear God. Where had all that money come from?

But he didn't ask.

"I need your help," he said earnestly. "At this point, you know more than I do. You possess an uncanny amount of background information that may lead to the discovery of the killer." He leaned back. "It's your personal vendetta that I'm worried about. I can't tell whether you are going to offer me facts or feelings."

"Why don't we begin with both?" I said tartly. "I am happy that he's dead."

"Mrs. Kelly."

"I'm surprised he succumbed to poison, actually. He was the type to consider himself immortal. Or at the very least, indispensable."

"You are not making this easy."

"Detective Fisher, if one of our staff wanted to murder a guest, he would never do it at the expense of his job. There are alleys for that. Unless they have a personal tie to the victim, none of the employees, including myself, have a reason to do something so public and foolish."

"Agreed. We'll focus on the table of suspects. Seven in all."

"And I don't think for a moment that the Reverend and his entourage somehow found out where I am and dropped a very good life in Minnesota to come all the way out here and try to frame me for murder."

"No."

"But I do think someone at the table did it, hoping to pin the blame on the hotel. Especially since it appears the reverend conveniently turned everyone's attention in that direction."

My words came faster and faster, and it was impossible to tell whether I was trying to divert him from the elephants in the room or exploiting the opportunity to tell him what I thought before he shut me down and turned me out again.

"It was premeditated," I said. "Someone already had the poison in hand. Brought it to the dinner party. Waited for the perfect opportunity and the reverend gave it to them when he fussed over the dessert."

"But who do you think hated Reverend Olsen enough to murder him?" he interrupted. "Everyone seemed upset by his death."

"Have you ever heard of crocodile tears?" I sighed. "In truth, no one. The citizens of Waterford Township, Minnesota, are faithful to a man. Believe me when I tell you they don't tolerate anything bad spoken about their dear pastor. He's led the flock for two generations."

"Then maybe it was someone from the theater."

"Would they kill the golden goose?"

He nodded grimly. "I see your point."

"They had no idea I was here. None of them, actually. That's an advantage."

"It was." He stood and smoothed at his wrinkled jacket. "But now that you have thoroughly exposed yourself, perhaps you will remain in the background where you won't antagonize them to the point they won't speak to me."

"I knew it." I stood and threw my shawl onto the seat. "You can't stop me from investigating. I have everything at stake."

The officer in the doorway turned around and watched us.

"We have established otherwise, Mrs. Kelly. And I need them cooperative, or I won't get anywhere."

"What am I supposed to do, then?"

"Stay away from them. Once I've questioned everyone, you can tell me what you think. Your insight is the key to finding the killer. I'm certain of it."

"Flattering. That sounds like doing things the hard way. Let me stand in the room and listen. They wouldn't dare lie with me staring them in the face."

He raised an eyebrow and crossed his arms. "Why do I feel like this is something you've done before? With them?"

I paused to collect myself. With a perfectly calm voice, I said, "I can't tell you."

"Your past is your business," he said, "but if it has anything to do with the present..."

"I don't see how it could. Their choice of hotel was perfectly random."

"In that case, you'll have to respect me enough to cooperate. Let me do the work up front and help me sort it all out when I'm done. At the moment, what they do not know is your relationship with me. Hopefully, I made it perfectly clear that you are a main suspect. At the very least, fired from your position and in my bad graces."

"That's good?" I crossed my arms to match his.

"It will make the killer complacent. Think he got away with it. Slip up and drop a clue."

"Am I supposed to stay home and knit, then?"

A smile crept into the corner of his rough cheek. "How about this? What if you attend the theater tonight?"

"Are you talking about the California Theater?"

"The very same. I can get you a ticket and an introduction to Madame Fabbri's inner circle. Perhaps you can discover something that will help the case."

"They weren't even at the table when it happened."

"Mr. Sims was. Find out why they were discussing a dagger."

"You remembered."

He patted the notebook in his breast pocket. "Everything you say is in here."

"Everything?"

He smiled at the apprehension on my face. "I'm going to let the hotel know that we don't hold anyone on their staff accountable for what happened. And tell Heyes to go home and get some rest."

"Do you think it will be enough to save their jobs?"

"If I promise the culprit will be caught soon."

"That's a big promise. What if you can't keep it?"

"I can't fail. I've got you." He held out his hand. "Colleagues?"

His confidence was unnerving. He was right, though. He had me right where he wanted me.

I gave him my hand, and he gave it a gentlemanly shake.

"Try to get some rest today," he said, moving toward the doorway. "I'll send your ticket around later."

"Send two," I said, collecting my shawl.

He paused and turned. "Two?"

"It's Becky's day off."

He nodded and left, taking the officer with him. I only gave the coffee service a glance before leaving it behind. Pearl was upset with me, and I decided to steer clear of the kitchen until we had answers.

I snorted, still in disbelief at her reaction, and stepped into the Grand Courtyard. Now well into the morning, guests strolled the warm hotel arm-in-arm between giant potted palms or sat in little cafe chairs sipping espresso. Although bunting still draped from balconies, all traces of last night's gala had been cleared away and I couldn't find so much as a single flower petal on the ground.

The dining rooms were closed and the ballroom silent. No carriages circled in the drive. At the other end of the front promenade, an elevator rose like a suspended gilt cage with two women twittering inside. All was serenity in the Palace Hotel, oblivious to the winter rolling past her windows. I imagined most of the guests had not yet risen from their feather beds.

There was no sign of Detective Fisher.

The crisply uniformed doorman was too well trained to show surprise at my appearance or the utterly inappropriate wrap around my shoulders. He opened the door for me and stood at attention as the wind whipped at my loose hair and slapped my skirt against my ankles. Thoroughly awake now, I moved briskly down the walkway on Montgomery Street, trying to outpace the cold.

My only advantage was disappearing with every passing hour. There was never a chance Mrs. Berg or Mr. Nilsen would have allowed me to question them about Reverend Olsen's death. They'd already had enough of that last spring.

But the new widow Olsen hadn't. She'd never met me. And unless I hurried, they'd turn her against me, too.

I needed to find out what had happened after I'd run away from home.

Hurrying around the corner onto the narrower Jessie

Street cut some of the wind, but I was fast going numb in my feet and fingers. It was welcome. San Francisco had embraced me from the moment I'd arrived, with balmy days and foggy evenings. I'd basked in the temperate weather, looking forward to the year-round luxury.

What was I doing hiding indoors from a little cold?

I should have smelled the snow coming.

San Francisco was a city full of surprises. Corrupt lawmen, violent socialites, or extravagant bordellos, the city offered a wondrous display of eccentric and unexpected humanity. Neighborhoods were made up like one of Aunt Mary's patchwork quilts, each with its own block of skin tones and colorful layers of clothing, meals, and languages. You knew exactly which sidewalks made up the seams.

And, while crime was rampant in the shadows of this place I now called home, and men killed each other every day, I'd been promised its weather could not. Head high, the tears on my cheeks dried as they formed.

I sidestepped a slushy puddle and turned onto Annie Street. Nearly an alley, yet easily passable for the delivery wagons and guest carriages that pulled into the underground entry beneath the hotel block, it mercifully buffered the wind. The basement embraced me in scents of home. Hay and manure from the stables mingled with oil and grease from the hydraulics in the bowels of the building and sawdust and lumber from the innumerable goods and produce that filled underground pantries.

The wind vanished altogether and the cold eased by a degree or two, but I moved through the unusually quiet space with determined strides until I reached the door leading to the apartment. It took three tries before I could release my cuff and slip the key into the lock with my shaking fingers.

Locking the door behind me, I ignored the interior door that led to Becky's glove shop and climbed the tiny staircase. I hadn't reached the landing before hearing Becky's relieved voice crying, "There you are! I've worn a path in the rug, pacing!"

She dropped a newspaper onto the chair as she jumped up to greet me. The gray tabby tumbled from her lap and slunk beneath the table in reproof. I gave her a brief and uncharacteristic hug that made her blink.

I still had Becky. But I would have to fight to keep Pearl, and fast.

"Why, you're frozen! Were you outside? Dressed like that?" She took the shawl from me. "Get those shoes off and your slippers on. I'll pour you some tea and bring the quilt out."

She hung the shawl on the hat tree, and I went directly to the *Chronicle* and picked it up.

"Karine, don't!"

"I'm in a hurry, Becky. I need to know what they're saying before I go out again."

She went to the kettle. "You have no business that can't wait. Let's get you warm and rested. I couldn't believe the nerve of Detective Fisher when he rapped on the door. It wasn't even dawn! And him saying you'd been up all night and had still more to do before I should expect you." She poured boiling water into a teapot.

I rubbed a hand over my eyes and forced them to focus on the tiny print. "I see the snow made the front page," I said, skimming over the columns.

"It's a great shot," she said, bringing cups to the table. "I guess there was just enough for sledding on the hills. Shame it didn't last long."

It was beneath the fold. "New Year at Palace Hotel Rings in Tragedy," I read. "The Palace Hotel's grand New Year's Eve gala, a glittering spectacle of San Francisco's finest, took a dark and tragic turn at the stroke of midnight. Amidst the splendor of satin gowns and lively waltzes, whispers of unease rippled through the crowd as word spread of an untimely death discovered in one of the hotel's private dining rooms. The victim, whose identity is yet to be confirmed, was found under mysterious circumstances, prompting the immediate presence of the city police. Guests carried on with dancing and dining, as officers discreetly questioned hotel staff and certain attendees, in defiance of an air of unease that could not take away from the joyous welcome of 1883..." I turned a page. "It goes on to describe the party. That was all they said about it?"

Becky draped a quilt over my shoulders. "Was it terrible? Detective Fisher refused to tell me what happened."

"He must have done a great job with the reporters, too." I handed her the paper and laid the quilt on my chair. "Obviously the staff are taking the details to their grave if it means their job."

"You're here now," she said, resuming her seat. "Sit

down and tell me. Why did you have to stay?"

I'd already gone into my room. "I have to change into something dry and dark," I said through the open door. "Something proper and somber. I'm going up to call on the widow."

"What widow?"

It was a small comfort to step into clean, fresh clothes, but the fancy corset was no friend of mine.

"She was married to the man who died last night."

"Why are you intruding? Will she receive you? Oh, dear, do you know her?"

Why did dresses have so many little buttons?

"I knew the murdered man. He's from my hometown in Minnesota. A reverend in the church there."

There was a long pause while I finished adjusting a dry pair of stockings. "Murdered?"

"For all I know, the widow killed him."

She gasped and the room was silent while I buttoned my shoes.

"Mrs. Kelly. What are you going to do?"

I pulled out a hairpin. "Help me with my hair, will you?"

Chapter Seven

M Y CHEEKS WERE still pink from the scrubbing I'd given them, I was lightly scented with rose water, and I carried a fresh lace handkerchief. If we were back in Township County, I'd have a casserole in my hands.

Regardless of which floor one chose, rooms along the west corridor overlooked Jessie Street, perpetually in shadow, and the stark wall of the tall building on the other side. In contrast, interior rooms were larger and had the Grand Courtyard balconies to enjoy. Although care was taken to furnish them as sumptuously as any other rooms, the feeling of being tucked away and turning inward to ponder one's own company reduced the rate by a fraction.

I was not surprised to find a row of rooms trimmed with discrete black grosgrain ribbon there.

Short, narrow halls branched from the main corridor and led to two different room doors. If guests had a single room, this was their only way in and out. Larger parties who wanted to share interior doors and combine two rooms could do so, but anything more, involved moving through the exterior halls, which was almost never done.

I paused in the corridor, trying to decide which rooms

were whose. If they'd paired off two by two, then logic dictated the son would share a room door with his parents in one hall, and Mrs. Berg and Mr. Nilsen would take the other hall with rooms of their own.

The hour was fast approaching noon and, though I was weak with weariness, I hoped the party had all gone to their own rooms to sleep, otherwise it was likely I would find them all together again.

It was all or nothing if I rapped on a door. Had Pearl been speaking to me, she could have saved me the angst.

When a door opened, I startled and moved quickly out of view, praying it was no one who would recognize me. I was torn. If I ran down the corridor, I was safe, but if I stayed close enough, I might hear who was inside.

"Yes, ma'am, sorry ma'am." A maid exited the hall backwards, bobbing to whoever stood at the end. Holding two large pillows in her arms, she said, "I'll bring them directly, ma'am."

"We paid an unconscionable amount for these rooms." Mrs. Berg's voice carried all the way into the corridor. "Why would you have lumpy pillows?"

"Yes, ma'am. That is, no, ma'am." The harassed maid spared me a glance.

"Don't bring them for an hour. I'm going to sleep if I can and whatever you do, careless girl, don't disturb that door, either. We are in mourning."

The maid bobbed again as the door slammed.

"The other door," I asked. "Is that the widow's room?"

She looked me over and nodded miserably. "I'm supposed to deliver coffee, but don't know how I'm supposed to do it now. Can't anyone make up their minds around here?"

"I'll take it in." I assumed an air of authority and empathy. "She's expecting me. Bring two cups, please."

The maid scurried away, and I wandered down the hall, taking note of the room numbers, then turned the corner and made a loop along the Grand Court balcony. No orchestra filled the hotel with music today, but the view was pleasant.

Until I noticed Detective Fisher speaking with Heyes in the courtyard. Peering around a column and over the balustrade, I caught Heyes's nod and watched him leave through the main entrance. Detective Fisher looked up and nearly saw me. When I peeked around the column again, he'd vanished beneath my balcony. A minute later, I heard his low voice and the elevator doors close.

I looked up and down the corridor, frantically debating. Where was he headed? Did I want to be caught in the one place he didn't want me?

As the elevator rose, I moved along the corridor and peered around the corner. The back of Detective Fisher's dark suit showed through the open latticework door. The cage continued its stately ascent, and I counted floors until it reached the top of the building.

He was paying Lina a visit. Perfect.

I met the maid at the top of the staff staircase and took the coffee tray from her grateful hands. Treading softly, I balanced the tray with a hip and put my hand out to knock. Thinking better of it, I lowered it and tried the knob. When it turned, I smiled and let myself in.

The room was dark, and it took a moment for my eyes to adjust. The drapes were drawn and lamplight glowed from the adjacent bedroom doorway behind me, casting the parlor room into soft shadows. I shifted a vase of flowers aside and set the tray on the low central table, mingling the rich aromas of coffee and roses.

A prostrate form on the sofa shifted and a small voice said, "Thank you. Leave it on the table, please."

"Allow me to pour for you, Mrs. Olsen." I dragged an ottoman to the table and perched on it. "I'm terribly sorry for your loss."

Lying flat out with her light hair down and flowing to the carpet, the woman had only the corner of a blanket still over her, showing that she hadn't yet changed out of her party dress. If one could call it that. Nondescript in the pall of the room, I recalled it being a dull wine color but with no flounces or trim. A dress that would command attention back home but fade immediately into San Francisco's wallpaper.

"You are all so nice here," she said without moving, "with the coffee and the flowers. Eli said it would be posh, but he didn't prepare me for the kindness." She sniffled. "I've got a terrible headache and the powders I took aren't touching it at all."

I stirred in plenty of sugar and placed a cup in front of her. "Perhaps the coffee will help. Shall I bring you a pillow so you can sit up?"

"I can manage." She shifted and brought her stockinged

feet to the floor but winced and rubbed the back of her neck. "I must have dozed off."

"You've had a shock," I said. "I won't stay long, but allow me to be useful while I'm here. Do you have any questions for us?"

I tucked the handkerchief into my sleeve and sat ramrod straight. If she thought I was a maid, so be it. I had no problem representing the hotel if it meant I could get answers of my own.

"Yes." Sitting up seemed to hurt her. She stared at the cup and slowly picked it up. "Where is my husband?" The coffee sloshed in the cup and dripped into the saucer before she brought it to her lips.

"I believe he is in the morgue," I said. "But not for long." I hoped she hadn't noticed the second cup. Or my question. "What are your plans?"

"Send him home, of course. To his congregation. His people."

"Not yours?"

Her lips pressed together, then she said, "I cannot in all honesty say so. We are newly wed, the Reverend Olsen and I. This June." She wiped her cheek with the edge of the blanket. "My family are all in Maple Grove. Outside of Minneapolis." Her tears fell in earnest, and she set her cup down.

"I see," I said, fidgeting with the sugar bowl. "You'll return to them instead?"

She frowned and blinked. "No. Never! This is all their fault."

I held my breath and waited.

"Do you know what it's like to have a dream?" she asked, staring into her coffee. "To know from childhood what you were born to do? Your one true purpose? I have always known my destiny." She turned her eyes to mine. "I can sing. The good God gave me a voice, and I intend to use it."

She took up her cup and drained it.

"My parents called it a gift until they decided to call it a curse," she said. "I sang in the church my whole life, and then two years ago, I started getting offers for positions in the city. Singing jobs." She hung her head. "You can guess how far that went."

I had some very good guesses. "Your family must be very devout."

"It's the same music," she said with some heat. "The same voice. When did I go from saint to sinner?"

"You couldn't," I suggested, and poured her more coffee.

"I had offers of marriage too. None were good enough for Papa. This summer, he decided our family needed revival. We packed the wagon and toured through Minnesota."

"Your father is a preacher?"

She coughed into her hand and winced again as the cup wobbled. "Yes. And the only man good enough to marry me was going to be a preacher too. He met Eli in Waterford Township." Her voice wavered. "And they discussed me like a mule for sale. The next week, we held the wedding, and my family moved on without me. As far away from Minneapolis as they could dump me."

I was quickly adding two and two together. "Your husband—Reverend Olsen—he loved you, though?"

Through her tears, she said, "Yes. Yes, I believe he must have." She shook her head. "Once he heard me sing, he declared me an angel. He was incensed when I told him the truth about my family. God only knows what my papa told him, but when dear Eli knew my heart's desire, he decided then and there to make my dream come true. We came to San Francisco. My family would never find me here."

Her voice faded and she looked at me. "I don't know why I'm telling you all of this. It's just that no one understands what I've lost." She set her cup down and used the corner of the blanket to wipe her damp cheeks.

All things considered, it seemed she'd gained. If Reverend Olsen had married her on a whim and decided to leave hearth and home for the great and wild unknown to make a complete stranger's dream come true, I'd eat my hat. The poor woman had leapt from the fry pan into the fire and now the fire was out. She was a free woman.

With a hefty inheritance, possibly.

"I heard that you met Madame Fabbri." I tried to sound comforting, as if seeking to cheer her up, but it was dangerous, leading her like this. If she'd been in her proper state of mind, she'd have shown me the door for my impertinence.

"Delightful woman." She brushed the hair from her ravaged face. "Understood me immediately. Eli and I were going to be patrons of her theater."

"Have you seen it?"

Now her face softened. "No. Oh, I can't bear to think

we'll all go back again before I've even set foot inside."

"Perhaps you won't have to."

"I don't see how. Mrs. Berg would throw a fit, and you haven't seen a fit thrown until you've seen hers."

The hint of humor decided me.

"Mrs. Olsen, you've just lost your husband," I said gently. "You're bereft and so is Madame Fabbri, you see. You can't leave without telling her farewell, can you? It would be seen as quite rude. After all, it is within your rights to conclude your husband's business on his behalf."

"I hadn't thought about it like that."

"We can provide a carriage this evening, once you've rested, if you like. The hotel can secure tickets to tonight's performance, and you can speak with Madame Fabbri yourself."

"Tonight? Alone? No."

"A companion would accompany you, of course."

She thought it through. "I suppose I could ask Mr. Olsen," she murmured.

"But if not, a female companion is perfectly appropriate. The hotel can provide a chaperone."

"I'll want one even if he's going," she said. "Especially if he's going," she added.

I pondered the look on her face. "You have a staunch friend in Mrs. Berg," I suggested.

She shook her head fiercely and the blanket dropped to her lap. "She was adamant about not coming out here. She nearly changed his mind. I know the church is a tight-knit group, and Eli's been a pillar in the community his whole life, but I've never seen such a to-do. Actually," she said with a sudden thought, "they may…" She inhaled sharply. "They may blame me. Oh, I can't go back if they do, but he must be laid to rest in his own cemetery, mustn't he?"

"There now," I said, standing. "Don't upset yourself like this! They're good people, and I'm certain they loved Reverend Olsen."

Heavens above, I was standing up for the devil. What had come over me?

Her face grew frantic. "He's been poisoned, they say. Killed! It never would have happened if I hadn't persuaded him to come to such a sinful and wicked city. They'll say what Papa kept saying. That pride goes before a fall. And they'll say it was my pride that caused his fall. If we'd stayed in Minnesota, he'd be safe right now!"

"He certainly would." The voice behind me chilled the room.

"Oh," Mrs. Olsen said with a start, "Mrs. Berg. Come in. There's coffee."

"Edith, if I've told you once, I've said it a hundred times, you have no discretion. We mustn't share our troubles with the servants. You may go, miss, and not a word from your lips or I'll personally see that you lose your position."

I dipped a fast curtsy and, keeping my face well down, turned away from Mrs. Berg in silence to dash through the open door.

"One moment!" Mrs. Olsen called. "Send for Mr. Olsen, please. He's the next hall over. Thank you."

I reached for the door knob.

"I'm sorry, Martha," Mrs. Olsen said as I closed the door after me. "But they are all so kind here."

It was interesting that the two women shared a hall. That Mrs. Berg was a more welcome neighbor than the son, Mr. Olsen.

I marched down the corridor and stopped the first maid I found. "Follow me," I said. "This will only take a minute." Pointing to the second hall, I said, "Knock on these doors and find a Mr. Olsen. Tell him Mrs. Olsen in room 412 needs him immediately."

The implications were not lost on me as I gave the directions. Why had he come to mind as her chaperone to the theater instead of Mr. Nilsen, the one who handled the finances and could no doubt conclude the formal withdrawal of their partnership? But if Mr. Nilsen and Mrs. Berg had teamed up against the widow on religious grounds, it made sense that the worldly-wise son might be a more comfortable person to go with.

I removed myself some paces down the corridor while the maid knocked.

If what Mrs. Olsen had told me was true, and she still felt so starved for kindness six months after her marriage, the good reverend was back in my bad graces. He had not married her for love. He had not even given her kindness.

He did not upend his life and bring her here, no matter what proof of love that may have seemed to her.

Voices in the hall lured me closer, and a moment later, Mr. Olsen stepped out and went around to the ladies' doors. I arrived at the hall as the maid turned from a door, nodded at me, and left. This was his room, and it was currently empty.

I grinned to myself in recollection. No one locked a door in Minnesota.

More fool he.

Chapter Eight

M R. OLSEN'S ROOM had been done up in greens and dark wood, and a coal fire warmed the room from the fireplace grate. He could return at any moment. I had to be fast.

The drapes were tied back, allowing the gray midday sunlight to brighten the tidy room. The *Chronicle* lay open on the parlor table, on top of three other newspapers and a magazine. A half-empty bottle of scotch and a damp glass sat to one side. A quick look through the tiny desk revealed unused stationery and a thin diary containing several New York addresses that did not appear in any way connected to each other.

The entirety of the diary, however, was undecipherable. Dashes, curls, and dots filled pages with gibberish, even in his calendar. It had to be some form of communication. But why encode his personal notes?

I lingered a moment, recalling his mother, the Reverend Olsen's first wife, a sweet-faced and shy young woman who'd succumbed to measles. It could not have been easy, to be raised by a father who rained fire and brimstone at the slightest opportunity. Although every family, including mine, had helped nurture the child, Josiah Olsen had eventually rebelled and been sent away to school immediately thereafter.

He could be anyone and anything now.

I began with the bureau, moving as carefully as possible. A pair of gloves, Rowland's Macassar hair oil, tooth powder, soap tablets, and a comb were laid on top. A box with felt lining held a gold tie stickpin and three sets of cufflinks. The top drawer revealed neck ties, cuffs, and stiff collars. Cotton and linen shirts filled the next drawer, and the last held a set of long johns. I ran my hand along the sides, hoping to bump into the second earring.

A wet shaving cup and blade on the rail in the small lavatory suggested his latest activity and his wrinkled clothing from the party had been tossed into the bottom of the wardrobe. And Detective Fisher had already checked those.

Hangers displayed two jackets with trousers and matching waistcoats, and a fine cutaway coat with a cleaning ticket in one pocket. A heavy, knee-length topcoat with a fur collar hung to one side. A walking cane stood propped in the other corner next to a shined pair of laced brown shoes.

On the top wardrobe shelf, a silk top hat and a serviceable bowler sat beside his—presumably empty—suitcase.

There was no time to find out, and the small trunk at the foot of his bed was locked. A scattered handful of paper labels on its side proved him to be a traveler, at least along the East Coast.

Frustrated, I turned in place, taking in the room.

The bed was made up and I looked again at the sofa. The

pillows were well rumpled just now, which made sense if he were lounging with the paper, but had he slept there? Or had he allowed maid service and the morning to proceed like any other day? Men did not display grief in public the way a lady might, but I could not believe a man this functional to be entirely in mourning, despite his wails and tears of the night before.

I searched the entire room for the other earring. But had he? Had he even noticed the first one missing? If the second earring was here, he'd taken care to put it well away. And I doubted they had anything to do with Lina.

The thought sent me to the door, wondering if the seed I'd sown with Mrs. Olsen had taken root and I would have the unbelievable luck to have both to myself this evening. The Reverend's San Francisco murder had roots in Minnesota, and though I could trace them too well, only these two newcomers could tell me what I'd missed. Would it help me to share the parts of the story I knew, or would it alienate them as much as it had everyone else?

I'd opened the door several inches when Detective Fisher said, "I have a few questions for you."

Freezing in place, I watched the back of his suit step through the door on the other side of the hall.

"Yes, sir." Mr. Nilsen's deep voice rang with memories.

He'd used the differential phrase with Reverend Olsen, meek and mild and eager to be of use. The handyman for years, he'd roofed the church more than once, repaired graves in the cemetery, painted walls, and varnished pews. And suddenly, he wasn't. He was Reverend Olsen's secretary.

He'd taken Aunt Mary's job.

I let myself out of the room and made certain the door was properly closed, then hurried through the fourth-floor corridor and down the grand staircase.

This time, when I presented myself in the apartment, Becky was ready for me.

"I've got the kettle on," she said, leaping up, "and you are going to bed if I have to lock you in your room."

"Yes, mother hen." I dropped into my chair. "I'm afraid you win this time. I need to lie down."

"This is the longest day off I've ever had," she said, bustling about me. "You told me just enough to tease. What's this about being partners with Detective Fisher? And you knew the murdered man?" She clapped a cup onto the counter and the teapot rattled. "At least you aren't mixed up in the suspect list."

I cleared my throat and settled deeper into my chair. Spoon wrapped himself around my ankles.

"You know I don't drink tea, Becky."

She ignored me and dropped her quilt on my lap. "Did she see you, then? The widow? Oh, you must tell me what happened."

"Becky, I have more questions than answers now." I glanced out the window. Gray was dismal, but ever so much better than white. "Yes, she saw me, but she didn't know it was me." Where to begin? "Have I told you about my Aunt Mary?"

She nodded and perched on her chair. "You told me she cared for you, and you loved her. She died before you left to come here. Wish I'd met her."

"She named me as her only heir. I inherited a great deal of money from her."

"Right." Spoon leapt into her lap, and she gave his ears a rub. "And you didn't find out until you were here, so you stayed." She smiled. "I, for one, am terribly glad you did."

The kettle whistled and she rose.

"I knew that she and her husband had acres to the east," I said. "A farm of their own before I was ever born. When she became a widow, she didn't have the heart to keep it up and sold it and came to live with us. I was already a young lady raising eight wild brothers, but she wrapped around us like a silver picture frame."

"Don't cry over spilled milk," Aunt Mary said.

"I'm not crying," I said with a sniff and fished in my pockets for a handkerchief.

"Oh, Karine," Becky said, pausing to pat my shoulder. "You all were the children she never had. Of course you miss her."

I fumbled in my sleeve and came up empty. "So, naturally, I assumed the money she left me came from the sale of her farm."

"Your dairy farm was very prosperous, you told me." Becky came around and offered me a cup and saucer. "But this came from her personal money?"

Becky was good with numbers. Her skills kept her shop running well and discussing finances, while an unladylike faux pas in higher social circles, was one of her keen interests.

"Yes. The dairy farm profits had to remain with the

family, of course. I'd never have taken a dime of it with me. I had enough to take the train west and my new husband was going to care for me after that." I checked my other sleeve, leaving Becky standing with the cup. "She knew all of this. I can't imagine she thought I'd need a pile of money from her."

"She loved you." The statement was simple and profound.

"She argued with me." I meekly accepted the tea. "She was the only one I told about my plans to leave. To be a mail-order bride. And she couldn't see any sense in it." I blinked up at her. "She died a year ago. During a blizzard. And no one believed me when I suspected murder."

Becky stood rooted to the floor. "What?"

"I think she was killed, Becky. I still do. But no one listened to me because…"

She waited.

"Because," I said, "I blamed the church for it. I think the reverend knew what happened to her and refused to confess. Whether he did it or he was protecting the one who did, he's every bit as guilty."

"Oh, my."

"And he is the man who died downstairs last night."

She fell into her chair. "Oh, Mrs. Kelly!"

"And this time, he was murdered without a doubt. Poisoned. And Detective Fisher knows I know the people and wants me to tell him as much as I can, but…"

"What a horrible thing to go through!"

"Six months I spent trying to get to the bottom of it.

The police said she was caught in an unexpected storm and froze to death. Becky, when you've lived in a place all your life, you know when it's going to snow. You know how far you can travel, and common sense keeps you alive. She would never have been so foolish."

"I believe you."

I gave her a thin smile. "You are the only one who does. The congregation began to shun me. A word against the clergy is a slander against God, I guess. I was chastised for unladylike behavior and accused of being obsessed about bringing shame on the church. Reverend Olsen threatened to excommunicate me. Then, finally, one day in May, I told Peter I was leaving."

"Your brother?"

I nodded. "He likely was glad to see me go, at the end of it. He was shocked to hear I'd been planning all along to go west and marry, but it paled next to his shock at the way I pursued justice for Aunt Mary."

"He only wanted me to rest in peace," she whispered.

"So do I," I said.

Becky looked at me uncertainly.

"After she died, I considered staying. Honoring her last wish for me. But by then, home was no longer home. It was a chance to start over. I never told a soul where I was going or why, unless Peter told after I was gone. I'd like to think he kept my confidence."

She shook her head. "He must have told. Why else would that reverend come here?"

"Peter doesn't know which city." I shrugged. "The theater people said he was here on their account, and the widow corroborated it. They had no idea I was here."

"If it's nothing to do with Aunt Mary, then why was he murdered?"

"I'm trying to find out. His secretary, his son, his wife, and her companion are all staying in the hotel on the fourth floor."

"Goodness! You went up there! Right up to the lion's den! What did they say?"

I yawned in her face and didn't have the will to cover it. "So far, the two who already know me aren't speaking to me and the two who don't … still don't know who I am. I rather like it that way."

"You're frightened. I don't blame you. Can I ask you something?"

I drank down half the cup in one go and nodded.

"Why did you blame the reverend for Aunt Mary's death?"

"She volunteered for him. She was his secretary for two years and the closer it got to Christmas last year, the stranger she behaved. She was gone more than usual, worked odd hours, and grew very distracted. I thought it had to do with my wedding. Then I wondered if she had some secret or other planned for the holiday. But after she died, I was certain it had to do with the church. She mentioned the ledgers once. I never forgot it."

"If there were nefarious doings at the church, it must have followed these people out here and they had it coming." She squinted at me. "But there's something else worrying you, isn't there?"

The tea was cold, and I pushed the nasty brew away. "I'm not certain where the money came from. The money I inherited."

"You said she sold her farm."

"Ages ago. And I never inquired. Why would I? But…"

"You don't think it was hers?"

"What if she … it's impossible, but was she somehow involved with a scandal?"

"Now, Mrs. Kelly, you know better than that."

"We have sewing bees and church suppers and quilt raffles. Collections were taken for a belfry and a bell," I said. "And it was supposed to be built in time to ring in the New Year. It was one of her pet projects, but it never happened. I forgot about it until today. If the belfry wasn't built, where did the money go?"

"Why does it matter now?" Becky rose and took my cup. "It's all behind you. You're exhausted and distraught. Go to bed and sleep. You poor thing."

"He all but came out and said so." I felt utterly bleak. "Reverend Olsen said she'd been punished for her sins and had the audacity to forgive them and deliver her straight to the pearly gates at her funeral."

"I've never attended a funeral, but I doubt a preacher is supposed to send folks any other direction."

"Becky, something very strange is going on, and I'm going to find out what it is. It didn't end with Aunt Mary."

She shook her head. "Please, Mrs. Kelly. I don't see any reason for it, only more heartbreak for you."

"That's what Peter kept saying."

"Then why are you doing it?"

"The earrings."

She glanced at the beautiful jewels in my ears.

"A week before Christmas, Aunt Mary put a gift under the tree for me. She died two days later."

"Oh! That's what you had against celebrating with me!" She slumped against the wall.

"And I did not open it until weeks later, when I thought I could bear it. These earrings were in the box." I gently put a finger to one. "I did not have pierced ears. The only thing that made sense to me was that she had reconsidered her arguments about my marriage and wanted me to have something lovely to remember her by after I left."

"They are what a fine city lady would wear," she said with approval.

"Exactly. No one in Minnesota pierces her ears. It's prideful and wasteful and several other impractical considerations. These earrings were her way of giving her blessing on my dream."

She hesitated. "But you don't think so now?"

"Last night, Detective Fisher pulled an earring out of Reverend Olsen's son's jacket pocket. It is an identical match to mine."

We sat in uncomfortable silence, and my eyes closed.

Where did the money come from, Aunt Mary? And how did you get your hands on earrings like this in isolated Waterford Township in deep winter?

There was no answer.

And more to the immediate moment, my handkerchief was gone.

Chapter Nine

B ECKY WASN'T THE least bit pleased about my relentless pursuit of justice or the fact that I'd gone right back out again. Several hours of sleep had done wonders for my spirits, however, and the envelope that waited for me on the side table when I woke gave me the first spot of hope I'd had in months. Two tickets to the evening performance.

Dressing in a modest dove gray gown was a far cry from the fancy blue-violet gown and new hat trimmed in peacock feathers I wished to wear, but traveling with those in mourning required tact and sympathy. In the guise of an impartial hotel employee, I planned to blend into the shadows and learn what I could.

Becky would never have guessed I was on my way to the theater. And I didn't tell her.

Mrs. Olsen's dress was so severely plain and black that I was convinced she'd borrowed it from Mrs. Berg. Mr. Olsen had been pressed into accompanying her and his black suit was at least tailored and crisp. The two were not currently speaking to one another. The three of us swayed in a rocking carriage as it made its way over the cobbled streets to 414 Bush Street and the California Theater.

Detective Fisher had secured front row seats, but I attributed my growing excitement to the fact that I would soon have five of the seven suspects close at hand. There was also some small smugness involved that I studiously ignored and held my tongue, content to observe my fellow passengers.

The widow Olsen kept her eyes on her hands in her lap and said, "Mr. Olsen. Can you give me any idea of whether Mr. Nilsen did or did not, in fact, sign the paperwork?"

Mr. Olsen continued his vigilant staring out the window, even though he couldn't see much between gas street lamps. "Again, Mrs. Olsen," he said, "I am not privy to your late husband's financial records. Mr. Nilsen is not forthcoming. Six months was not time enough to secure anyone's trust, although you know how hard I worked at it."

She pressed her lips together for the rest of the short drive. Turning right at Lotta's Fountain, Kearny Street took a mere three blocks before a quick right onto Bush placed us in a line of carriages moving slowly up to the theater.

Three stories tall, the building was in the Corinthian style, with columns and glowing arched windows. Richly dressed ladies and dapper gentlemen strolled the sidewalk and disappeared inside. I tried to place a finger on the opinion I formed. While it was as equally and impressively welcoming as the Palace Hotel, the theater was a bit turned down in the heel when one looked beyond the face.

Its false front was only noticed when searching around the corner into its alleys. The Palace maintained its grandeur on all four sides of a city block. The Theater, squatting between two disparate buildings in the middle of the block, seemed to give one a wink and remind them that they weren't here to stay, and that was the point. No one was supposed to look in the alleys, beneath the makeup, or behind the scenery and spoil the fun. Leaving their luggage behind, its guests were meant to wander into another world entirely, if only for an hour or two.

By the time the carriage door opened and I was handed out by the valet, I'd made up my mind. I was quite happy to pretend the Palace and its murder, the past or the present, did not exist. I passed between a pair of street lamps and waited next to a column at the open front doors.

Mrs. Olsen came next, and she stood aside as her stepson exited the vehicle. He offered his arm as the carriage rolled away and she took it with ill-concealed dismay, leaving me to follow meekly behind them into the theater.

They made a handsome couple, I thought, if her face hadn't been so ravaged by emotion and his clouded by dark thoughts I was determined to uncover. Once in the brightly lit front vestibule full of theatergoers, they gave their tickets to the collector and coats to the coat check. A discreet sign pointed up a broad, sweeping staircase to the dress circle seats and the boxes. Another pointed down to a saloon and the toilet rooms below.

"Miss?" The ticket collector held out a gloved hand.

"I'm sorry, no." I shook my head as Mr. Olsen turned and he froze, stunned.

He'd seen my earrings, as I'd waited for him to do. Casting my eyes down to conceal my glee, I said, "I'll wait for them here, sir."

Deserting Mrs. Olsen, he approached with an affable smile and said, "I say, Miss…"

"Mrs. Kelly." Our eyes locked.

"Mrs. Kelly." He turned to the ticket man. "She's with us, sir. I'll gladly purchase her ticket."

The collector was not amused. Dryly, he pointed to a window, saying, "Standing room only, sir."

"Indeed." I let Mr. Olsen steer me by the elbow toward the ticket window.

"There's no need for it, sir," I said. "I can wait with the carriage until your business is concluded." I raised an eyebrow and jiggled the earrings.

He blinked, and his smile vanished. "I believe I won't allow you more than two feet from my side until *our* business is concluded," he said grimly.

"You can hardly ask Mrs. Olsen to stand in the back of the theater alone."

"No." He stared at the earrings as if to be sure. "But I shall stand and watch the both of you. Don't be so foolish as to disappear."

"Nor you," I said coolly.

An usher escorted Mrs. Olsen and me to plush seats in front of the stage. We were on the main floor to the right of the orchestra pit, and the soft sounds of instruments warming up for the performance floated past. A glance over my shoulder was rewarded with row after crimson row of velvet tilting chairs that led all the way back to the cheap stools and standing areas. I counted three boxes on each side and the edge of the balconies snaked above us like icing on a layer cake.

The painted ceiling, arched high above the crowd, glittered with a thousand prisms from a pendulous chandelier. Elaborate murals of San Francisco graced the walls, and the curtain over the stage was done in a panoramic view of San Francisco Bay.

Mrs. Olsen's face turned in all directions as well, and when I finally drew breath, I asked, "Isn't it lovely?"

Her eyes were huge as she turned them to mine. "It opened a dozen years ago and cost a quarter of a million dollars to build."

"Truly?"

"We learned as much as we could about it. It's the first theater on the West Coast to use limelight." She pointed at the stage. "Calcium light with parabolic reflectors, aimed from the house, to light up the stage."

"That sounds fancy."

She nodded and some color came to her face. "It is." So far as I could tell, Mrs. Olsen did not recognize me as the maid from her room earlier.

I opened the playbill. "Do you know what Madame Fabbri does? She retired from the stage, didn't she?"

"Yes. But now she organizes the productions. She was a glorious opera singer." Her smile faded and I left her to her thoughts.

The playbill was fascinating. Tonight was one of the final farewell appearances of the Famous Colville Opera Burlesque Company. Done in two acts, with a generous intermission, the show, *Ill Treated Il Travotore, Or, The Mother, The Maiden, and the Musicianer*, starred Miss Kate Everleigh, with Mr. Robert Graham, and Mr. Ed Chapman.

"Last night's performance was a benefit," I said, reading. "For an actress. Miss Roseau. I wonder what ails her?" I turned the page. "And there's a violin concert next week. A matinee. How lovely." Mrs. Olsen remained lost in thought, so I continued. "It says the Company is leaving the California Theater after many successful seasons. How very exciting it must be for Madame Fabbri to audition the next cast."

Mrs. Olsen gripped my arm with more strength than I credited her for. "It's to be me," she said with a look so intense it captivated me.

I lowered the playbill. "You?"

She nodded fiercely. "It was part of the arrangement. Our patronage. For me on the stage. If the contract got signed, I shall stay!"

"Ah."

It was as far as I got. The lights flickered and dimmed, and the orchestra began the overture.

When the notes faded into the rafters among thunderous applause, the curtain rose on a rotund gentleman in a cutaway jacket.

"Esteemed ladies and gentlemen," he cried, "J. T. Maguire at your service!" The applause continued to roll through the building. "We present tonight, a new and elegant opera by the Colville Burlesque Company. Cast with its full strength and promising to be the most exquisite as well as the most popular of any of the productions that have emanated from this remarkably talented company."

His opening remarks were lost to the crowd, and I shifted uneasily in my seat. Were audiences usually so full of ginger? I hoped it wouldn't continue during the production. To my relief, the clapping stopped as a gentleman in a tall top hat and long jacket came forward and recited a poem with rich feeling and perfect elocution.

He was swallowed by the curtain dropping again, but the orchestra took up the gap and within moments, the curtain rose on the opening scene. A young woman strolled onstage in a tight ruffled jacket with puffed sleeves and a high, frilled collar. The costume included a short cape, a pair of tight stockings, and pants so brief they left nothing to the imagination.

The audience howled with appreciation and a bouquet landed at her feet on the stage as she sang the first bars of her song. The short curly hair in no way fooled us. A corset beneath the costume and her graceful movements said she could have played the mother or the maiden. But Kate Everleigh was, apparently, the musicianer.

"Oh, dear!" Mrs. Olsen did not bother to lower her voice.

"What?"

"This is not opera…"

"No." I held up the playbill. "Operatic burlesque. It's a comic take on a serious opera. A farce."

She stood and was immediately chastised by the people behind us.

"This is not what Eli was told!"

I tugged at her arm. "We'll sort it later. Sit down, Mrs. Olsen. Please."

She pulled free and moved down the aisle, her skirts crowding into each person's face as she passed. Torn, I cast a forlorn look at the stage, then gathered my skirt and hurried after her, ignoring the angry hissing of our neighbors.

An usher lunged for her, but she made it through an exit. The audience spilled into the lobby and were none too pleased with the disturbance Mrs. Olsen continued to create once we reached it.

"Mrs. Olsen!"

She did not stop until we neared the ticket window and the man on the other side of it listened with interest.

"Opera," she said, a hand to her heaving side, "is refined. Madame Fabbri. Has entirely. Misled us." She pulled out a handkerchief and coughed into it.

I searched the bodies lined up along the entries of the auditorium, but there was no sign of Mr. Olsen.

Mrs. Olsen wiped her tears. "Not this. This den of iniquity."

A thunderous ovation from the theater drowned the sound of her weeping and by the time Mr. Olsen finally fought his way through the crowd, it had turned again to coughing. He shot a keen look from her to me and took her elbow.

"Which way to Fabbri's office?" he barked at the man in the ticket window. "Where is it, man?"

Directed to a hallway, Mr. Olsen glared at me and said, "Follow us."

Wild horses could not have kept me away.

The hall took us to a plain staircase that led to an up-stairs door. He hauled Mrs. Olsen up and did not pause to knock. "We are here for one purpose," he said. "And then you are returning to your rooms." He pushed her into the room ahead of him.

"I beg your pardon." Madame Fabbri's tone was icy enough to be a social snub.

"Excuse our intrusion, madam," he said. "We have urgent business that cannot wait." With a scowl, he turned and saw me, but I evaded his grasp and moved past him into the room and away from him.

"I think, detective, that the answers to your questions have just arrived." Madame Fabbri sat behind a large teakwood desk in a frothy silver creation of a gown and what I very much suspected was a wig. Not a hair out of place, she nearly glowed in the soft light and, with alarming speed, had rearranged her face with its unfortunate nose into calmer and far more flattering lines.

Mr. Olsen closed the door as a man rose from a side chair. Notebook in one hand and a pencil in the other, Detective Fisher kept his own face inscrutable as he took in the three of us.

Mrs. Olsen approached the desk and placed both hands on it. "I want the contract," she said. "Now that my husband is dead, our business here is terminated."

She shook her noble head, taking care with her wig. "That is not how it works, my dear."

"I did not sign anything," Mrs. Olsen said. "You may as

well destroy your copy."

Madame Fabbri glanced at Detective Fisher. "I have a contract signed by her husband, who, as you know by law, can make legal arrangements on behalf of his wife. And it was cosigned by his secretary, Mr. Nilsen. I'm afraid it's binding."

"You deliberately misled us!" Mrs. Olsen straightened and brought her handkerchief to her eyes. "In her bare stockings! Opera is a classic form of entertainment. Education. The costumes are regal and tasteful. You cannot make me stay! Oh, I knew it was too good to be true."

"I say," Mr. Olsen interrupted, "anything on stage is a charade, you know. Not the true person."

"And you!" She turned on him. "You are no better! Chasing women and drinking and carousing the minute we arrived! You were never going into the ministry! Eli was right about you!"

He bristled. "I am guilty of leading a normal life and nothing more!"

She turned a woebegone face to Madame Fabbri. "How can you have such a thing in your theater? With your reputation? I've looked up to you for inspiration for years!"

"I am flattered, of course," she said, sounding anything but. "Your husband thought you had potential or you wouldn't be here. Take courage, child. We will make you a star yet."

"But—"

Madame Fabbri rose, commanding an audience even from her desk. "The first thing I will not have, is you abusing your voice this way. Your throat is the most vital instrument on a stage and the only thing of yours I value. Cease this caterwauling at once."

"But—"

The office door crashed open once more and a man entered, waving a gun, shouting, "Stop there, you!"

Detective Fisher drew his gun. The Olsens leapt into each other's arms. And Madame Fabbri rolled her eyes to the ceiling and said, "Not now, Sims."

Chapter Ten

MR. SIMS FUMBLED the gun and his words. "Inez! What's happening?" He looked around the room. "I was told you had intruders. Are you harmed?"

Detective Fisher peered at him over their guns. "I had some questions regarding the New Year's Eve murder."

The Olsens untangled themselves and Mrs. Olsen put a steadying hand on the desk.

Mouth gaping, Mr. Sims lowered his gun. "Timing, sir! And during a performance, when she's needed ten other places at once?"

"Timing was my point." Detective Fisher holstered his gun, and I didn't miss his quick glance in my direction. "It rather helped that you all would be in the same place at the same time."

"Put that away, Sims," Madame Fabbri said. "If I had a situation, I could handle it myself." She motioned for Detective Fisher to resume his seat. "His gun is a stage prop. Mine is not."

The intrusion seemed to have shocked Mrs. Olsen out of her train of thought.

She blinked rapidly and said, "I must lie down."

"Take her outside," Detective Fisher said to Mr. Olsen. "Call for the carriage and wait there for me."

Mrs. Olsen swayed, and Mr. Olsen caught her by the waist. She leaned on him heavily as Mr. Sims showed them through the door.

"Mr. George Sims, indulge me for a moment and then I shall leave you both to your business."

I hadn't moved and took a moment to scramble through my list of reasons for being here. I would need them soon, I was certain.

Once the door closed, Detective Fisher wasted no time. "Madame Fabbri, I need to see your copy of the contract you signed with Reverend Olsen."

"Of course." She sat and opened a drawer.

"Do you have any reason to think Reverend Olsen was going to break his agreement with you?"

"No." She laid a sheaf of papers on the desk. "We toasted to it over supper. Everyone can attest to it."

"Did the wife have any doubts at the time?" He flipped quickly through the contract but did not sit down.

"None. I rather assumed the whole thing had been her idea. She penned all of their correspondence."

Detective Fisher slid the papers back toward her, apparently satisfied.

"As you can see, her husband made it abundantly clear that her opportunities were part of the patronage. Without proof that she could deliver or not, I agreed. We need the money."

"And if she could not?"

"I see no reason why that might be. I was told by many that she sings like a nightingale. After a great deal of hard work and tutelage, I have no doubt she will be an asset to our theater."

"If you don't mind," he said, "I'd be curious as to why you said you needed their money."

She sighed. "Detective, the first year we opened, the theater cleared $100,000." She let that sink in. "Over the years, we've had to compete with every other entertainment in this city." She let that one sink in, too. "Do you have any idea how much revenue one needs for props, scenery, and costumes? Upkeep of the building and refurbishing velvet seats? Ticket sales were down until we brought in the Colville troupe. They've kept us afloat."

"And they're leaving," Mr. Sims said. "Miss Kate Everleigh took a contract with the Savoy Theatre in London. She's jumping on the wildly popular Gilbert and Sullivan train. You've heard of them? It's not great opera, but it isn't quite so risqué as the burlesque, I think."

"Burlesque pays the bills," Madame Fabbri said. "When I was lead soprano and Nellie Melba graced this stage, fine opera was *de rigueur*." She sniffed. "But the Bank of California failed in '75 and Mr. Ralston went for a swim and did not resurface…"

"There now, Inez." Mr. Sims tutted.

"The theatre has been in a slow decline ever since." She paused to rally herself.

"I see," Detective Fisher said, opening his notebook.

"Oh, Al would love to get his hands on this place!"

"Who?" His hands stilled.

"Mr. Al Hayman," she said. "He operates the Baldwin Theater at Powell and Market. He's offered to buy this place before and been cut for his impertinence. Said he'd put the whole theater in electric lights. Can you imagine? Electricity is so vulgar. The light flatters absolutely no one."

"Madame," Mr. Sims said, "Mr. Edwards was unable to appear on account of illness tonight, and John Vesey has taken the role." He glanced at Detective Fisher. "And the bar is missing a crate of rum."

Madame Fabbri pursed her rouged lips.

"And your husband, madame," Detective Fisher said, perusing his notes. "Mr. Muller. What is his role here?"

"Baritone. He is my second husband and my rock. Jacob sings on occasion, but does not make the business decisions and will have little to tell you."

Detective Fisher nodded and turned a page. "Mr. Sims, there was something mentioned at the dining table immediately before Reverend Olsen died. An argument. Something about a dagger. Can you tell me who said what and why?"

I leaned forward.

Mr. Sims pushed his spectacles higher on the bridge of his nose. "Yes. I believe so. Reverend Olsen had no concept of how a theater is run. His secretary was there. Mr. Nilsen. He was questioning expenses, which a patron has every right to do, of course, but not accepting my answers. The cost of a dagger that glints in the theater lights and of a quality that demands belief when used to dispatch a villain meant nothing to him." His lips pressed into a thin smile. "We paid a lot of money so you would think my revolver was real, didn't we?"

Detective Fisher looked the man up and down. "And do you share your accounts with all of your patrons? Is your ledger an open book, Mr. Sims?"

Mr. Sims took hold of his waistcoat lapel. "Yes. Patrons need to feel needed. We have nothing to hide."

The detective closed his notebook with a snap and said, "Thank you. That's all for now."

"For now?" Madame Fabbri stood, her irritation clear.

"Yes." He moved to the door and Mr. Sims got out of his way. "For you." He opened the door and waited for me. "I, however, am far from being done for the evening."

I considered curtsying to Madame Fabbri, but I'd been standing still so long that my knees wouldn't bear it. Avoiding everyone's eyes, especially Detective Fisher's, I left the room and went down the stairs.

He caught me at the bottom and steered me into a corner near the coat check. Creating a respectable distance between us, I braced for the inevitable.

"What are you doing with the Olsens?"

"Enjoying the tickets you gave me. Thank you."

The audience in the lobby erupted in cheers.

"And where is Miss Smith?"

"Home with a headache."

"You gave them to the Olsens, didn't you?" He started to run a hand through his hair and stopped himself.

"And a good thing I did."

"Fight fire with fire," Aunt Mary said with approval.

"They think I'm a hotel employee—which I am—and let their guard down. There's something going on between them. That much is plain."

"You were supposed to question Madame Fabbri."

"So I was told." I narrowed my eyes at him. "Yet there you were."

"You were supposed to watch the show while I was up there getting answers."

"Madame Fabbri wasn't supposed to have anything worth questioning," I said. "And the Olsens know everything I don't. Of course, I was going to find a way to get close to them."

His hand raked through his hair. "We could have compared notes after."

I unclenched the fists at my side. "You and I have different ideas on how to go about this. You can approach them directly with the law on your side and I can circle behind them and collect the gossip. We are the perfect team if you would cooperate."

"Only if we are working together, not gallivanting around, hoping for the best. What if Mr. Sims's gun had been real? We must organize, Mrs. Kelly. Colleagues collaborate."

"Is that what they do? Sounds like something a man made up. Women get to the bottom of things faster than you can tie your cravat."

The audience clapped and roared at whatever had happened on the stage.

"I don't wear a cravat," Detective Fisher had to shout.

"And I wasn't shot at," I shouted back.

We waited for the crowds and our tempers to settle.

"I am a paid detective on the police force," he said when the air cleared. "Not a highly paid one, but still. It's my duty to pursue the killer until I have him or her behind bars. Because you are a…"

"Volunteer," I provided.

"Yes. Because you are a volunteer, I also have a duty to protect you and any other civilians. My job is doubled if you are involved."

"Only if we are collaborating."

"What do you mean?"

"If you go about your duty and I go about my day, who's to care how the villain is apprehended?"

"Mrs. Kelly, you're going to be involved no matter what I say. Please work with me and not against me."

He had a point.

"Then no more tickets to a show?"

"And no more headaches for Miss Smith?"

We shook hands on it.

"They're waiting in the carriage," I said, turning toward the exit. "We may get something from them yet."

"Who do they think you are?" he asked as we walked through the vestibule.

"A very helpful employee representing a very sympathetic hotel."

He cut his eyes at me. "Mr. Olsen attempted to shove you into the room up there."

"He is under the illusion I have something of his. That I

know something I don't."

He stopped short of the main doors. "What?"

I touched an earring. "He recognized them. I let him think I, as a maid, found his missing earrings. Or stole them. It doesn't matter which. The point is, he is eager to have a conversation, and I can't wait to hear it."

"If they represented anything innocent, he'd have mentioned them to me." He stopped. "Or accused you outright to me. I thought you were off enjoying the theater and instead you were taunting a murder suspect."

"He wasn't in the room!" I stopped.

My voice had gone up again and the doorman openly stared at us.

"We both know that's irrelevant." With tightly constrained manners, he handed me through the door into the chilly night.

Our carriage waited at the lampposts, and the valet opened the door for me. Mrs. Olsen sat on one side, and Mr. Olsen on the other, their disdain for each other and impatience to be off, palpable in the closed space.

"I'm sorry for the delay, ma'am," I murmured to Mrs. Olsen, sliding in beside her.

If they were surprised when Detective Fisher clambered in and sat beside Mr. Olsen, nothing was said. We rode back to the hotel in a dark, stuffy, and uncomfortable silence.

Arriving in the Grand Court of the Palace Hotel as a lady was something I'd never experienced. When our carriage pulled up in front of the lobby and the valet handed me out into the sparkling, warm light, the surprise on his face was an extra treat.

"Just back from the theater," I said breezily. "Thank you, Jack."

Ignoring the looks on Detective Fisher and Mr. Olsen's faces, I left them all with a demure curtsy and vanished among the palm trees. There was no legitimate reason for me to be a part of their group, but that didn't stop me from following them at a discreet distance.

They took the elevator, and I swiftly ran up the staircase, irritated that I might miss their conversation. Relying on my colleague was like having an itch I couldn't reach. The three moved down the fourth-floor corridor, and I stopped at the corner, straining to listen.

"Dare I be happy?"

"You have dared this far."

"If Eli thought for one minute that she would allow me on stage in such a costume…"

Mr. Olsen's voice was heavy and patient. "That is burlesque. Not opera."

A door opened. Mrs. Berg cried out. "Just look at you! I knew you oughtn't to exert yourself so. The very idea, going into that den of vice. Can we all rest in peace now and go home tomorrow? Is the nasty business concluded once and for all?"

"Oh, yes, we're finished!"

A door slammed.

Several minutes later, Detective Fisher wandered around the corner, not at all surprised to see me.

"She gave Mr. Olsen a look that damned him straight to hell and slammed the door closed in his face," he said.

"She does not approve of his wild ways." I turned toward the stairs, and he fell into step beside me.

"Why should she care?"

"I would say it makes the family look bad, but neither of them are much invested for all that they are Olsens."

We slowly spiraled down past each floor.

"Are they romantically involved?" he mused.

"I cannot imagine such a thing in the reverend's home. The son was not welcomed. Or trusted."

"What happened in the six months you were gone, then?"

"Mrs. Olsen trusts me, as far as I can tell. I'll bring her breakfast in the morning and see what I can find out."

"It might go faster if you tell her who you really are."

"And she might throw me out on my ear."

He glanced at my ear. "Speaking of that, I want you to avoid the son until I can decide who he really is."

I paused. "Who he really is? It's plain as day who he is. I knew him as a boy."

"What was your impression of him, then?"

"He used to be quiet. Not shy, but observant. He asked too many questions about the deity, and by questions, I suppose I mean doubts." I continued down the steps. "We weren't surprised to hear he'd gone off to school."

"Where to?"

"Now you ask, I never got the details. The rumors only said east somewhere." I sobered. "The Reverend Olsen was a man who never spared the rod or spoiled the child. I would have left much sooner."

He grunted. "Then the son is a suspect. What are your thoughts on Madame Fabbri's story?"

"She is either a liar or a fool. And a woman does not rise to her position by being a fool."

"Where is her lie?"

"If she recognized the first stages of consumption, she did not want us to know. Why?"

He nodded. "Mrs. Olsen doesn't seem to understand what her cough means. She truly seems determined to sing on the stage, poor woman."

"Her marriage was arranged. An unloving family foisted her onto the reverend. She was convinced he loved her because of this trip. This chance for her to sing."

"Is the widow a suspect?" he asked.

"That depends on why the reverend married her. I can't imagine he didn't know about her condition. So why would he go through this charade of bringing her out to be an opera singer?"

"I think those answers must lie with Mrs. Berg and Mr. Nilsen."

"They won't talk to me."

He smiled. "But they'll talk to me."

I absent-mindedly scratched my elbow.

Chapter Eleven

THE FOLLOWING MORNING brought the same thick gray clouds and biting wind. Outside my window, Market Street peddlers pulled their hats low on their faces and a few lucky working horses wore blankets. It was the kind of day that made you happy to stay indoors with a hot water bottle tucked into your lap quilt and the Tuesday morning *Chronicle* in your hands. But Becky had a glove shop to tend, and I had a murder to solve. I turned the situation over in my mind as I fastened my hat—the blue one Becky admired—firmly to the blonde twist of hair on my head with a long hatpin.

There was no sense in being shy now.

The Olsens thought I was a hotel employee. A maid, perhaps. Mrs. Olsen had confided in me, thinking never to see me again. And if she was to transfer over to the theater, she would not, although I would know exactly where to find her if needed. The widow had arrived at her destination and secured the contract that would make her dream come true.

If she'd gone to the theater to confirm what she surely must have researched—that the theater catered to the less than pure arts—then her reaction could have been a farce itself. Was she an accomplished actress as well as a singer?

Had she hoodwinked an unsuspecting Reverend Olsen into marriage and moving and then killed him once her goals were realized? Or before he could change his mind? Was the marriage of convenience the preparation for a widowhood on the stage?

I shook my head, and the feathers in my hat waved back in the mirror over my bureau. Her grief seemed as genuine as everyone else's. If she'd thought me an insignificant maid, then it didn't make sense that she would perform on my account.

But why confront Madame Fabbri and try to get out of the contract? Remorse? There was more information to be had from her, but as it appeared the contract would keep her in San Francisco indefinitely, I needed to concentrate on everyone else first.

Mr. Olsen was likely to hunt me down today. Especially if the family party were preparing to return to Minnesota to bury the Reverend Olsen in the bosom of his long-suffering congregation. I would beat him to it.

I needed Mr. Olsen to confide in me. But I intended to take the upper hand with a man who pushed women around. If I told him my true identity and that I knew all about his past, then perhaps we could meet in the middle with mutually beneficial information. Going as a maid would never do.

Turning in front of the mirror, I checked that every hair was in place and reached for my gloves. Becky was right. The hat made my eyes dance. The deep blue-violet underskirt of my dress sported a striped and flounced overskirt that swooped up to the bustle behind with a long, trailing bow the width of my hips. With a matching jacket and tall, black-buttoned, calfskin shoes, it was a shame I couldn't complete the look with a parasol.

But the earrings, stunning and perfect, made me a woman to be reckoned with. Aunt Mary had left them to me for a reason and it hadn't been Christmas or even my wedding.

More and more, I'd decided they were a message she'd left behind. In case. And she'd counted on me to understand it sooner or later.

If I hadn't run away, first.

"It is the honor of kings to search out a matter," Aunt Mary said in approval.

Mr. Olsen could ask for me by name, and any employee would point me out. All I had to do was dangle the bait.

Slipping down the stairwell and passing through the murky basement, I let myself up the steps behind the elevator shaft and entered the east promenade toward the Grand Court. I didn't make it past the ballroom.

Coming to a stop, I locked eyes with Mr. Olsen at the other end of the promenade and smiled. By the time he'd crossed the drive, his white-gloved fists were clenched and a deep line drawn between his noble brows.

Without showing myself in the open court, I retreated a few steps. This quickened his pace, but before he could take hold of my arm, I raised it and put a finger to my lips.

"Mr. Olsen," I said quietly.

He paused, taking a moment to scrutinize both my outfit and my earrings with growing confusion.

"If you please," I continued, "I'd like to take a turn in the conservatory with you this morning."

I pointed to the elevator.

"Mrs. Kelly." He gave me a curt nod and kept his hands stiffly at his side. We turned and stepped into the elegant redwood-lined rising room.

"Seven, please," I said to the driver. We rode up in silence and I scanned the area through the gilded grid as we climbed, relieved to find no trace of Detective Fisher or anyone else we knew.

The top floor of the Palace Hotel wrapped around the open court beneath the glass ceiling. Steel girders crisscrossed overhead and inlaid patterned tiles lined the hardwood floor along the four sides. Instead of columns, the top balustrade supported fern-filled granite urns interspersed with frosted globe lights, and glass panels at waist height between them. White marble statues graced each of the four corners.

We exited the elevator and followed the path as the car descended slowly out of sight.

Mr. Olsen's voice was low and menacing. "How very changed you are this morning. I should hardly have known you."

"Today is my day off," I said, pausing to peer over the rail.

"It will be your last. You've stolen those earrings. They're mine. You've made a terrible mistake, Mrs. Kelly."

"I am not a thief. These are not yours."

He whirled to face me. "Tell me why I shouldn't turn you in to the police right now. I lost one of those the night of the murder." His face grew red. "Either you are a maid who had no business digging through my things or you are someone I've been looking for all these months. I want answers and I want them now."

My chin rose. "Do you? I spent the first half of last year demanding answers from your father and getting nothing for my pain." I poured an accent into my words from the mother tongue. An accent I'd worked hard to remove. "So, Josiah, you needn't be quite so bellicose."

He leaned back in surprise.

"I recall you as a shy boy, but very inquisitive. You've changed a bit, now you're a man."

"Who are you?"

"Your neighbor. From Waterford Township. I watched you grow up from across the way. The Langland dairy farm. Hill House."

His face had gone from red to white, and a bead of sweat appeared at this hairline.

"You can't prove it."

"When you were ten years old, our old bull chased you through the pasture and I had to feed you a full dozen gingersnaps before you were calm enough to head home."

He blinked. "You. You are…"

"Miss Karine."

"And you work here? Or have you followed us from Minnesota?" He'd taken a step back.

"I left six months ago and came here. Alone. But my aunt, Mary Halvorsdatter, died last winter and left this pair of earrings to me." Our eyes remained locked. "And my question for you, Mr. Olsen, is what are you doing with my aunt's earrings?"

It was a minute before he drew in a shaky breath. "Your aunt bought them?"

"So far as I know."

"And where are mine?"

"I have no idea. More to the point, I have no idea about any of this. I'd like some answers of my own, if you don't mind." I cut my eyes down the hall where I knew Lina's rooms were. "For example, where were you when your father was poisoned?"

His eyes narrowed. "The same place you were, as I recall. You're the maid in the hall who screamed at Mrs. Berg, aren't you?" His head tipped to the side. "I assumed you'd been arrested. But you were also with us last night. And now you're here dressed like this. Who in hell are you?"

I raised an eyebrow, but he crossed his arms and refused to apologize.

With a sigh, I said, "She recognized me. And so did Mr. Nilsen. But I'm investigating the death of your father, and I can't do that until I know what happened in Minnesota over the half-year I've been gone."

"Investigating? You're with the police?"

"No one is supposed to know that. Not even you."

"There's more to it. There has to be. Tell me."

I turned the tables. "Who have you been looking for all these months? Who did you suspect me to be?"

He rubbed his chin in thought. "You and I may be on the same path." He pointed at the floor, and we continued our stroll. "I came home after years away. I can't tell you what happened at the church during those years."

"You don't have to. I was there until the beginning of June."

"I arrived in June."

"Why did you come back?"

He shook his head. "All of that will be revealed this evening. Detective Fisher asked Mr. Nilsen to open and read my father's will. Nilsen fought him on it."

"Do you expect a problem with it?"

"Mrs. Olsen and I debated over it yesterday. By law, everything passes to me. But he'd disowned me, you see, and in the short time I was back, I don't know that his opinion changed, regardless of how much I repented." He scowled at the floor. "I kowtowed to him for six months."

"So, you have no idea what's in it. Which explains your odd behavior last night."

We stopped. "We are both in the dark. Madame Fabbri was the only one who could tell us whether the contract was finalized or not. That blasted, tight-lipped—I beg your pardon—Mr. Nilsen refused to tell us anything, and if the police weren't involved, he might never have agreed to read the will and share its contents. You don't have to do such things in the backwoods of Minnesota, you know. It's all very assumed and family ties and knowing nods."

His eyes held the pulpit fire his father had once perfected, but I wasn't about to tell him so.

"Our plan was to throw a fit and demand answers from Madame Fabbri. I'm happy Mrs. Olsen got to the bottom of it, or I would have had to escalate. That would not have ended well with the detective in there."

"No. His gun is real."

"And so is her grief, if you doubted it. Oh, she can act. On the stage! But we were both gobsmacked when Reverend Olsen died. She loved him for bringing her out here and in some twisted, obscure way, I suppose he cared for her, or he wouldn't have done it."

"They were going through with it, then?"

He nodded. "May have burned a few bridges behind them, too. His flock was devastated when they got the news they were leaving."

"Then why did the shepherd abandon his sheep? Who took his place when he left?"

His laugh was bitter. "He thought I was taking his place in the pulpit."

"How could he have believed that?" I looked him up and down. "I don't know what you are, but clergy, you are not. Are you that good at acting as well?"

What scheme had the two Olsens cooked up?

"Isn't that what a preacher is? It's all an act. My father acted like he was born with a halo around his head, but he was as mortal as the next man." He frowned. "Nilsen must have started to glow at some point. I had it on good authority that Mr. Nilsen went from handyman to secretary in a single day."

"He did."

He met my eyes. "Apparently, a Mrs. Mary Halvorsdatter left a vacancy."

My breath caught in my throat, and I laid a hand on the rail.

He had the decency to look down. "I apologize for the rough way I handled you. It was part of the act, you see. And I thought you were a thief."

"The Palace Hotel does not hire thieves. If one of our staff puts a toe out of line, they are not only sacked, but no hotel in the city would hire them on."

"I believe you. I'm sorry."

"Why did you come home?"

"I—had news of something. So, I came home to find out if it was true. I told my father I regretted our breach and was home for good. But the harder I tried to get information from him, the further he retreated. He was trying to cover something up and no way in hell was he going to let me know what it was. Beg your pardon."

I felt his frustration bubble up in me. I'd done the same. "What did you think you would discover?"

"Corruption."

"Not murder?"

He pursed his lips. "Do you think it has something to do with your aunt?"

"I'm certain of it."

"Those earrings are part of it."

"They must be."

"We must speak with Edith right away. Mrs. Olsen," he corrected. "She was as close to him as one could get and it's our belief that Mr. Nilsen resented the idea of either one of us using our familial ties to uncover the past."

"If Mr. Nilsen or Mrs. Berg are with her, she'll never see me."

He smiled and offered his arm. "They have no authority over anyone. They couldn't bear the thought of their beloved reverend leaving Waterford Township and chose exile to be with him."

"If he still wears a halo in their eyes," I said slowly, "they must not be privy to Reverend Olsen's dark secret. They would not know where to look, even if they suspected it." I looked him in the eye. "Did either of them have a reason to kill your father?"

He was amused. "Kill the cash cow? The highly beloved? Mr. Nilsen's highly lucrative position and Mrs. Berg's deep devotion tell me no."

"You realize that leaves you and the wife as suspects?"

This time, he barked a short laugh. "Mrs. Kelly. Mrs. Olsen got exactly what she wanted. No motive there. And I have not as yet obtained anything I wanted. If I am all you have left, may I remind you that until today, I knew nothing of your aunt's death or your subsequent investigations. Not to mention"—he added with a wink—"I've tipped my hand to you."

Considering he'd admitted to lying to every person in Minnesota, that wasn't saying much. If Mr. Olsen had come home to dig for answers of his own, and Mrs. Olsen had declared herself useless, my suspicions rested firmly at her doorstep. As a wife, she would have had access to her husband's personal effects. Even if he hadn't shared, she could have found a way to investigate.

The woman knew something she hadn't shared with anyone. I smiled and took his arm.

"That's settled, then," he said. "We will go to Mrs. Olsen and tell her what you know and show her the earrings. She must have the missing puzzle piece. Something she can tell us about the reverend that only a wife would know."

Either that, or she would deny everything. We made our way to the elevator.

I was surrounded by actors. And I was going to yank back the curtains.

Chapter Twelve

MR. OLSEN PULLED out a pocket watch and checked the time as we walked down the fourth-floor corridor. "Nearly noon." The dull glint of gold flashed as he returned it to his waistcoat pocket.

"You'll forgive me," I said, "if I noticed an air of discontent between the two of you last evening. Anger that must have been part of the act? If you were working in tandem."

He gave a noncommittal grunt.

"You did quarrel, then."

I felt the sudden tension in his arm. "We disagreed. I proposed waiting until the will was read. She was determined to approach Madame Fabbri for answers. Impatient."

Thinking back to my discussion with Mrs. Olsen in her room, it rang true. I had opened the possibility for her. But what if I hadn't?

"She doesn't trust Mr. Nilsen?"

"I doubt she trusts anyone." His pause intrigued me. "But there is something else," he said with some reluctance. "Someone has been in my room. I found a lady's white handkerchief on the floor. I thought it was the thief. You." He glanced at me, but I kept my face forward as we approached Mrs. Olsen's hall.

"Who do you suspect it was, then?" I asked.

His voice dropped. "I think Mrs. Olsen has been in my room."

"And why would she do that?"

No answer.

"Are you certain she is innocent?" All of my suspicions raced through my head.

The handkerchief was mine, of course, but if there were cracks in the Olsens's story, this was one way to discover them.

He swallowed and said, "I cannot believe her capable of killing her husband after all he did for her."

We stood before her door. "As you said, she now has everything she ever wanted. And I can't imagine her wanting Reverend Olsen." I shuddered.

I could not imagine anyone wanting him for anything. Ever.

He straightened and rapped on the door, his face grim. "It's far past time for answers."

The door behind us opened and Mrs. Berg stuck her head out. "Hush there! Have you no respect? We're resting!"

Mr. Olsen turned. "Is Mrs. Olsen inside with you?"

Her eyes grew round and she cowered behind the door. "What's she doing here? I thought she was in jail!"

"How do you do, Mrs. Berg?" I tipped my head and let the earrings sway.

She watched them, mesmerized.

"Go away!" she hissed. "Have you no shame? You are

nothing but trouble."

"Mrs. Berg," Mr. Olsen said patiently, "we are looking for Mrs. Olsen."

"She's resting."

"In your rooms?"

"Of course not. After all we've been through? Edith told me she isn't taking callers all day. She didn't even want my company. Why don't you wait until tonight when Mr. Nilsen summons us?"

Mr. Olsen turned and rapped on the door again. Mrs. Berg shot me a dark look. "I don't know what you're doing here with *him*, but good riddance to you both. We leave at first light for home."

She shut her door in my face.

"She is every inch as charming as the day I last saw her," I said.

"Acrimony is not a complexion enhancer." He rapped harder. "Mrs. Olsen! It's me!"

I touched his arm with a finger. "She may be indisposed." Despite my automatic surge of aggression at Mrs. Berg, she did have a point.

Mr. Olsen looked stubborn. "Unless she's already taken on theater hours, I can't imagine her asleep at the luncheon hour."

"However." I touched the doorknob, but it did not yield. Surprised, I turned harder. "That's odd."

"How so?"

I removed my hand and bit back the words. I didn't want him to consider my insight regarding Minnesota manners.

He gave the door a resounding thump. "It's Josiah. This is important!"

"You don't suppose…" I glanced over my shoulder at the empty hall. "You don't suppose she's simply left? For the theater?"

Mrs. Olsen had just moved to the top of my suspect list, if so.

He renewed his attack on the door. "Mrs. Olsen!"

Fearing Mrs. Berg would come storming back out, I went to the corridor, and relenting, Mr. Olsen reluctantly followed.

"We have to know," I said, "and the lobby could tell us whether she's checked out. But I have a faster way."

The racket had brought a maid running and I accosted her immediately.

"Apologies for the ruckus," I said with a glare at Mr. Olsen, "but there was no answer to our discreet rap on the door." I marched her to Mrs. Olsen's hall. "Please unlock it for us."

The girl quaked in her shoes and rolled her eyes at me. "If it ain't your room, ma'am, I'm not supposed to do it."

"Pearl knows all about this," I reassured her as she pulled her keys out. "We've already ordered up coffee, but have arrived ahead of Mrs. Olsen, it seems. We'd prefer to wait for her inside, not loitering in the corridor."

Whether she was listening or not, she unlocked the door. I wondered whether mentioning Pearl's name had been a good idea. And if Pearl was still employed.

My hand met Mr. Olsen's on the doorknob. "Allow me,"

I said. "If she's here, she may be in a delicate state. A woman's job."

The maid hesitated, watching, but he nodded and stepped aside.

If Mrs. Olsen had fled, I wanted a first look at her room. Entering swiftly, I noted that the room was made up properly and the drapes were open. No fire in the hearth made for a chill in the air, and the uninspiring view added to a room without welcome. "She's gone," I called, and Mr. Olsen joined me.

I moved to the bedroom door, wondering how long she'd debated before breaking completely from this crazy lot and forging forward to her destiny. She was either a very courageous woman or a deeply wicked one.

A peek into her boudoir immediately disabused me of the ideas.

Mrs. Olsen was still in bed, hair scattered over her pillows, bedding rumpled and tossed by her sleep.

I froze. Nobody slept through the pounding Mr. Olsen had given the door.

Reaching for the light switch with rising nausea, I said, "I think ... oh, dear. I think she *is* gone."

"What?" Mr. Olsen pushed his way in and stood over her, a hand in midair, as he stopped himself from reaching out to touch her. His breathing filled the room in great, ragged heaves.

Beside the bed, empty powder sachets scattered around a small brown bottle, tipped over, with the stopper removed. A water glass. A spoon. Dizziness caught me and I leaned against the wall.

Behind me, the maid screamed.

Mr. Olsen took up a limp hand and felt along the wrist.

I whirled to the maid. "You must run for the police and a physician! Hurry! Ask in the lobby!"

Mr. Olsen shook his head as I joined him beside the bed. "It's no use. She's stone cold. Clammy." He laid Mrs. Olsen's hand gently on the quilt and stifled a small sob.

It made no sense.

"There." He pointed to a sheet of paper near the foot of the bed. It appeared to have fluttered and landed softly near her knees. A single crisp white page bearing the hotel crest. The stationery provided in every room.

"Mr. Olsen." But it was too late. He'd lurched for it like a drowning sailor for a rope.

Holding it to the lamplight, he scanned the few written words quickly and then once more. When his eyes closed and he groaned, I placed my hands over his and gently removed the paper from his grip. Mr. Olsen sank to the floor and buried his face in his arms.

"I cannot," I read aloud, "follow through with this. Sin upon sin. My pride has led to destruction. God be merciful. I've killed my husband and secured my fame at the price of my soul. I go to meet him and beg his forgiveness. Edith."

After replacing the letter where it had been on the bed, I bent over the bedside table without touching anything. She'd mentioned headache powders. A hesitant sniff over the bottle told me it had once held laudanum. If she'd taken the whole bottle at once, it would have done the job.

"Edith," Mr. Olsen said, muffled by his arms. "No."

Careful not to topple over, I hovered above Mrs. Olsen's face. Her eyes were closed and her jaw slack. Her blue lips, parted in death, smelled faintly bitter.

Suicide from a woman who had everything to live for? A full confession?

I didn't believe it for a second. And seconds were all I had. Swiftly, I slid open every drawer in the room, from the bureau to the wardrobe. The reverend's clothes were still orderly, and I found no signs that Mrs. Olsen had begun packing any of their things. She was in her nightclothes in the bed. How long ago had she died?

Moving into the parlor room, I ran an eye over the dusted mantle, the spotless table holding a lush bouquet in a silver vase, and perfectly placed pillows on the sofa, and decided she'd gone directly to her bed after last night's theater trip.

Two sheets of hotel stationery were in the narrow top drawer, and an inkwell and fountain pen sat in their niche at one corner of the simple desk. A desk pad and blotter beneath a small lamp completed the tidy ensemble.

Frustrated, I paced, watching the open door, waiting for the first person to arrive.

Praying it was Detective Fisher.

If he'd already questioned Mrs. Berg and Mr. Nilsen, then this sudden turn of events might point directly at one of them for Mrs. Olsen's murder. We could end this now.

I paused, mid-stride, and blinked at a painting hung near the door. The twinkle came and went as I moved closer.

Balanced on the top of the heavy wooden frame, an earring dropped into my searching fingers.

It glittered in my palm, an exact replica of the two in my own ears. The mate to the one Detective Fisher had fished from Mr. Olsen's pocket. But how did it get there?

"Mrs. Kelly!" Pearl stood in the doorway, panting and holding her side. "What are you doing here? Missy said—"

Her words were cut off as Mr. Olsen staggered in and raved, "Mr. Nilsen did it! The beast!"

He made for the door and slammed directly into Detective Fisher, who took him by the shoulders.

"Let me pass!" he cried, twisting out of Detective Fisher's hands. "He'll get away! He'll take the will and burn it!"

I gasped as the two wrestled a moment, then Detective Fisher had Mr. Olsen's arm twisted up behind his back and said quietly, "Drop to your knees before I have to hurt you."

Anguish in his face, Mr. Olsen did as he was told as Heyes ran in with two valets and the sobbing maid trailing behind them.

"Take him," Detective Fisher told Heyes, and moved directly into the bedroom, passing me without so much as a look.

I tucked the earring into my narrow bodice pocket as Mrs. Berg pushed into the room.

"What in tarnation is going on?" she cried. "A body can't get rest no matter how she tries! Come out of here at once, all of you!" She fixed an eye on Pearl, who stared right back at her.

"Fetch Mr. Nilsen," I told a valet who'd nervously

backed toward the door. "The next hall over, room 409. Tell him he's needed immediately."

Mrs. Berg looked at me. "You." How she managed to instill a single syllable with so much venom was a gift.

Detective Fisher returned and said, "Mrs. Berg. Sit on the sofa, here, please."

"Why? What's the trouble?" Mrs. Berg asked. "What are you doing here? Where is Mrs. Olsen?"

"I sent for Mr. Nilsen," I said.

Detective Fisher turned to me with a frown. "That was presumptuous."

"Were you going to?"

His frown deepened. "What are you doing here?"

Mrs. Berg moved to perch on the sofa's edge, straining to catch our every word.

"We came together, Mr. Olsen and I, to speak with Mrs. Olsen. We found her in her bed and sent for you right away. The maid can tell you so."

He glanced at Pearl, who nodded and said, "Missy." She dragged the maid from the room.

"You came in anyway?" Mrs. Berg interjected. "And she was in bed? For shame!"

"I don't think this is what it looks like," I said, ignoring her.

"She's dead!" Detective Fisher was as shocked as Mr. Olsen had been, but where grief had brought Mr. Olsen to his knees, Detective Fisher's anger rose every minute. "It looks exactly like that, Mrs. Kelly!"

Mrs. Berg wailed, Mr. Olsen groaned, and Detective

Fisher hauled me out into the corridor.

"You are supposed to be working with me," he began.

"I am!" My voice echoed into the court.

"No more gallivanting off with my suspects. From now on, you go where I go."

"She belongs in prison, so that's convenient." Mrs. Berg stood in the doorway, tears on her face and twisting her hands together, watching.

"Mrs. Berg." Detective Fisher was fast, but not fast enough. She ducked into the room with a sob before he could pretend to escort her there.

"Karine Langland." Mr. Nilsen appeared in the corridor with the valet. "I am not at all surprised to see you once again in the center of mayhem." Disapproval radiating from him, he passed me and entered Mrs. Olsen's room.

Rooted in place, I watched Pearl send the sobbing maid away with the valets, then turn to me.

"Mrs. Kelly," she said grimly. "I know you didn't do it. But if the good Lord keeps placing you at the feet of the dead, you can't stay here. Missy did something that will cost her job on account of you."

"Pearl, I'm sorry. If there had been any other way…"

She walked away and I nearly reached for her. Instead, I called, "Please don't! Tell them we locked ourselves out! It wasn't her fault!"

"Are you asking me to lie, Mrs. Kelly?" she snapped over her shoulder.

She turned the corner and was gone.

When I turned, Detective Fisher was behind me. He

took in my new hat. He paused over the earrings. Our eyes met.

"I never lie," I said.

"Then you have a prodigious amount of explaining to do."

I raised an eyebrow.

"Suicide." His voice dropped. "Three suspects in there."

"Suspects?" I gave him a small smile. "You don't believe it's a suicide any more than we do."

"We?" He squinted.

"Mr. Olsen and I."

He slowly looked over my new dress. "And we trust Mr. Olsen because…"

"He confided in me this morning. Told me about Mr. Nilsen and the will and how neither he nor Mrs. Olsen were able to win anyone's confidence after six months of being family."

"Mr. Nilsen was going to open the will this evening."

"It may be too late now." I glanced at the open door. "It may be too late for any number of things."

Chapter Thirteen

WHEN WE ENTERED the room again, the air was thick with emotion. Mrs. Berg cried into her handkerchief, Mr. Olsen sat in rigid anger, and Mr. Nilsen, standing with parted feet and hands folded behind his back, presented a wall of defensiveness. But I saw fear in his eyes as they darted from person to person.

Heyes stood in the doorway to the bedroom, facing us with hands on his hips, waiting for instructions.

Detective Fisher stopped me from closing the door. "Watch for the physician. Mr. Lees is on the way too."

It had been Sergeant Ross who'd come for Reverend Olsen. The coroner himself was coming for the wife.

I added my own shock and disbelief to the mix, trying to avoid Mrs. Berg's eyes and telegraph sympathy toward Mr. Olsen. Detective Fisher marched into the center of the crowded room and Heyes pulled out his notebook.

Mrs. Olsen did not commit suicide.

The enthusiastic woman who'd confided in me about her dreams might have used her husband to get what she wanted. She might have begun the diva life last night as she saw the stage for the first time. She might even have killed Reverend Olsen.

But she had every reason to live her dream.

And the woman was taking the key to her husband's murder, and possibly Aunt Mary's, to her grave.

I grew furious at the thought.

The earring sat tight in my pocket, a sharp reminder that someone had wanted her dead.

Detective Fisher's chin shifted as he worked his clenched jaw loose.

He turned to Mr. Nilsen first. "Mr. Nilsen, you're going to read the will now. I want every piece of paper in your room here on this table."

"All of it?" Mr. Nilsen shifted on his feet, a deep furrow between his eyes.

"Heyes, go with him and search the room thoroughly in case he's misplaced something."

"Yes, sir." Heyes handed the notebook to the detective and gave Mr. Nilsen a nod toward the door.

I stepped aside as they left and Mrs. Berg cried, "But what's happened to her? That nasty man wouldn't let me anywhere near Edith!"

"There's no sign of violence, Mrs. Berg," Detective Fisher said, opening the notebook. "It appears she went to sleep and never woke up."

She sucked in a hiss and turned to Mr. Olsen, half-rising from the sofa. "You were the last person she was with! What have you done to her?"

"Anyone could have been in here today!" Mr. Olsen rose swiftly, quivering.

"You stayed!" she countered. "You seduced her behind

the reverend's back! Do you think he didn't notice?"

Detective Fisher was fast. He pushed Mr. Olsen back into his chair and said, "Mrs. Berg, I warned you yesterday. You speak when I am ready to hear you and only answer my questions."

"I told you so!" she said, fluttering her handkerchief. "Everyone knew not to trust him! The reverend almost never let her out of his sight. He was that wary. And who wouldn't be? This—man—shows up out of the blue claiming he's reformed. The prodigal son, no less! And did you think your father would come running out to meet you? Ha! He wouldn't even let you in the house." She looked at Detective Fisher. "He made him sleep at Mrs. Astor's."

"You know an awfully lot about something that is none of your business," Mr. Olsen growled.

"And you know next to nothing," she said. "You're a shiftless, drunken, carousing fool, and your father was never going to let you take over the ministry. The moment you came with us, I knew. I'll wager you've never worked a day in your life, let alone prayed."

"Mrs. Berg." Detective Fisher's voice held an edge of danger.

"Look at his hands," she said. "Soft as a baby's. You killed your own father to have his wife, and when she refused you, you ... you..." She broke down and sobbed.

Mr. Olsen took hold of the armrests and glared up at Detective Fisher. "I don't know what pack of lies she's told you, but I have never been anything but kind to Mrs. Olsen. She is a pious and virtuous woman." He swallowed. "Was."

"Don't let this get out, detective, please!" Mrs. Berg wrung her hands. "The good people in Minnesota don't need to know their cherished reverend was anything but a victim of a degenerate city. He strayed. He wandered far from home. But don't sully his good name."

Detective Fisher ran a hand through his hair, and I wondered whether he'd ever hit a lady. It seemed like a logical time to attempt it. One of them was going to snap, and it wasn't going to be Mrs. Berg.

"Your indiscretions preceded you, Josiah Olsen."

"Watch your tongue, old woman!"

She raised her wet chin in defiance. "Then where did you go when you stormed out of the dining room? Where were you when your father was murdered?"

"I won't give you one more thing to chew over, you gossiping old hag!"

"How dare you!" She threw her hands in the air. "No, and you won't have to! There's only one place a drunk and wicked man goes in the middle of the night!"

This last to Detective Fisher with a knowing look and he took advantage of her dramatic pause to say, "Mrs. Berg. Mrs. Olsen committed suicide. She killed herself."

Thankfully, we were all spared her stunned reaction when several men entered the suite.

Mr. Lees gave me a brief nod and said, "Mrs. Kelly." He led his men into the bedroom.

Mr. Nilsen followed, carrying a large, leather briefcase in both hands.

Heyes came behind him and closed the door. "We could

hear you all the way down the corridor," he said.

Everyone glared at Mrs. Berg.

She startled and leaned back when Detective Fisher grabbed the low table in front of her and dragged it to the center of the room. He moved the flower vase to the mantle, saying, "Mr. Nilsen, if you would please leave it there and take a seat?"

Mr. Nilsen put the case on the table and sat stiffly on the sofa with Mrs. Berg. Detective Fisher tossed the notebook back at Heyes and shook his head.

"Let's try this again," he said wryly. "Mr. Nilsen, as you are currently the most cooperative in the room, can you tell me if Mrs. Olsen had any reason to kill herself?"

"She did?" Mr. Nilsen's long fingers gripped his bony knees, and the trousers puckered beneath them.

"Yes. Why?"

"I don't know, sir."

Detective Fisher pressed his lips together, but the moment he noticed Mrs. Berg's mouth open, he said, "Were the Reverend and Mrs. Olsen planning to make a new life here? In San Francisco?"

Mr. Nilsen pushed at his spectacles, then ran a hand down his beard before putting his hand back on his knee. "It was my understanding that they were going to look for a house here in the spring. After the thaw."

Heyes snorted.

"We do not have a winter here," Detective Fisher said. "Despite evidence to the contrary, it never snows in the city."

I rolled my eyes.

"And would you say their marriage was felicitous?" he continued.

Mr. Nilsen frowned.

"Happy," Detective Fisher said.

Mr. Nilsen pondered it. "It was an arranged marriage of sorts," he said. "Not, um…" He actually turned red.

"He doted on her," Mrs. Berg said. "Simply loved her the moment they met. He was too good for her, and that's a fact. She never so much as smiled at him."

"Mrs. Berg."

"She led him astray! That's what comes of marrying a wanton woman! Lured him from his faithful flock!"

"Mrs. Berg."

"She loved him, and he hated her." Mr. Olsen said. "I just can't prove it."

"What makes you say that?" Detective Fisher asked, turning to him.

Mr. Olsen crossed his arms and looked at the table.

"She rejected you!" Mrs. Berg was triumphant. "After all those months of teasing."

Detective Fisher stepped up and towered over Mrs. Berg, but to her credit, she held her ground and met his eyes.

"Enough," he said. "Silence. Mr. Nilsen, can you tell me how the Olsens financed this trip? How they planned to financially endow the California Theater Company? Surely the ministry is not so lucrative a profession?"

Mr. Nilsen nodded. "They got a generous parting gift from our congregation. For the hotel."

"And becoming patrons of the arts?"

"You will have to consult Madame Fabbri and Mr. Sims," he said. "The contract has an amount to be paid out, and I've prepared a check, but it's not my place to ask questions like that."

"He never spent a dime in his sixty years of service," Mrs. Berg said. "He scrimped his whole life." Her tears started up again. "To think of that woman taking his last penny."

"Did you not come with her as her companion?" Detective Fisher's question made her pause.

"Detective, I gave my life to the church when my husband died, Gott rest his soul, and if the dear reverend wanted to take another wife, then I was surely committed to caring for her as tenderly as any mother might. I hoped against hope that my suspicions were unfounded. Why would I want to hurt the reverend if she were false to him?"

Her bosom heaved in righteous indignation. "But when he died, I feared the worst. I'm ashamed of myself. I thought perhaps she'd done something drastic." She turned to Mr. Olsen. "But it's as plain as the nose on my face. You killed him. You brought enough shame to Edith that she took her own life over it. And you'll burn in hellfire for it."

For once, I was not the target of her vitriol. I nearly gave her a standing ovation.

Detective Fisher walked away from her. "Mr. Nilsen, pull out the reverend's will and let's finish this farce."

While Mr. Nilsen rifled through the briefcase, murmurs from the bedroom stopped. Mr. Lees stood in the bedroom doorway and beckoned to Detective Fisher. All eyes followed his men as they carried the limp body of Mrs. Olsen, wrapped in the sheet and bedquilt, through the room and out.

"We're done," he said quietly. "I'll leave two men for you outside. Come down when you've finished here." With a last nod, he left and closed the door behind them.

"Mr. Nilsen," Detective Fisher said, "I am aware that neither of us are lawyers, but as all interested parties are here and I cannot allow a delay after two murders, I must insist."

Mr. Nilsen sat erect with a sheaf of papers in his steady hands. I'd seen him walk the ridge of the church roof, hammer in hand, to make repairs. He'd fished a timber rattlesnake from beneath a pew and convinced a skunk family to move out of the church basement. He shared a sofa with Mrs. Berg. Clearly, the man was unflappable.

But now he blinked rapidly and handed the papers to Detective Fisher.

"If you don't mind," he said, removing his spectacles and pinching his nose between closed eyes. "The light is too dim." He sniffled.

Detective Fisher read rapidly to himself. Heyes had made a few notes but waited now with the rest of us.

"It's a new will," Detective Fisher said after a long, uncomfortable silence. "Dated two months ago. The son gets the land. And the church, it seems. The buildings, cemetery, groves, and so forth." He looked up at Mr. Olsen. "On the contingency that he remains in Waterford Township as clergy. Is that your intention?"

Mr. Olsen turned pale. "I was under the assumption that I would not be mentioned in the will at all."

Detective Fisher returned to the will and said, "The money, or whatever funds might be attached to the reverend's estate, is settled on his wife Edith Olsen. On the contingency that she apply it toward the patronage and remain fully employed with the California Theater in San Francisco, 414 Bush Street and so forth."

This time, he glanced at me.

"She was rich," I said.

"For one day." Detective Fisher skimmed over the rest of the papers. "The contract? Mr. Nilsen, do you have a copy of it?"

Silently, Mr. Nilsen replaced his spectacles and dug into the briefcase.

Mr. Lees had been thorough. Through the bedroom doorway, it was clear he'd taken everything from the bedside table and left only two rumpled pillows on the bed. A momentary image of the reverend sharing the space with Mrs. Olsen made me turn away sharply and stare out the window.

Detective Fisher exchanged papers with Mr. Nilsen and looked over the contract. After a quick scan, he said, "Everything seems to be in order. Dates. Signatures."

"They can't hold us to the contract now," Mr. Nilsen said. "Not if ... she's dead."

"It belonged to the church in the first place," Mrs. Berg added. "It should go right back home with us."

Detective Fisher handed the contract back. "The will does not specify what the money does if his wife's contract is rendered null. That assumes the heir, Mr. Olsen, gets it all."

Mrs. Berg looked aghast. "The church will never accept him!"

"I say," Mr. Olsen said, shaking himself from his reverie, "am I so very abhorrent to the fine people of Waterford Township? I grew up there and recall you were a shrew from the day I knew you. You don't speak for everyone."

"Train them up in the way they should go," Mrs. Berg quoted. "But the good Lord knows a bent tree will grow up twisted. It was too late for you, Josiah. Everyone could see it. It was for the best you were sent away to school and even better when you did not return."

"But I am here now." He stood, and Detective Fisher kept a wary eye on him. "And I say I won't leave until I find out which one of you murdered Edith Olsen."

"Have you no respect at all for your father or his memory?" Mr. Nilsen asked. "Do you not want his will to be done?"

"I've heard enough," Detective Fisher said. "Each of you will remain in your room until I can ask more questions. You won't be returning to Minnesota until I catch the person or persons responsible for killing the Olsens."

Everyone rose.

"You can't—" Mrs. Berg began.

"The funerals—" Mr. Nilsen stuttered.

Mr. Olsen put a hand over his face and wept silently.

"Now, if you please," Detective Fisher said, and opened the door. "Heyes, escort the gentlemen and once they are safely tucked inside, post a guard at the end of their hall and send one here. Not to fear, Mrs. Berg," he said, jumping ahead of her imminent tirade, "room service will see to your every need."

Mr. Nilsen reached for the briefcase.

"No, sir. Leave it. And all of you will have your rooms searched again."

They departed in various states of shock and grief, leaving the room cold and empty.

Detective Fisher watched Mrs. Berg close her door without a backward glance.

"Was she always like this?" he asked.

"Worse." I lowered my voice. "You never told them what the note said."

"I wanted them to draw their own conclusions."

"None of them accused her of killing her husband."

He looked around the room. "I find that interesting."

"None of them suggested offering a reward to find the killer, either. The one Mrs. Olsen offered you."

He met my eyes. "No. No, they did not."

Chapter Fourteen

THERE WERE A few things I'd learned to depend upon with the San Francisco police department. The first was that you couldn't depend on them. With a cavalier and somewhat vigilante attitude, Chief Crowley and Captain O'Meara spent more time shaking hands with Mayor Blake and attending public galas than worrying over the everyday crimes and common horrors of the city streets. Detective Fisher and Sergeant Ross, with their focus on Chinatown and the Barbary Coast, were fast to spot potential problems and eager to keep an always-seething cauldron of immigrant unrest from blowing sky high.

But with a force low on funds and lower still on manpower, a citizen was well advised to consider any expedient method available to solve one's own problems. The police seldom arrived and if they did, had little to offer. Bribes, threats, or politics were your only hope.

And, more often than I wanted to admit, people got away with murder.

When Mrs. Olsen died and took her reward with her, I paced the room, desperate to find a way to keep Detective Fisher on the case. It was unreasonable to think he'd care about a murder among tourists. But it was far too personal for me. I was committed. I'd follow them back to Minnesota if I had to.

And the Minnesota police had already laughed me out of hearth and home.

No, I thought, coming to a stop. It had to end here. I would not let it happen twice.

A knock came from the hall and Pearl stuck her head inside. "Detective Fisher?" She glanced nervously over her shoulder at the officer at Mrs. Berg's door. "Management would like to see you down in the lobby, sir. When you've time."

"Yes. I'm certain they would." He looked around the room again. "Let's go." Detective Fisher turned out the lights and ushered me out of the suite. Without meeting my eyes, Pearl locked the door behind us and followed at a discreet distance.

With the detective in his usual work suit and me in my finery, we could almost pass for guests as we moved confidently through the hotel. Heyes met us in the corridor, but after a look at our faces, he fell behind and walked silently next to Pearl. I ran a finger along the slight bump over my corset where the earring was hidden, debating whether this was the time to tell him about it.

Whether it mattered anymore.

Taking the staircase gave me time to think it over, but when we marched into the grand lobby, I was no closer to a solution. The space was open and cavernous, nearly two stories tall, with arched entries and alcoves, and a nearly domed ceiling full of electric lights. Potted palms were tastefully grouped over a patterned tiled floor. Guests sat in deep leather chairs around a long concierge desk. Valets and bellhops in crisp uniform lined one wall, watching for incoming carriages or outgoing luggage.

The west dining room could be seen through one large arch, and a peek down its corridor toward the two private dining rooms sent a chill up my spine.

The arch had been roped off. An elegant sign read, RES-TAURANT CLOSED.

Detective Fisher had not offered me his arm, but this was hardly a social situation. I hurried to stay at his side as he went directly to the massive dark-wood front desk. The furniture behind it nestled between columns and extended upward into a large brass clock that gonged the hours and a vast array of tiny drawers, hooks with keys, and cubbyholes full of detritus. Gas lamps reflected brightly from the polished countertop. A procession of gleaming brass spittoons lined the bottom.

"Detective Fisher!" Mr. Sedgwick hurried along the other side of the counter with a finger in the air.

From the look he gave me, he'd already recognized, passed judgment, and hung me in effigy.

"Thank you, sir, for coming. If I may have a word..." He looked up and down the room. Two men stood at the far end, smoking cigars, and a guest was checking out on the other. "In the gent's reception room?"

With neither wallpaper nor carpet, the bare plastered walls echoed with muffled voices.

"I beg your pardon?" I said, pointedly.

He raised his eyebrows and glanced back and forth between us. "Indeed," he said at last, "the telegraph room, then, perhaps? We must tuck you away before the reporters arrive." He moved swiftly to the end of the desk and strode across the lobby. Heyes went with us.

Pearl watched us go.

"Mr. Brant," Mr. Sedgwick said as we entered a small room off the lobby. A man seated at a complicated-looking console looked up in surprise. "You may wait for me in the lobby."

"Yes, sir." He took in the three visitors with frank curiosity before closing us into the room.

The hotel manager's hair glistened beneath the electric light, as did the sweat forming at his temples. It was not a pleasant sight in such proximity. A buzzer sounded from the console, but he ignored it.

"I kept my distance," he began, "when the diner met his unfortunate demise. I let you do your job so that I could do mine." He ran a finger along his stiff collar. "But today's scandal may ruin us! We are the finest hotel on the West Coast, Detective Fisher, and our guests do not die. No, sir. We care for them as if in our own home."

Detective Fisher shrugged. "You can't expect to prevent death with wealth."

"Death, no. The elderly and the infirm are cradled in luxury to ease their discomforts and someday, death will come for us all. But murder!" His eyes bulged. "We will not stand for it! I insist you catch the villain immediately."

"We are needed everywhere in the city at once, Mr. Sedgwick. You know this. I've only had twenty-four hours to investigate. You will have to be patient."

"What am I to tell our guests?" He nearly hopped on one foot. "They will not stay with us."

"Surely you are seeing it far out of proportion," I said soothingly. "No one would think ill of the hotel over a single incident."

"The diner died at your hand!" His mustache bristled forward as his mouth thinned. "There is no way out of the scandal, Mrs. Kelly. We've had no diners today. None. We closed the dining room early with great humiliation. Our guests have all gone out to eat."

Considering the bad weather, this was noteworthy.

"I sent all of the staff home," he continued. "And they are not to return. Our guests must be assured that every precaution was taken." He looked at the console. "We are preparing a statement for the press. And will hire all new staff. It will take us a fortnight. Do you understand?"

"The kitchen is empty," I said, "and the food—"

"Is thrown out!" he cried. "To the dogs! We've turned deliveries away and closed the doors. But that was nothing! Nothing! Compared to this!"

My knees quaked, thinking of the repercussions of Reverend Olsen's murder and the damage it was causing, but Detective Fisher was amazingly calm. "What do you mean?" he asked.

"A guest died in her suite." The man met Detective Fisher's calm with slow, ponderous words, fraught with emotion.

"And not by her own hand. I have it on good authority. Had that been the case, we could bill the room as haunted and raise the fee. No." He shook his head and glared at us. "If you do not provide the one who is killing my guests, then we must close entirely. Because now we must dismiss all of the room staff. Collect every key."

His short laugh edged toward madness.

"Which is good, yes? Since all of our guests are slowly checking out. Leaving us. Even those booked through next week for the holiday. They are going to other hotels. Hotels where they are safe. Hotels with professional staff who don't open doors for demanding guests."

Resentment rolled from him in waves.

I held up my hand and stopped his tirade. "Give us twenty-four hours more," I said. "And if we cannot find the killer beyond a shadow of a doubt, then I will turn myself in and save the hotel."

Chin high, I stared at him as the room went still.

"Mrs. Kelly—"

"This is nothing to do with you, after all, Detective Fisher," I said. "This trouble followed me, and I'll take care of it. None of the staff will suffer on my account. Once the public knows you've caught the killer, Mr. Sedgwick's hotel will be safe. You won't waste time or money. More than you have, that is. I'm sorry."

Mr. Sedgwick squinted at me. "You know who it is?"

"She does not," Detective Fisher said. "And she won't be your key to convenience. Yours is not the first hotel to experience a crime, and it won't be the last. The papers will soon be on to the next scandal."

"I know it isn't any of the staff," I said firmly. "So does everyone in this room."

Mr. Sedgwick was thinking so hard you could hear it over the console buzzers.

"I have a better idea," he said quietly. He glanced at the closed doors. "I was to offer you a reward, detective. A hefty incentive to be fast. To save the hotel. But Mrs. Kelly presents us with another way. It is faster yet."

"No." Detective Fisher's face hardened.

"Let Mrs. Kelly be arrested for both deaths," he said. "Tell the papers. I will bring the staff back and open for business immediately."

"Except for the part where she is innocent," Detective Fisher said, "it would work out well for all of us."

Heyes cleared his throat.

"Meanwhile," Mr. Sedgwick continued, "you will accept my very large incentive and capture the real villain. Also, immediately."

"And if I cannot?"

Three men looked at me, and I laughed in their faces. "But you can. You have me."

"You realize you could be charged and hung for murder?" Detective Fisher was livid.

"But I won't," I said sensibly. "Because I have you."

He looked away, his face full of conflict.

I turned to Mr. Sedgwick. "It's winter. They need their jobs. They have families. Of course I'll do it."

The buzzers in the console hadn't stopped and the lobby

sounded as if it had filled with people. From the other side of the closed door, Mr. Brant said, "No. The police are inside, and they'll talk to you when they're good and ready. Back off, now."

"Heyes, do you have a pair of handcuffs?" I held out my wrists.

"Does anyone remember that I'm in charge here?" Detective Fisher growled.

"You'll have to make it look real," Mr. Sedgwick said anxiously. "I need them to believe it."

Heyes adjusted the heavy metal cuffs around my gloves. "If I make them any looser, they'll fall off," he said apologetically.

"It's fine." I kept my hands lifted. "I won't disgrace you. Wait until Mrs. Berg reads the evening paper." I smiled at Detective Fisher. "This will set her up for life."

His eyes were hard. "I need a key to the Olsen suite, Sedgwick. All four rooms off limits. Room service assigned to the three remaining guests. Consider them under house arrest. I have them guarded."

Mr. Sedgwick's mouth opened to protest, but Detective Fisher cut him off.

"I don't give a good damn what your other guests will think. We've saved your precious hotel, and I'll hold you to that incentive. The jail needs an overhaul." He glanced at me. "I seriously doubt it will keep Mrs. Kelly contained."

Mr. Sedgwick's eyebrows rose into his hairline. "But she must!"

"Then don't let me down. Because when I haul in the

actual killer, I don't want him getting loose."

"No! No!" He nearly bowed.

"Then, let's get on with it. I want a closed carriage to the jail." Detective Fisher shoved at the door and a body on the other side momentarily resisted. Mr. Brant recovered his feet as Detective Fisher and Mr. Sedgwick walked out together.

Heyes, apparently having done this before, took me roughly by the arm and hauled me after them.

I briefly considered shrieking and resisting and exclaiming over my innocence for the benefit of the dozen or so reporters gathered in the lobby. They surged around us, shouting questions at the men up front and staring unabashed into my face, as if memorizing every feature and every inch of my frock.

The impulse to slap the nearest leering face was strong.

"This her, then?" the man said, his pencil scribbling madly in his notebook. "Both murders, you say?"

"A real peach, that one!" This man's breath was thick with garlic.

"Aye! I think the lady in blue is our girl!" A man actually ran the flounce of my ribbon between his fat fingers.

"Where you from, sweetheart?" Stubble. Gray.

"Why'd you do it? Love triangle?" Missing teeth.

"There's the bit." Young. Cocky.

"He says poison! An elegant weapon for an elegant lady."

"What's the name?"

"Mrs. Kelly. Irish, is she?"

Numb with shock, I gave up listening to the cacophony of insults. We'd finally crossed the eternal wasteland of a lobby and stood in the Grand Court at the curb. Guests had gathered on the balconies above us. I hazarded one look over my shoulder toward the kitchen and saw Pearl's dark form, alone, watching.

"There is a friend closer than a brother," Aunt Mary said.

When I turned back, a camera flash went off in my face.

The carriage pulled up and a valet opened the door.

Detective Fisher continued to answer questions.

Heyes shoved me up the step and into the seat. He followed closely as I tried to arrange my skirts out of his way and prevent the bustle from crushing. The cuffs did not slip off, much to my annoyance, and hampered all attempts at dignity. When Detective Fisher joined us, I scowled across the carriage at him.

The door closed and the carriage lurched forward. The light dimmed as the noise faded and the smooth drive of the Grand Court turned to the rough cobbles of Montgomery Street.

The temperature dropped swiftly.

"Enjoying yourself?" Detective Fisher asked.

Heyes held up the key and I gave him my hands.

"Immensely." I rubbed my emancipated wrists. "You'll have to pull around to the basement. Becky will be beside herself."

The chuckle was soft and his face impossible to discern. "We're off to prison, Mrs. Kelly."

"Only in theory," I said. "No one needs to know where I am so long as I'm not seen."

"You made a bargain. What's that you say so often?

What's done is done."

"You aren't one bit funny." I tried to see out the window, but the sun was nearly gone. "Take me home."

His form stretched out on the seat, and he folded his hands behind his head. "Mrs. Kelly, you're under arrest for the murders of the Reverend and Mrs. Olsen. It's my sworn duty to put you in jail. You wouldn't want a reporter to come by for a morning cuppa and not find you repenting behind bars, would you?"

Heyes gave a soft whistle and said under his breath, "It's going to be a long night."

Chapter Fifteen

"**H**OW AM I supposed to solve a murder from a jail cell?" My words bounced around the Broadway jailhouse entry, a sparse, dismal area with a long, decrepit bench against one wall and a long, decrepit desk against the other.

Mr. Samuel Merrill, the district attorney, did not work with the police, but as he'd hired the coroner, Mr. Lees, and Mr. Lees's morgue was quite literally six feet beneath our shoes, he spent his time working from behind the jailhouse desk and thus managed to keep a finger on the pulse of city crime.

Mr. Merrill, thin and haggard in a gray suit with a drooping mustache that failed to disguise a weak jawline, pushed his wire spectacles higher onto his nose and watched me with interest. He'd prosecuted several policemen for corruption back in the day, and Mr. Lees had fired them when he'd been chief of police before losing reelection to Crowley. It was a mistake to underestimate them. The two teamed up as a formidable, if usually behind-the-scenes, wall of justice behind Detective Fisher's arrests.

My only hope was to get Mr. Merrill on my side, and I

had just the leverage to do it.

I turned to him with a smile. "Sam, the idea is to keep the Palace in business, but not at the expense of justice."

"The idea," Detective Fisher interrupted, "is to keep Mrs. Kelly locked up so that justice can be served."

Mr. Merrill blinked at us. He wore his overcoat with a fur collar and the scent of a brazier told me he had coals near his feet. How any of them worked like this, I couldn't fathom.

Heyes had roped Wilson into standing with us and promptly disappeared. Whether he'd had enough of us for one day or he was off to fill my jail cell with creature comforts, I missed his empathetic presence. Where I considered Heyes the brains, always taking notes and making good observations, Wilson was the muscle. Perhaps I was more of a menace than I gave myself credit for.

I tipped my head and showed my peacock feathers to full advantage for Mr. Merrill. "He's teasing. I'm not dressed for prison tonight. You know what's happened. I must help where I possibly can."

He gave me an uneasy look. "I saw Lees bring her in," he said to Detective Fisher. "Guess he's waiting for you downstairs."

Detective Fisher nodded. "Right. After I lock her up, I'll see him. Do the paperwork, will you?"

After a pause, Mr. Merrill shuffled items randomly around on his desk.

"On what charges?" I asked.

"Murder. Both."

Mr. Merrill looked up and I rolled my eyes.

"We all know that's impossible. Send me home before Becky faints with worry. Miss Smith, I mean." I smiled at Mr. Merrill again. "Ever since you last saw her, I've thought her more delicate. She speaks of your bravery with glowing praise, Mr. Merrill. I'd be obliged if you came around and called on her. To boost her spirits, you know."

Streetlights beyond the front door windows could not penetrate the room, as the front entrance was technically a floor above them, approached by a set of wooden stairs and a landing. And though overhead bulbs cast more shadows than illumination, Mr. Merrill's face had gone undeniably red.

"That's enough of that." Detective Fisher took my elbow. "This way, if you please, Mrs. Kelly. Mr. Merrill, I expect the paperwork on my desk within the hour."

Without another word, he tugged me into the bowels of the building with Wilson trailing us.

"You can't possibly mean it," I said, yanking my elbow and failing to break his grip. "I'm fairly certain colleagues don't lock each other up."

The dank corridor led to an iron door. Beyond it, I knew, was another corridor that ended with a jail yard nearly embedded into the base of Telegraph Hill. On either side of the passage, duplicated another story up, were rows of prison cell doors. Solid metal doors with thick, locking crossbars and a shuttered, barred window near the top. The heavy doors showed extensive corrosion, and hinges were rusted nearly off. There were seldom more than a handful of prisoners held at any one time.

"Shouldn't you save your good cells for the truly desperate scourges of society?" I asked.

"And you aren't desperate?" We stopped at the staircase, a debate crossing his face. "Wilson," he said, turning, "I need strong coffee and two cups upstairs." He paused again. "And send down to Ling's. Two orders of chop suey. And tell him to use actual chicken this time."

"Sir."

Though his grip remained on my elbow, the stairs weren't quite wide enough for us both, and Detective Fisher allowed me a half-step ahead of him. I'd been to his office before and knew the way. Every inch of the building was of the same gray, unyielding stone. It made prisoners think twice, I imagined, but what did it do to those who worked in it year after year? Did they become as implacable? As dull?

The office lights flickered on, showing Sergeant Ross's desk, a chair behind and before it, two cabinets and a bookshelf. A cold grate full of ash was in the fireplace. Tall, narrow windows, arched at the top, looked out onto Broadway Street and down into Chinatown, a strategic move that lent speed to a dangerous job.

Releasing my skirts, I entered the office, and Detective Fisher dropped his hand. "You left me no choice," he said, closing the door behind us. "But at least we can speak without interruption here."

I walked to the window and looked out on the lights of Chinatown, picturing it covered in snow. "People are dying," I said. "We're out of time."

"You think there will be more?" He looked at the desk,

then dragged the chair out from behind it. "Let's sit."

"What?" I asked archly. "Not in a cell?"

"Drop the charade." He placed the chairs facing each other at the front of the desk and sank into one with a sigh. "If we don't figure out what's happening, you're the one who's going to pay for it. You've put your neck in it, now, Mrs. Kelly."

Considering his obvious lack of propriety in front of a lady, there was the smallest hope he was treating me as a colleague. Not an equal, I supposed, but a long sight better than a prisoner.

"Other than the fine print," I said, summoning a regal stroll to the chair and sitting primly at its edge, "this plan is perfect."

He pinched the bridge of his nose and, eyes closed, inhaled deeply. "We don't have a plan. It's out of my hands now! If this goes to trial, you'll be found guilty. Men have swung for far less, let me tell you. You cannot charm your way out of this one."

The door opened and Wilson entered with a coffeepot and two cups. He dropped them onto the desk without ceremony and left again.

We both looked at the pot. There was, at least, some steam coming from the spout. With a slight shiver, I reached for it. Detective Fisher scowled and rose.

"What is it?" he asked. "What is so important to you that you'll risk your life for it?" He wrestled out of his coat. "You hated the reverend. You only met Mrs. Olsen a day ago." The rough wool of his coat fell over my shoulders, and I nearly dropped my cup in surprise. "The hotel is one of many, none of which are exempt from failing." He sat down again. "And you don't need the job."

I took a long sip of bitter coffee, letting it bite its way into my roiling stomach.

"I think, Mrs. Kelly, that you must do something very courageous." His words were careful, but I recoiled from them. "You must divulge your personal life to me. Your past. The source of this conflict between you all. I can see no other way of saving you."

"He was going to ask sooner or later," Aunt Mary said.

I glanced at the window. It never snowed in San Francisco.

"I am sorry," he said. "I know it causes you pain."

Drifts of white. Trees covered in it. Only rooftops visible. Frantically digging to find the path.

"I respect you, Mrs. Kelly. That won't change."

A lady's boot half buried. The truth, and the rest of Aunt Mary, hidden beneath it.

I drained my cup and vowed not to cry. Detective Fisher poured himself a cup of coffee and sat back in his chair. His face was void of emotion. A professional mask that was prepared to hear the plaintiff impartially.

"Aren't you going to take notes?" I asked.

"No. I'm asking about a different case in a different state that I can't do anything about."

"Well, there we are equals." I put the cup on the desk and tried to decide where to begin. "The first thing you must understand is how different Waterford Township is from this city. Back home, everyone for miles and miles shares the same heritage. The grandparents still speak the language of their ancestors, and they settled Minnesota as a group, bringing a single way of life, a work ethic, a religion, family expectations. We all run dairies. Their children married neighbor children and the grandchildren all resemble each other."

"A tight community, even if spread out."

"Yes. So, everyone is Lutheran, and we all consider pastors like Reverend Olsen family, and we defend each other completely, warranted or not."

"We have our communities here," he said. "Packed into city blocks, but they behave the same."

"None of them are Norwegian."

"I'm certain we could find some."

"At any rate, my Aunt Mary was widowed young, and for a while, she kept her husband's farm, but she loved our family and after my mother passed, she sold her farm and moved in with us. She was everything to me."

"Eight brothers, you've said."

"Yes. My only sister, Marte, died when she was four."

He waited while I debated a second cup of the vile coffee.

"Aunt Mary volunteered as Reverend Olsen's secretary. She was busy and happy and quite sharp, even at her age." My voice was testy now and it was more welcome than sadness. "She could run numbers in her head faster than I could. She was in no way impaired or confused."

"I'm not questioning it."

"Well, many did. After. What I know is that Christmas was two days away, and she was leaving for the church. We could smell the storm coming, but the road wasn't long, and we'd traveled it since birth. There was nothing more worrisome on my mind than the supper we were planning. She was on the front porch and Peter brought around the sleigh."

I poured myself another cup after all.

"She told me the ledgers didn't make sense. That's it. It was all I had to work with. She never came back."

"Why was she working instead of staying home with you? So close to Christmas, I mean?"

"Reverend Olsen was supposed to get a new bell for the church. For our New Year's celebration. It distracted her that nothing had been done about it. She didn't have to go. But when she had a wild hair, you didn't get in her way."

"True." Aunt Mary listened eagerly for the rest of the story.

"The storm blew in and we were stuck home that night and all the next day. It was Christmas Day before we could dig our way out to the barn, but we didn't truly worry. Any one of our neighbors would have taken her in and shown her a lovely time, waiting out the storm. For all I knew, she was baking *brune pinner* at the reverend's home and telling him to wipe his feet before coming to the table."

"Pearl said their group especially requested your presence after admiring your desserts."

I shrugged. "To them, it was home. Our home."

"How old was your Aunt Mary?"

"Sixty-seven and tough as nails."

"I believe you."

"I offered to go with her after the holiday. To help her. She was offended. Told me to stay away from the church and her business."

"Offended?"

"I know. Now I think she was warning me away for other reasons. Christmas Day was a gathering at the church. Everyone who could come did. The pews were full. But no one had seen Aunt Mary. By the end of the service, I was beside myself and several of us went person to person, asking after her. Reverend Olsen confirmed she'd come two days before but left long before the storm arrived. He acted as perplexed as any of us."

"Was her sleigh found?"

"Yes. It was in the churchyard stable."

"He said she left, but he couldn't have seen her leave if she hadn't driven away." He was leaning forward, as involved as I was.

"No. And I made certain to establish that fact later." I shuddered and got it over with. "We found her buried in a snowdrift several yards away, between the church and the cemetery. She was up near a woodpile, or anyone would have discovered her, driving through on the paths. The police insisted she'd gotten turned about and tripped. Bumped her head and laid unconscious as the storm blew in. Froze to death. A tragic accident."

"But you don't think so."

"She had scratches on her face and hands. A huge gash on the back of her head. And she was out there without her coat. Her clothes were dirty and soggy and she was a mess once we dug her out, but we never found her coat. Anywhere."

"And what does the rest of your family believe?"

"As the police turned their back on it, and Reverend Olsen denied knowing anything about it, they've laid it to rest along with Aunt Mary."

He waited.

"Christmas services were the last I attended. Reverend Olsen knew something. He was nervous and testy and once he realized I wasn't going to walk away from it, he encouraged everyone to shun me. Do you know what that is? To have everyone you've known and loved for a lifetime slowly step away? I wasn't welcome at the community gatherings. None attacked me, but none spoke to me."

"You attacked their reverend."

"Yes. And in doing so, I neglected the farm. I stopped cooking for my family. I suppose I was obsessed with needing to know why."

"Did you get a look at the ledgers?"

"Absolutely not. Suddenly, Mr. Nilsen had them all under lock and key. The handyman! He was next to useless when I asked him questions. The other women who volunteered about the place threw up a wall around Reverend Olsen, and that was that."

"You sound cynical."

"Only of the church. Not of God. Morality is being faithful. Not necessarily loyal."

Aunt Mary wound up for a sermon, but I cut her off and

said, "I know right from wrong, Detective Fisher. Aunt Mary did not get justice. Her killer still walks. What I want to know is whether her killer walks here or is still in Waterford Township."

He nodded.

"And now I have even more questions," I said in a rush. "Where did my earrings come from? Where did my inheritance come from? Because, as hard as it is for me to think of her being murdered, it's harder yet to think of her being involved in something ... corrupt. Something so big that she could be killed over it."

There. It was out. I swiped at a tear with a gloved finger.

"Do you think she did something wrong?" His question, while gentle, cut deep.

I stared into my empty cup, unable to answer.

Chapter Sixteen

OFFICER WILSON BANGED through the door and we both jumped in our seats.

"Here it is," he said, carrying the large basket to the desktop and dropping it with a rattle. "Ling used nice bowls, so put 'em back in the basket when you're done. Told him I'd bring it all back later tonight."

"Thanks, Wilson." Detective Fisher was already on his feet, digging into the basket with enough enthusiasm that I wondered whether he was eager to shelve my story or truly famished. I took the opportunity to remove my gloves and dry my face.

"Have you eaten this yet?" he asked, as Wilson walked out. "We try to keep our eyes open down there. Stay close and personal with the shopkeepers. They don't poison us, and we don't arrest the first Chinaman we see." He handed me a hot bowl with a flourish. "Chop suey. Means a little of this and a little of that. Never the same dish twice."

"Thank you," I said, letting it warm my hands and taking a deep sniff. "Chicken?"

"It'd better be." He sat and took a bite. "Probably."

I fished a linen napkin from the basket and laid it over

my lap. "Bamboo shoots." My nose took in the details as I poked at it with a spoon. "Onions. Peppers. Mushrooms."

"Odds and ends." He ate faster. "I like it with shrimp. Easier to identify."

I ate thoughtfully, appreciating the distraction as much as the food. What was he going to do with me? It was late, and I was tired and my new hat felt rather foolish at this point.

"Detective Fisher," I said after a few minutes, "I found something in Mrs. Olsen's room earlier."

He looked up and stopped chewing.

Slipping a finger into my pocket, I said, "The other earring, assuming you still have the one from Mr. Olsen's pocket." I pulled it out and it twinkled as I laid it on the desk. "It was up on the top of a framed painting in her parlor."

His supper recommenced, but he stared at the jewel.

"It's an odd thing to have," I said. "For anyone in Minnesota."

"They aren't all from Minnesota."

"You mean Mr. Olsen." I hesitated. "He inherits everything, you said."

He nodded and ran his napkin over his mustache. "The probability was nearly one hundred percent. No one leaves an estate to a wife. Especially if a son is present. Despite his words, he had to have expected it."

"Couldn't a reverend leave his worldly goods to his congregation?"

"Maybe. I find it odd that the reverend would, instead,

force a reprobate son into a ministry he'd nurtured for sixty years."

"He wouldn't have. I can't imagine he believed it for a second. So why put it in the will? For that matter, I find it odd that the reverend would force a young wife into the theater, even if she demanded it. The theater! I'd as soon believe a pig could fly."

His smile was too brief, but it did pleasant things to his face.

"What if she'd changed her mind?" I added. "She nearly did."

"It's too late to question them," he said, finished with his bowl. "And I understand that you made some conversation with the young and dashing Mr. Olsen, but I'm not pleased to hear you trust him. Now that we have a complete set of earrings, I have some hard questions for him."

Had Mr. Olsen used smoke and mirrors on me? After our conversation, his empathy for my own story had gone a long way toward my believing his. He'd gone so far as to doubt Mrs. Olsen, and I'd eagerly pushed him there.

Detective Fisher stood and began to reload the basket. "I agree with you. We're running out of time. Your past is trespassing on the present, which is a problem. It's distracting. We have to focus on these murders. Here. Now."

"They may be one and the same," I murmured, and stood to stretch my back. His coat came with me, its bulk wrapping over my own small jacket, but I didn't offer to return it.

My mind had caught on something and wouldn't let it

go. "You said something earlier. A wife would never inherit if there was a son. The first wife died young. She never had a second child. What if Reverend Olsen's hasty marriage was the result of his prodigal son's return?"

He closed the basket and turned his attention to me.

"I took Mr. Olsen's word for the timeline he suggested. What if the reverend panicked," I said, "thinking of his grown son getting his hands on the ministry and decided to marry and have a child to replace him? Have a suitable heir?"

"It's been done before, I suppose."

"But that leads to…" I bit my lip.

"Yes?"

"Well, you found an earring in his pocket, and I found the other in her room. One might infer…"

"That they were romantically involved."

"And if she were … in the family way…"

"Who would the father be?" He sat down.

I twisted my gloves in my hands. "What if there was? The promise of another son? If she was with child? Would that be motive for murder?"

"It wasn't her husband who killed her," he said grimly.

"But perhaps it was the hope of a second son that made him write what he did in the will." It made sense. "What if he was referring, not to Josiah Olsen, but to an unnamed next son? I doubt Reverend Olsen had any intention of dying. Not for several decades yet."

"That's a solid reason for Mr. Olsen to kill his father." He leaned forward. "It changes the motive from money to passion. And he wouldn't have killed Mrs. Olsen if he thought she was carrying his child."

"But … would he have killed her if he thought the child *wasn't* his?" I leaned in to ask.

"And how would he know for certain?" Detective Fisher suddenly straightened, and his mouth fell open. "I'm sorry, Mrs. Kelly. For a moment, I forgot myself and to whom I was speaking."

"It's a bit late to be squeamish," I said. "Your question is a valid one, if delicate."

He eyed me in speculation.

"I am not the delicate type," I reassured him. "And I think we both know where to find some answers."

A brow went up.

"The morgue," I said. "Downstairs. Mr. Lees will have some things to contribute by now."

He nodded, rose, and swept the earring from the desk and into his pocket. "After you, Mrs. Kelly."

It took me all the way down the stairs to slip my gloves back on. The temperature dropped with each step, and by the time Detective Fisher paused to call out to Mr. Merrill, I was grateful to have absconded with his coat.

"The paperwork, Merrill?" he asked.

"Done." Mr. Merrill leaned over his desk to see us in the corridor. "But I'm not handing it over. I don't know what you two are doing, but it's highly irregular. Don't ask me to participate, Fisher."

"Too late." Detective Fisher opened a door and motioned me down the stairs. "Mrs. Kelly is sleeping in the back room tonight. Have Heyes light a fire and rustle up some blankets. Tell Wilson the basket is ready for him."

"I'm going home," Mr. Merrill retorted. "Ask them yourself." His eyes lingered on mine.

"Mr. Merrill," I said, "if you would be so kind as to inform Miss Smith of my whereabouts, I'd be eternally grateful."

He pushed his spectacles up the bridge of his nose. "If you think she will answer her door at this late hour."

"She's up pacing, no doubt," I said. "I cannot have her distressed all night! You really must."

Buttoning his coat, he said, "I will. But I cannot promise the news will make her any less distressed."

I shrugged and gave Detective Fisher a look of surrender. "Apply yourself, Mr. Merrill. Everyone else must believe that I am a desperate criminal."

The two men exchanged a look, and I pushed forward and down the steps into the morgue.

If the Broadway jailhouse was stark, the morgue was outright desolate. Without windows, and approached by the steps, the other door was at the far end of a cavernous and exposed room. And it led directly to more jail cells.

Bodies wrapped in sheets were piled in rows, awaiting the undertaker. Shelves displayed strange and menacing instruments. Jars of ointments and acids released odors into the air. And a pile of rags in a corner came from the dead, who no longer required them. Clothing and shoes that the poor were welcome to salvage.

The space confronted one with the inevitability of death and doubled whatever hopelessness they'd entered with.

Mr. Lees turned rheumy eyes on us. Bundled in a coat and heavy boots, he had wrapped an apron over all of him and it was not clean. Bare bulbs overhead cast him in a gruesome light full of flickering edges.

"Mr. Lees," Detective Fisher said, "how are you doing this evening?"

"How do you think?" His voice was hoarse. "It's colder than a witch's…" He blinked at me through swollen eyes and yanked out a handkerchief to wipe his raw nose.

Though I understood that a morgue had to be kept cool all the year round, I agreed with the man. Even the refrigerated room in the Palace kitchen seemed a desert oasis by comparison.

"Merrill is on his way out," Detective Fisher said, joining me near the tables in the center of the room. "I expect you'll be on your way home to a roaring fire any minute?"

"Indeed." He sniffled and cleared his throat.

I pulled Detective Fisher's coat tighter around me.

"The jailhouse was a mistake when they built it," Mr. Lees said to me, approaching the other side of the table. "Drainage from Telegraph Hill. Water flows downhill, an engineering fact that was overlooked at the time. The walls are always damp, and the morgue floods if it rains more than three days straight."

He sneezed into the handkerchief. "Mold," he mumbled around it.

"We won't keep you," I said. "We have a question."

He cocked his head at the word *we*, but said, "About these two?" He pointed at the bodies, each on a table and covered with a sheet.

"The Olsens," Detective Fisher said.

"I have a theory," I said. "That Mr. Olsen killed the reverend—his father—in a fit of jealousy because he learned Mrs. Olsen was with child. He thought it was his own. But afterward, she told him that it was her husband's child, so he killed her too."

"You assume," Detective Fisher said, "that they fell in love during those six months. Almost immediately after the wedding."

"Or they met before it. But it would explain their working together and then her sudden coldness the night of the theater. If he confessed to her and she was horrified instead of impressed, then he had to cover his tracks."

"Would she not have turned him in to me for murder?"

"Not if she had religion. Not if she wanted her husband and child to be untainted by an affair. If she simply left, then no one would be the wiser. The Minnesota congregation would support her and the child without question. The theater surely wouldn't. No wonder she wanted out of that contract."

"Rather a coldhearted tale from you, Mrs. Kelly. He seduced her. Then he killed her. I thought you trusted him?"

Mr. Lees watched the two of us volley back and forth, suffering with his head cold.

"I admit, I hardly know anymore. For all we know, the child was his and she denied it for fear of having to marry a murderer."

"Say for a moment that he did it," he said. "Where is the

poison? How was it administered? He wasn't in the room when his father died. And no one was in the room when Mrs. Olsen died."

"My food was not poisoned when it went into the dining room. That means either someone added poison at the last minute—and how is that possible in a room full of people— or he also swallowed something else. Something the son planted before he left the room. As for Mrs. Olsen, how do you know she was alone?"

Mr. Lees interrupted me. "Why are you certain they both died by the same hand?"

"They were both poisoned," I said. "The killer is truly unoriginal."

"Not entirely." Mr. Lees sniffed. "The reverend died from cyanide poisoning and the wife died from a laudanum overdose. The first is rather more violent than the second."

"Mrs. Olsen's death was rather more obvious," I said. "Bottle in plain sight."

"Let's not prolong Mr. Lees's discomfort," Detective Fisher said. "Lees, was Mrs. Olsen expecting a child?"

The direct question caught him off guard, and he looked entirely put out.

"You may speak freely before Mrs. Kelly. What is it?"

Mr. Lees cleared his throat and rubbed hard at his jaw. "No. She wasn't." He pointed at her body. "She, uh. Well, Fisher, she wouldn't unless she'd … um." His face had gone slick with sweat. "She'd never…"

Suddenly, I understood. "But she was married."

"Nevertheless," Mr. Lees said.

"Thank you." Detective Fisher moved for the steps. "We'll get out of your way."

With both men so obviously uncomfortable, I hurried to follow. We left the Reverend and Mrs. Olsen united in death and I imagined, as I climbed the stairs, that the people of five counties would attend their funeral.

"That changes things," I said, joining him in the front office. "If there was no child, there was no love triangle."

"No." He ducked behind the desk to add coal to the frieze on the floor.

"Mr. Olsen didn't seduce anyone. I feel strangely comforted by that."

Detective Fisher motioned for me to follow him and led me down a short hall that opened into a room not much larger than a cell. The rag rug on the floor and the threadbare blankets on a saggy bed were poor compensation for the men stuck here overnight. A basin and water pitcher on a chest with a mirror on the wall above them raised my doubts, and the rack full of rifles displayed over rows of ammunition confirmed them.

"It's better than a cell, isn't it?" he asked blandly.

He went to the hearth and knelt to build a fire.

"I'm grateful," I said. "I'm not certain it's necessary for our charade."

"Unfortunately, our bluffs were called." He struck a match, and the wood momentarily smoked.

"Our?"

"You bluffed about going to jail. I bluffed about keeping you here. Both are now a reality. We're stuck together, colleagues or not." The fire crackled and he rose and brushed his hands together. "And we have to find the killer. Fast."

"You'll interrogate Mr. Olsen?"

"And the others. Perhaps he had an accomplice at the table."

"Mrs. Berg? She hates him. Mr. Nilsen refuses to speak to him."

"No. Someone else. One of the theater people. Mr. Olsen makes no secret that he's a man of the modern world. A liaison in that direction is more logical. Good night, Mrs. Kelly. Please call out if you need anything."

"Are you staying as well?"

"Someone has to guard the prisoners."

"How many are there?"

He smiled, and his eyes were weary. "Full house."

Chapter Seventeen

I WOKE THE next dawn, stiff from sleeping in my corset and groggy from a very unrestful night. The door closed but it did not lock, and the collection of firearms was too close for comfort. It was not a pleasant thought that if there was a coup or a raid or a jailbreak at midnight, I'd be the first to find out.

The fire still blazed in the hearth, and I vaguely recalled having uneasy dreams about winter back home. Visions of Mrs. Olsen's room, gloomy and heavy with death. And though my eyes had flown open at every strange sound, I'd managed to miss whoever had come in and draped my own clothing at the foot of the bed.

While I'd taken down my hair and braided it for sleep, I'd only removed my jacket, shoes, and outer skirt with its ridiculous bustle. My lovely blue hat perched on an old trunk like a little lost bird. My finest costume was worse for the wear. Frustrated, I smoothed helplessly at my skirt wrinkles after changing quickly into the serviceable black dress that had magically appeared. Another look around the room told me Detective Fisher had reclaimed his coat.

It was no loss. Mine fit better, anyway.

I silently thanked Becky as I pinned my hair into submission. She'd even sent my black hat with its mourning veil. Subtle.

What had transpired between her and Mr. Merrill last night? I couldn't wait to find out.

"Mrs. Kelly?" A rap at the door accompanied Heyes's voice.

"Come in," I called from my spot before the warped mirror. Another two hairpins, and I was done.

Heyes opened the door and entered, bearing a cup and saucer. "For you. I've been practicing for two hours."

I stepped close and inhaled the scent of coffee. "Bless you, Heyes." The first sip warmed me all the way to my toes.

His smile went from ear to ear. "Made so much coffee that the boys are all hiding from me. Made 'em drink their weight in it."

"You've gotten the knack of it, I think." I gratefully took another sip. "Where is Mr. Merrill today? Detective Fisher?"

"Neither here this morning." He slid his hands into his trouser pockets and rocked back on his heels. "Just a few of us officers holding down the fort."

"But where have they gone?" It was early, but a glance out the window didn't reveal the time. I wondered if we'd ever see the sun again.

"Fisher's at the hotel, I believe. Sam's gone to meet the mayor at City Hall."

"Detective Fisher is working without me?" I tried to keep the disappointment out of my voice. After what he'd said last night, I'd assumed we were a team.

"I don't rightly know. All he told me is I'm to be available to you while he's busy. If there's anything you need, I'll fetch it."

"That's fine, then." I smiled brightly at him. "It's just that I thought he would head directly for the theater first."

He shrugged.

"I do have some errands to run, though." I handed him the empty cup. "The pharmacy."

"Tell me what you need," he said, nodding eagerly. "I've got some emergency funds we can spend." The idea seemed to tickle him. "It's not every day we host a lady here, Mrs. Kelly."

I pursed my lips for a moment and dropped my eyes. "I'm afraid I can't send you, Heyes, but thank you. I'll have to go myself."

"Nothing doing. You can't leave the jailhouse. Orders from the top."

"But Heyes…" I tried to work up some color in my cheeks but only managed a wince. "It's a female situation. Delicate."

It would never have worked with Detective Fisher. Officers were exposed to the base degradation of humanity all the time. I was certain Heyes could draw his own conclusions, but just how fragile and dainty he considered the situation was hard to predict.

"No offense," he said, "but you're accused of two murders. I saw the papers. You're a desperate criminal. We've already had three reporters come by the desk and refuse to leave until I told 'em you were locked up here. It'd be my job if you walked out the front door."

"I understand. I do." I clasped my hands together. "That's exactly why there's a problem. I'm not at home among my own things. If there was any help for it ... but perhaps you have a wife who might run the errand for me?"

His face colored prettily. "You know I don't."

"Well, then, be sensible. I'm wearing black," I pointed out. "My hat is veiled. It's a quick ride to a pharmacy and no one need ever find out. You'll be with me the entire time."

I considered his silence a good omen.

"We can leave through the back," I said, reaching for my hat. "No one would see us climb into a buggy there."

He looked over his shoulder into the empty hall. "We can't go anywhere near the Palace. Or more than ten minutes away."

"Of course not." I adjusted the hat and began draping the veil. "You can drive us where you please. Why not across the street in Chinatown? There are several herbal shops quite close."

"How do you know?" Suddenly suspicious, he caught me off guard.

"I shop everywhere, remember? For ingredients. I know all the shopkeepers in Chinatown."

An exaggeration maybe, but I had one particular place in mind, and he didn't need to know that. He stared into my face, squinting through the veil. "And what if the shopkeepers know you?"

"Do you think a Chinaman is going to care about a prisoner? Who's a woman? Do you suppose they read the

English papers? Would they come running to report me?"

He straightened. "You have a point."

"I'll be quick as a wink. Thank you, Heyes. You're a real gentleman."

"Reckon we'd better get on with it, then," he muttered. "But you won't make me a fool, will you? If you disappear, Fisher will run me out of town. After he shoots me. No funny business?"

I crossed my heart, and he helped me into my coat.

Satisfied, he stepped aside and allowed me to exit the room. "We don't have any patrols running Pacific Street right now," he muttered, more to himself than to me. "Too early. Should be all right."

The small hope I nurtured kept me company through the jail, past the bleak cells, into a small buggy, and down to Dupont Street. It was nearly impossible to see through the veil in the murky gray morning, but the sounds and scents of Chinatown led us unerringly to the largest shop on the corner of Washington Street.

Wagons rumbled past or stopped in the road, delivering or picking up produce, dry goods, fowl in crates, baskets of spice, or barrels of meat. Whether one required eggs, fish, bread, or herbal medicine, it could be found within the corner grocery. Shoppers at this hour were either servants of fine houses or cooks from restaurants. Both sides of the building opened to the outside air and apartments rose above the shop for three more stories.

Mr. Song would tell me what I wanted to know. His son ran the flower shop next door.

"Will this one do?" Heyes asked, reining in the horse.

"Yes. Thank you." I gripped my skirt, but he said, "No, Mrs. Kelly. Wait for me."

The bustling tradesmen paid no mind to us as we stepped inside. A glance here and there at Heyes was natural. No one wanted business with the police, and they all kept a respectful distance as I moved directly for the counter near the back of the shop. Mr. Song was in his place behind it, reigning benevolently over his little kingdom.

It took only a moment before his face creased into a smile of recognition. I flattered myself that I was one of his favorite customers, but perhaps he made everyone feel that way.

"Good morning, Mr. Song," I said. "I need several things."

His head bobbed up and down. "Yes, Mrs. Kelly. All you wish."

Hesitating, I bit my lip and gave Heyes an uncomfortable look. Taking the hint, he wandered away and turned his back to me to inspect a pile of potatoes. He'd placed himself between me and the door.

Unnecessary.

I leaned closer to Mr. Song. "I want fresh ginger, raw honey, a lemon if you have one, and turmeric."

"Yes, Mrs. Kelly." He signaled to a boy who'd evidently been eavesdropping in a corner and the boy scurried away.

"I also want to know if your son sent the usual floral delivery to the Palace Hotel this week."

He nodded. "Yes. Usual."

"Can you find out whether there were other deliveries? Orders for a bouquet. Roses. Monday. I want to know particularly who ordered it."

"To Palace?"

"Yes."

He pondered it, and I looked around to check on Heyes. "I am working at the jailhouse today. You can send word to me there."

His smile vanished.

"It's no problem," I assured him. "A boy can leave a message at the door, can't he?"

The boy in question arrived and placed my purchases on the counter between us. He didn't linger. As he left, a figure across the shop caught my eye. Small, dark, and arguing fiercely over a basket of almonds.

Pearl. I rubbed my suddenly icy hands together and turned my back to her.

"There's something else," I said, lowering my voice further yet. "Someone purchased poison in town in the last…" I calculated. "Either last Friday or Saturday. Shops were closed on Sunday, were they?"

One fast nod as he listened intently.

"Cyanide," I said. "And laudanum. This person asked for them both. At the same time. An odd combination. Should be easy to remember who made the purchase once you discover who made the sale."

"Maybe not in Chinatown." He crossed his arms and looked down his nose at me.

"No. But you will find out," I said.

This was a man who could find any fruit or vegetable out of season. Who had once presented me with an herb grown only in China. He'd find a needle in a haystack if the price was right.

"A white man or a woman," I whispered. "Not from here. Heavy accent probably, and no idea where to purchase them in the first place. They would have asked around."

"Ready to leave?" Heyes was at my side and reaching into his pocket.

"Yes, thank you." My veil fluttered as I looked back at Mr. Song. "Give him a generous tip, Heyes. He was most helpful and will send around the last item I need later today."

Heyes was in a hurry and handed over nearly double what my small items cost, but the look in Mr. Song's eyes said it was enough. Collecting my package and bidding him good day, I hurried toward the door.

The hiss came from behind a stack of crates and froze my feet to the floor. Heyes nearly bumped into me and cursed under his breath.

"What are you doing here?" Pearl asked, horror written clearly across her face. "You were arrested."

"She still is." Heyes took my elbow with a frown.

"They say you did it," she whispered. "Your face is on the front page of the newspaper. The hotel opened up like nothing ever happened."

I nodded, not trusting my voice. My throat was thick with emotion. Seeing her back at work made my gamble worthwhile.

She glanced around us, then said, "Those people are still locked up on the fourth floor, though. Detective Fisher is still meeting with them. So, I don't know what to think."

"Think about doing your job," Heyes said. "And let me do mine." He steered me to the door.

"Pearl?" I called over my shoulder. Heyes paused but strengthened his grip. "Did the hotel purchase flowers for Mrs. Olsen? As a condolence or some sort of apology? When she was widowed, I mean. Not when she…"

"Flowers?" she asked.

"A bouquet. It was in her room. On the table. She said it was from the hotel."

"We don't do that." She stood in the aisle, and I left her there, full of unasked questions.

I'd piqued her curiosity, but it was clear Heyes was ready to throw me over his shoulder. I let him help me into the buggy, and we drove away without looking back.

The Palace Hotel, while known for its extravagance, did not furnish fresh flowers in each suite. Wine, chocolates, or a complementary pot of tea, on a special occasion. But Pearl confirmed it. Flowers were too expensive and perishable. The hotel did not place them in her room.

Then who did?

"The flowers could have been from her husband," Heyes growled. He gave the horse an impatient slap with the reins. "Obvious, don't you think?"

I would have, had they not been so fresh that I'd ignored them. Drooping, unwatered bouquets had a scent one couldn't avoid noticing. If Mrs. Olsen claimed they were courtesy of the hotel, she'd been either lying or lied to.

Hopefully, Mr. Song would be able to help me find out.

Meanwhile, if someone from Minnesota had gone out to purchase poison, I hoped they were awkward and obvious about it. It was hard to decide whether they would have approached the pharmacy right in the Palace Hotel shops, or gone somewhere full of dark corners and people who wouldn't ask any questions. Like Chinatown.

Heyes drove the buggy up Pinkney Alley to the rear of the jailhouse. I grew colder just looking at the place.

"Thank you, Heyes." The cells we passed on our way inside reminded me of the generosity I'd been shown, and I had a momentary stab of panic, visualizing what might happen if things went horribly wrong.

He opened the door for me with a sigh of relief. "We'll settle down for the day, shall we?"

"Indeed," Detective Fisher drawled from within.

Heyes and I exchanged a look of foreboding and walked stiffly toward the front office. Detective Fisher, in his coat and hat, sat behind the desk. He did not look happy.

"Officer Heyes," I said, "would you be so kind as to put on a kettle? I want to make some tea."

Heyes vanished.

I placed my parcel on the desk and unwound my veil. "Good morning, colleague. Have you broken your fast today?"

His voice was icy calm. "Tell me what in hell you just did." It was a tone that normally accompanied a drawn gun.

"Heyes took me around the corner for this." I laid my

veil next to the package. "We weren't gone ten minutes and I doubt anyone noticed."

"I will never leave you alone again."

I took it for the threat it was.

"In that case," I said with a smile, "I'm joining Heyes in that hole you call a kitchen and making us all some proper food. This package is for Mr. Lees. He's going to catch pneumonia down there if someone doesn't do something about it."

"You broke out of jail for Mr. Lees?"

"Yes. All of you must learn to live like civilized men. Thank the good Lord you clapped me in irons, Detective Fisher." I turned on my heel and left him.

It was proving a most productive morning.

Chapter Eighteen

S EVERAL OFFICERS MANAGED to fill their lean bellies with the breakfast I threw together. It was nice to be thanked in person over a fresh plate of biscuit, eggs, bacon, and gravy instead of standing at my station in the Palace Hotel making more, always more, for faceless diners I would never meet.

"Careful, Mrs. Kelly," Heyes said around a mouthful, "we'll never let you escape if you keep cooking like this."

"If I thought it would keep me from being hung, I'd throw in an angel food cake."

"What's that?" he asked, eyes wide.

"A type of sponge," I said, but I was interrupted.

"Something you better pick up and get to work with," Detective Fisher said. He wiped his mouth and added his plate and cutlery to a dishpan full of greasy water. "You and Wilson wash up. She has better things to do than play nursemaid to a bunch of deadbeats."

"They aren't," I said amiably as I removed the apron it took ten minutes to find. "How did Mr. Lees like the tea I made him?"

He led me to the front office, where a fitful sun attempted to break through the cloud cover outside, bringing a passable, if fickle, light to the place through the front windows. He took his time answering and watching him argue with his pride was entertaining.

"I reckon if it don't kill him, it'll cure him," he grumbled.

I bit my tongue on an acid reply and said instead, "It'll cure him, all right." I took a seat on the long bench. "If he keeps a flannel around his neck and drinks the entire pot, he'll feel better in no time."

He frowned at the door, sighed at the desk, then put his hands into his pockets and sat on the bench with me.

"It chafes you," I said. "To be a colleague. I confess to the same. But I truly see no other way forward. We must learn to cooperate with one another."

He eyed me. "You're right. I left without asking you, and you turned around and left without asking me. Not for a minute do I think you did it for Lees. And you aren't the spiteful type to do something to prove that you can. So, what were you up to on this fine morning?" He held up a quick hand. "I intend to return the favor, of course."

"Don't we need to take notes?"

"Be my guest." He waved his hand toward the desk, and I rose, walked around it, and sat in Mr. Merrill's chair. Detective Fisher merely raised an eyebrow and waited while I gathered the correct apparatus and wrote some preliminary words.

"My trip into Chinatown was merely to gather information," I said, writing down the fundamentals of what I'd put forth to Mr. Song. "I want to know where Mrs. Olsen got the flowers in her room. They were fresh and completely out of place."

"I still have the key to her room in my pocket," he said. "But I didn't go in this morning."

"No one else will go in, will they?"

He shook his head. "Mr. Sedgwick says I have the only copy."

"Good. I want a closer look at them. Now that we know about her … condition, it rather proves what I've said all along. They did not come from her husband. They would be wilted by now. And Pearl says they were not from the hotel—"

"Pearl?"

"Yes." I glanced up from my report. "She was in the market and knew me, even through the veil."

He ran a hand through his hair.

"Meanwhile," I continued, "if anyone's purchased the poisons in the last couple of days, the Chinatown grapevine will know. I've arranged for a boy to deliver the answer here later today."

"That fast?" He rose. "Why are they so cooperative for you? They've known me for years and not offered help."

Our eyes met and my smile only irritated him further. He very well knew why. Chinatown merchants appreciated my shopping skills and exotic curiosity, but the underground tongs owed me allegiance from a previous kerfuffle I'd helped them through.

Detective Fisher and I never discussed it.

Hastily finishing my notes, I waited expectantly for his.

He chose to pace. "I wanted to speak with Mr. Nilsen this morning. He's not the most cooperative man I've ever tried working with."

"You can say that again."

"He gives out one-word answers and other than drawing my gun, I couldn't see any way of finding anything out unless my question was direct."

"Obtuse."

"How's that?"

"It means you'd have to hit him in the head with a cross-beam to jog information out."

"Mm. Well, I've kept his paperwork locked in Mrs. Olsen's suite, and he's none too happy about it. He stands by his story that at least the four of them were here in the city to stay, and that the son, Mr. Olsen, was an unexpected and unwanted companion."

"He is the odd man out," I said, writing in the little book, "but the only one I think who would stay at this point." My fingers itched to turn the pages back and read what was already in it.

"I'm going back to the California Theater," he said, and his hands returned to his pockets. "You'll have to come, with the veil. Even that may not be enough at this point. Your photograph was on the front page of every paper in town."

I straightened. "Did you bring them?"

"Used them to start the fire this morning. You don't need to know what they're saying, since all of it is untrue." He shook his head. "Each story was more wild than the next, and none of them flattering."

"I see." Still. It would have been an entertaining read.

"Reporters are worse than lawyers," he said and went back to pacing. "At least if a lawyer loses, his victim can walk free. A reputation is maybe a harder thing to reclaim."

I shivered but blamed the weather. "In this town, a reputation is an asset."

"It isn't funny, Mrs. Kelly."

"What have I left, Detective Fisher, except a sense of humor? I'm the distraction. The bait. If it protects the people whose trust I value, and finds us the actual killer, let them talk!"

He'd stopped and stood staring through the window in the front door. When a face popped up on the other side, he quickly locked the door.

"Damn reporters," he muttered, and drew the blind.

"I cooked this morning," I said quietly. "No one refused to eat. Don't think I didn't notice. Even Mr. Lees trusted me with that strange concoction I brewed up for him. That means everything to me."

After clearing his throat, he said, "We best get moving. I'm ready if you are. I've sent the linens out to the laundry. The bed and toweling should be fresh by tonight."

"I'm not going home, then?"

"Mr. Merrill has offered to run between here and there when needed. It's all I can offer you."

He continued to stare at the door and I rose, resigned. I was a burden, not a contribution.

"Mr. Nilsen is taking too long," he said, finally turning. "Madame Fabbri will be swift. There must be more to their connection."

I handed him the notebook. "Then let's go find out."

Our drive to the theater was uneventful. It included neither guards nor small talk. Where Heyes had begged for my cooperation, Detective Fisher assumed it and made no motion toward me that he would not have afforded any lady in his presence. I sat behind my veil and determined to repay his trust.

Somehow.

As we pulled into the alley that ran behind the theater, he said, "Stay quiet and behind me, please. In order to avoid anyone looking you full in the face. There may be no help for it once we are in her office, but we'll address that when we come to it. Agreed?"

"Agreed." I let him hand me out of the buggy.

The surly brute at the theater's rear door was none too happy to see visitors, but once he understood the detective wanted to question Madame Fabbri about a recent murder, he hurried us into the silent building.

"She ain't awake yet," he said. "Can I rouse Mr. Sims for ye instead?"

"No." Detective Fisher was curt and put some steel into his voice. "I want her in her office. Now."

The place seemed eerily topsy-turvy as we moved through the backstage area where props and scenery stacked randomly among costume parts and rope pulleys. Here and there, a ragged boy slept curled in a corner.

We followed our escort down a hall with many closed doors before finding the one he wanted. It opened into the front vestibule, and the stairs across the way were familiar. "Up there." He grunted. "I'll get her for ye."

The place was abandoned. "Theater hours," I said quietly behind Detective Fisher. "She might have only just gone to sleep."

He opened the office door for me. "As you said, we're running out of time." I led the way into her showy, if stuffy, office and took a chair in front of her desk.

Detective Fisher sat beside me and pulled out his notebook. He'd read through a couple of pages before the door opened and an immaculate Madame Fabbri stalked into the room.

None would ever guess she slept. Without a wig, her lovely dark hair was coiffed into a simple chignon with silver combs and her face dewy and fresh. She wore her French-cut burgundy dressing gown like royal robes, and I caught a glimpse of silver slippers before she took her throne across from us.

"One does not enjoy the word murder at this ungodly hour of day, detective," she said. "I cannot imagine why you've returned so soon."

The door opened again, and Mr. Sims came in with a tray. The aroma of coffee wafted by as he set it on her desk.

"Although I can appreciate that you did not intrude in the midst of another performance." Rings glittered on her fingers as she raised a hand over a delicate yawn. "I trust you will be brief."

"I'm afraid it's all my fault," I blurted out. Detective Fisher froze. "I asked him to come. I wasn't in my right mind the other night, and I owe you an apology."

She nodded regally and Mr. Sims handed her a hot, steaming cup of coffee that he did not offer us.

With a wobble in my voice, I said, "My husband's death is still such a shock that even now, I don't trust myself to speak. But Detective Fisher here was very kind. He said we could see your copy of my contract. I'd like to read it for myself now that I am calmer."

I held my breath. Detective Fisher pulled out his notebook. The die was cast.

"As you please." She fumbled in the desk and slid the paperwork toward me. "I assume it is safe with him next to you. Detective, are you anywhere near finding that poor man's murderer, then? Such a terrible blow."

"It was," he confirmed. "I recall you mentioning Mrs. Olsen here wrote you several times before their arrival?"

I kept my head down and read the contract, taking care to lift the veil only as far as necessary.

"She did."

"Do you have any of those letters? May I have one?"

"You may as well. I don't need them."

Within moments, he was opening an envelope. I ached to look over his shoulder but focused on my part.

"I confess to being shocked by your behavior," she said languidly. "Your letters were nothing but eager, Mrs. Olsen."

"And so I am," I said. "After all, this is the first theater to use … um … limelight."

I affected distraction, but she leaned forward over her cup.

"Are you prepared to move in with us, Mrs. Olsen? There is a room all arranged for you at your earliest convenience."

"Thank you," I said, turning another page.

"Perhaps you will be ready to give me an aria or two once you're comfortable?"

"I've looked forward to such a moment my whole life. It was part of our arrangement, was it not?" If I was going to represent the dearly departed, I wanted her to look down and approve.

"Indeed." She sipped her coffee.

While they drew out the silence, I continued to read the contract. I stopped on the final page.

"This clause says that if I fail to perform my part, the money stays with the theater." I widened my eyes beneath the veil. "No matter what? What if something happens?"

"Whatever do you mean, child?"

"If I die?"

"How very tragic. Try not to. Whether you run away to marry or go mute after eating an oyster, the money stays. It was most explicitly stated, as you see."

"The patronage is secure, then, from every possibility?"

Her lips curved in an indulgent smile. "Child, what do you believe possible?"

"Consumption, Madame Fabbri."

She dropped back in her chair, and a line creased her forehead. "So. You know?"

I waited, and Detective Fisher slid the letter back into its envelope.

"My husband's will bound the patronage and myself equally to you. This contract was set up as the opportunity of a lifetime, but we both know it can never be."

Mr. Sims collected Madame Fabbri's empty cup and carried the tray away. I hoped he hadn't gone to get the morning papers.

"What happens next?" I asked.

She gave an elegant shrug and glanced at Detective Fisher. "You stay. I've been compensated for your room and board for as long as it's needed."

"A prisoner," I said. "Heartless, is it not?"

"Not for a woman who begged to be here," she retorted. This time she scowled, and I wondered what it cost her vanity. "Detective, arrest this woman at once."

He snapped to attention. "I beg your pardon?"

"I am out of patience. You appear to have her hair and fair skin beneath the veil," she said, eyeing me. "And you have an impressive way with accents. That's clear. But you forgot to cough, or at the very least, weep. I saw you both in the same room, I think, and you are not the flighty thing who wanted out of her contract. Who are you and why are you impersonating my protégé?"

Detective Fisher stood abruptly. "Mrs. Olsen is dead. She was found with a suicide note. Do you know anything about it?"

It took her a full minute to comprehend his words. "No," she finally said. "Perhaps she really did know about her condition."

"How could she have possibly not known?" I asked.

"She didn't. Her husband arranged for her to die happy. Is that a sin?"

"If the reverend and Mrs. Olsen are both deceased," Detective Fisher said, "you have all their money and none of their problems. Unless you destroy the contract."

We all looked at the papers on her desk and she slowly, deliberately, slid them back into her drawer.

"Business is business," she said. "I'm sure Mr. Olsen is content."

It took a minute to sink in. "Mr. Olsen?" I cried, rising. "Won't he contest the will now? Demand his rightful inheritance?"

"He's a cad if he tries," she said. "After all, he's the one who introduced them to my theater."

Chapter Nineteen

DETECTIVE FISHER REMAINED deadpan in the face of this bald statement. We stood in front of Madame Fabbri's desk, and I struggled to keep my mouth shut. After my masquerade and my angry outburst, I had to defer the next move to him if there was the slightest chance of maintaining our colleague status.

"Madame Fabbri," he said, "the entire party from Minnesota was at the New Year's Eve table with you. I understood that your Mr. Sims and their Mr. Nilsen handled the monetary details of the patronage."

She nodded her regal head.

"I also understand that Reverend Olsen and his wife were quite eager to make the arrangements you have before you in the contract."

Another nod.

"The other three, Mrs. Berg, your husband Mr. Muller, and Mr. Olsen, were not?"

"Only the woman was against it," she said. "If I had to guess. She seemed eager to agree to whatever the reverend wanted, despite her obvious personal distaste with the whole affair."

"Your husband's vote?"

"Why would he say no to anyone who offered to support our theater? His counsel was not requested."

It was Detective Fisher's turn to nod. "That leaves Mr. Olsen. The son who burst into this office. I was not under the impression that you knew each other before they arrived in San Francisco."

"Only through correspondence. He wrote an introduction for the late"—she glanced at me—"Mrs. Olsen. I continued the correspondence with her, answering questions and encouraging them to come out and see the theater for themselves."

"You had not met before the party?"

"No." She glanced at the door. "Sims!"

"He was the first to reach out to you? Not the Reverend or Mrs. Olsen?"

"That is correct. His initial inquiry regarded an audition for Mrs. Olsen, but it was soon followed with a generous patronage offer that we could not refuse."

Mr. Sims entered and positioned himself next to the open door.

Detective Fisher ignored him. "When did you know that your incoming protégé had consumption and would be worthless to you?"

A smirk played around her lips. "She was worthless to us, regardless. We are not in need of a new soprano. We are in need of funding."

"When did you find out?"

"Her husband sent the information with the contract.

My part was to encourage the woman and give her haven."

"And hope," I added quietly.

The room fell silent enough to hear the end of Mr. Sims's pencil tapping against his palm.

"Thank you, madame," Detective Fisher said at last. "We've kept you from your rest long enough. We will see ourselves out."

"Nonsense. Mr. Sims will escort you."

"One last question, if you please," I said. "There are a pair of earrings involved with their deaths. Blue pendants. Diamonds, perhaps. Large sapphires." I was reluctant to remove the veil and show her my set, but it was no matter, as she was already shaking her head.

"No." She patted her smooth hair with a delicate hand. "I know nothing about any jewels."

With a brief nod, I swept through the door Mr. Sims held open. Detective Fisher caught up to me on the stairs down but kept silent until Mr. Sims moved ahead of us in the vestibule and led the way out.

"What was all that in there?" he asked under his breath.

"It was a shame to waste these widow's weeds. Why can I never attend the theater in my best dress?"

"You were never meant to sit in an audience," he muttered. "You prefer the stage."

It might have pleased me more had not a part of me been shocked by the idea. I waited, but Aunt Mary did not have an opinion ready for such a contingency.

I shrugged. "Once Madame Fabbri reads the morning paper, I can't show my face here again." It was frustrating to see the doors closing so swiftly around me. "If anyone recognizes me now, it could be your job too."

"Keep the veil," he said tersely as we stepped outside of the dark building and into the alley's brightness.

Mr. Sims waited at the door while the brutish guard relinquished our horse and buggy.

Detective Fisher handed me up into my seat. "We're going to see Mr. Olsen immediately. I'm getting to the bottom of this."

Not him, I pleaded to myself. Anyone else. I waited until Detective Fisher came around and climbed in to say, "We must consider any of the three in the case of Reverend Olsen's murder. Not only Mr. Olsen."

"What is your allegiance to him?"

I faltered. "A gut feeling, is all. He may have done it for the inheritance, I suppose. Not for love, but to make certain his status was uncontested."

"If so, that begs a question, Mrs. Kelly." He slapped the reins over the horse's rump, and we rattled forward. "How did the son know there was anything to inherit? The church does not pay well and its leaders, as far as I know, are supposed to keep tithes circulating. Not hoard them. How did Mr. Olsen know there was anything worth fighting for, since he was never interested in the congregation or the location?"

I had no answer for that.

Swallowing the lump in my throat, I challenged, "And if Mrs. Berg killed him?" He scoffed, but I added, "To punish him for his wicked ways. She's a zealot. You might have noticed."

He was already shaking his head. "She was devoted to him. She's lived in Waterford Township her entire life but decided to come with the Olsens and support them. According to her, they were all she had left to live for."

I sat with a frown for a full minute. "She was widowed before Josiah Olsen was ever born. But her husband left her a comfortable living with the creamery. Spent her time running gossip between five counties for years. The entire grapevine likely collapsed when she left."

"Were you ever on friendly terms?" His question held doubt, and well it should.

"And withal they learn to be idle, wandering about from house to house; and not only idle, but tattlers also and busybodies, speaking things which they ought not," I quoted.

He glanced at me.

"Don't you own a Bible? First Timothy. No. Most of us had to do a day's work. Mrs. Berg spent most of her time at the church and never missed a gathering. I spent months trying to get information from her about Aunt Mary, but she absolutely wouldn't hear a word against Reverend Olsen. Tighter than a rusty lid on a pickle jar."

She'd played a big part in turning the congregation against me, but I thrust the bitter memories away.

Detective Fisher tactfully changed the subject. "Why couldn't you get anything out of Mr. Nilsen at the time? He's reticent. And loyal. But you are the persuasive type.

Surely the handyman and you got along in the past?"

My arguments seemed to melt faster than I could form them.

"Mr. Nilsen is the least likely person to have killed the reverend," I admitted. "We all liked him well enough. No local family. He came through looking for work many years ago and Reverend Olsen hired him on out of charity. While none were especially close to him, let me tell you, it was a shock to see him sitting at the dining room table in a tuxedo. He was never arrogant. A humble but quiet man." I cleared my throat. "Until Aunt Mary died."

"Does it strike you as odd that Reverend Olsen would ask a handyman to be his secretary?"

"At the time, we all wondered. But it's obvious now. Reverend Olsen was hiding something. He chose Mr. Nilsen completely on the strength of his loyalty and silence. Never were two more perfect people created for the job of protecting Reverend Olsen and hiding a murder."

"As far as I can tell," he said as we turned a corner, "their devotion resulted in their leaving the only home they had."

"And becoming wealthy," I said. "And coming to a big city in style and staying in a luxurious palace."

We slipped down Pinkney Alley and pulled to a stop in the jail yard. Officer Wilson stood waiting for us and took the horse by the halter.

I turned to Detective Fisher, bumping his knee with mine. "My question is, where did all that money come from? Neither my aunt nor the reverend should have had that kind of money in their pocket. Why would the reverend give it all away in one fell swoop? Why would Aunt Mary leave it all to me?"

He tipped his head, playing with the reins in his hands. "Two stacks of money. One is the reverend's and one is your aunt's. If we assume your aunt was involved. And we must because of the earrings," he added apologetically.

"Both stacks of money left Minnesota quickly and more or less at the same time," I said. "Permanently. And is now in someone else's hands."

"What were they going to live on out here?" he mused. "A third stack of money?"

"If the reverend's money was supposed to purchase a belfry and didn't, it would be fraud in the church. Something Aunt Mary tried to warn me about."

"And if he gave it to a theater instead, a reverend supporting a burlesque is a bit of ethical fraud, is it not? For a church."

"But that part happened after she died." I tried to put the timeline together. "And Josiah Olsen arrived afterward, as well." If he'd written to Madame Fabbri about Mrs. Olsen, had the idea been his? But what had prompted the letter of inquiry? I couldn't see him convincing Reverend Olsen to do anything as rash as take his fortune and his family to a sin-filled city and the stage.

A young, beautiful wife with a voice like an angel could have, though. What had she done to influence these two men, neither of whom had apparently ever shared her bed? And what had she done to deserve death?

I struggled with the fact that the suspicion had circled

right back to Mr. Olsen's feet.

"We'll piece the puzzle together at the hotel," Detective Fisher said.

"Mr. Nilsen's paperwork," we said at the same time. Then we looked down at Wilson.

"Sir," Wilson said, snapping to attention. "A boy's here to see Mrs. Kelly."

"Mr. Song's boy," I said, pleased that something had gone right.

I climbed from the buggy ahead of Detective Fisher.

"He's in the last cell to the right," Wilson called as I opened the door to the jail.

"What?" I spun around and Detective Fisher nearly ran into me. "Why?"

"He was skulking around the front landing," Wilson said. "Sneaking, like. We caught hold of him, but all he'd say was he was looking for you."

"Wilson!" Mr. Song would never trust me again.

"Half a dozen reporters was loitering there as well," he said, raising his voice. "I couldn't tell him you wasn't here, could I?"

"Wilson." Detective Fisher's voice cut into Wilson's tirade. "The key." He held out his hand and Wilson dropped a heavy key ring into it.

"He tried to make a run for it, fought coming inside where we could even try to get a word in, so we locked him up safe till you could see him." Defensively, Wilson looked back and forth between us.

Detective Fisher took the door from me and followed me

swiftly down the dank corridor.

At the final cell before the door leading into the building proper, Detective Fisher applied the key and turned the rusty lock. The door swung open to show a small space with only a bucket and a bare pallet on the floor. A boy had curled up with his back in one corner, knees pulled tight to his chest, and stared at us over them, his eyes wide with fear.

The boy from the market this morning.

"I am Mrs. Kelly," I said softly. I moved into the cell and lowered myself onto the pallet. "I'm sorry. You were not supposed to be in here."

Detective Fisher waited silently in the doorway.

My billowing skirts covered whatever was on the floor, but the scent of fear and cold damp permeated the space.

I would burn my dress later.

I held out a hand, hoping he would recognize me from the market. "Please. You're safe. We'll take you home."

Only the boy's eyes moved as he considered my words. And if he didn't understand all of them, I hoped he would understand my behavior.

Slowly, he unfolded himself, rose, and walked to me. His short trousers and long tunic were plain black and his battered cap perched above a long dark braid that fell softly over a shoulder.

"You have a message?" I asked, looking up into his dark eyes. "From Mr. Song?"

He withdrew a slip of paper from beneath his cap and laid it in my hand.

"It's a delivery order," I said, reading it. "A bouquet to be sent to the Palace Hotel. Delivered to room 412. Mrs. Olsen died later that night." I swallowed. "Signed for by Mr. Olsen."

"She told you it was from the hotel?" Detective Fisher sounded weary.

"She lied about him," I said, flummoxed. "But they weren't lovers."

"Is that all?" Detective Fisher stepped back into the hall. "Send him home."

The boy saw the offer of freedom but leaned closer to me. His small hand rustled in a trouser pocket. His feet were bare. He handed me a second receipt. It was impossible to decipher the Chinese characters across the bottom, but English words leapt between them.

"Laudanum. Two bottles. This is headache powders. Oh. It must be smelling salts here. It's a list of sorts."

"We brought all of those things in from Mrs. Olsen's bedside table."

My eyes stopped. "Cyanide. Two."

"Two?"

My hand dropped to my lap and the boy waited while I worried. "Why two?" I whispered.

"Come, Mrs. Kelly." Detective Fisher pointed at the boy and then over his shoulder. "You. Go now."

The boy gave me a last look, then darted from the cell.

Detective Fisher stepped inside. "Is there a date? A name?" He offered his hand, and I took it to haul myself up.

"No." I handed the slips to him as I walked out and shook my skirts hard.

"We must," he said, following, "at least consider that she took her own life."

"Did she finally admit to herself that she was dying?" I led the way into the front office, trying to outrun the cold and the frustration and the truth. "Did Josiah help her take a faster and painless way out?"

"Or did her dreams die with her husband? Or," he said with frustration, moving behind the desk and yanking open a drawer, "did she kill him and then herself, exactly like the note says? I've got it here. Let's go to the hotel."

"You're inviting me?"

He paused and scowled at the paper in his hand. "There's only one person between us and the room and he is in our debt." After opening and closing his mouth again, he shook himself and marched down the hall without looking back.

His trust galvanized my feet.

As we moved back among the cells, I said, "You kept one of Mrs. Olsen's letters."

"Yes. To compare with the signature on the suicide note. We'll study it in Room 412."

"Clever. But they won't match."

"Not likely. But I can't force any of our suspects to give us a handwriting sample."

"You won't have to." I yanked open the door to the yard, hoping the buggy was still hitched and waiting. "Every guest has to register at the hotel front desk. We can ask Pearl to show it to us."

He finally met my eyes. "Now, that is clever."

Chapter Twenty

WE FELL SILENT during the short, bumpy ride to the Palace Hotel. Not for a minute did I think my black dress and heavy veil would fool anyone who knew me. It might give me time to move between hiding places, though. And Mr. Sedgwick, I hoped, believed me locked up and would not register my form even if we passed in the hall.

Detective Fisher turned into the Annie Street alley and directly down into the basement. Groaning machinery, horse hooves, and the shouts of delivery men echoed through the dimly lit interior. I could detect mold, grease, hay, and apples slowly turning to cider in their crates beneath the scents wafting through from the kitchen upstairs.

Home was never so appealing.

"Detective Fisher, sir?" Mr. James stood at the horse's halter and stared at us; his dark face nearly lost in the uncertain flicker of an overhead bulb.

That he knew me was apparent, but Detective Fisher hopped from the buggy and said, "We aren't here. You did not see us."

"Yes, sir." Mr. James nodded and looked away from me as I clambered to the ground.

Detective Fisher leaned in and whispered into the man's ear, then turned and said, "We're taking the servant's elevator. Quick."

I fell in step with him. "You put Mr. James into a terrible place," I murmured as we headed for it. "He's Pearl's sweetheart."

"The staff owe you cooperation," he said tensely, stepping into the elevator. "You traded your freedom for their jobs."

"And here I am, abusing it." The weight of carrying both sides of the burden settled heavier on my shoulders and I squared them. "What if he tells Pearl?"

He took the elevator controls. "That's exactly what I asked him to do. We need her up in the room and I can count on her discretion."

"His. She's unhappy with me."

"Pearl has always been loyal."

I pondered that on our way up to the fourth floor, recalling the night of the murder and how swiftly she'd been able to produce him. She had always been loyal to him, more than once in direct opposition to my own agenda. Would that change now that Detective Fisher and I were colleagues?

The fourth-floor corridors were clear of guests when we marched quickly down to room 412. The sentries watching over the three particular guest rooms gave us a nod, but we entered the Olsens' vacant room unchallenged. Detective Fisher pocketed the key, and we left the door unlocked.

Removing my veil, I moved to the window, but he said, "Leave everything exactly as it is until we've taken another full look at it." He flicked on the lamps, and I paused, twiddling with the lace in my fingers, to take note that the curtains were still open and the window locked.

It was stuffy and cool but not cool enough to preserve the flowers on the mantle. They drooped, brown and wilted over the edge of their silver vase.

I left them in place and wandered to the bedroom while Detective Fisher examined the sofa, kneeling to glance beneath it and lifting the cushions before sitting down. The bed was rumpled and missing the sheet and coverlet they'd wrapped Mrs. Olsen in. The bedside table was cleared, but the bureau and wardrobe had not been emptied.

"We'll go through this systematically," he said, opening the briefcase. "Beginning with the signatures."

"I'd like to see the will," I said, sitting next to him and laying my veil between us.

He slid a handful of ledgers from the case and three folios.

"So much paper," I said, opening a thin book. "Is it everything from all of them? Or everything Reverend Olsen ever did at the church?" I gasped.

"What?" He looked over my shoulder.

"Nothing. Sorry." I blinked. "This is in my aunt's hand. Numbers. Tallies." I ran a finger over the elegant handwriting and waited for the feelings to pass.

"Good." He returned to the papers scattered over the table. "We have some history here. Let's put it in chronological order if we can."

Envelopes held bundles of receipts and our task quickly

grew overwhelming. "This will take time," I said. "Nothing's in order. It's like someone dropped the contents of several desk drawers into the luggage upside down."

"What's this?" He held up a slip of paper. "The patronage check." He examined it soberly.

"That's worth killing over." It was incredible to think about.

He grunted and tucked it away again. "Keep going."

"All is vanity and vexation of spirit," Aunt Mary sighed.

I'd stopped to read the contract when the doorknob turned, and Pearl stepped cautiously into the room.

"Detective Fisher?" she asked. "I'm glad you sent for me."

Our eyes met but she didn't look away.

"We need your help with something," Detective Fisher said, his eyes and hands still busy.

"Pearl?" It was one word, and I put all of my longing for reconciliation into it.

She shifted on her feet. "I thought about what you said in the market this morning."

We had Detective Fisher's attention now.

"About the hotel's regular flower order, and I asked around a little." Pearl slipped a hand into her apron pocket. "We've had special orders for each holiday. In the dining rooms. For the tables."

She pulled a small brown bottle from the pocket and held it up.

"This was in the bottom of one of those vases."

I was at her side in a flash, bent to examine it better.

"How did you find it?" The empty bottle was the size of my little finger and had no stopper.

"We reuse our vases," she said. "They were rounded up and the flowers changed out for fresh ones after the New Year's Eve party. I waited until the breakfast rush was over this morning, then I went from table to table and…" A nervous half smile came and went. "Pulled up the new flowers to look inside each vase."

"You didn't get caught?" Ida would not have approved.

Pearl shook her head. "If someone had noticed a small bottle anywhere in the room or among the flowers we discarded, we would have turned it in. The only place not checked at the murder was in the bottom of the vase."

She walked to Detective Fisher and placed the clue carefully on the table in the middle of the paperwork. "I can't promise it came from that exact dining room. It's been in water. The stopper must've floated out with the flowers. It may be of no use now. But it must be what the poison came in. Don't you think?"

"It's perfect, Pearl," he said. "Well done!"

She bit her lip, then said, "It was Mrs. Kelly's idea."

He leaned forward to examine it, but I went directly to the mantle.

"It must be here," I said. "We have to check." I picked up the vase, but the table in front of Detective Fisher was covered in papers. He rose as I set the flowers on the little desk instead.

"There. I found out today that they were ordered and delivered from the Chinatown florist on Monday. By Mr. Olsen."

Pearl's eyes widened and Detective Fisher said, "What are you looking for? Mr. Lees said she died of a laudanum overdose."

"Only one bottle of laudanum was purchased." I gently lifted the dead flowers. "And you have it. Where is the cyanide? The other bottle? One that matches Pearl's?"

"The other bottle?" Pearl whispered.

Mucky drips fell from the stems to the carpet, and Pearl quickly looked into the vase. "Nothing. Put them back before you ruin the floor."

"I had to look," I said. "If the killer did it once…"

"Oh, honey, it makes perfect sense." Pearl glanced over her shoulder. "You searched the rest of the room? You took the only key and none of us have been in here since then."

"Yes." Detective Fisher wandered back to the table and picked up the letter he'd taken from Madame Fabbri. "Thank Mr. Sedgwick for his patience. We can't keep the others locked up beyond today. We'll release these rooms as soon as we can."

I looked down to hide a quick smirk. I couldn't help myself. They were currently incarcerated, and I was not.

Then again, I might hang for something one of them had done.

"Detective, what did you want me for?" Pearl moved to his side and left me staring at the damp spots on the floor.

"I need something from the front lobby," he said.

The waste basket sat beneath the desk. It was empty.

"Is Mr. Sedgwick currently at work downstairs?" he asked. "I don't want to disturb or distract him."

"Pearl, how often are the waste baskets emptied?" I asked.

"No, sir," Pearl said. "He's not in today. We had too many reporters buzzing about." She glanced at me. "On Sundays."

Long before the suicide note could have been written.

Detective Fisher pulled the note from his other pocket. "I need to see the guest registry. Specifically, the signatures of these guests on the day they checked into the hotel."

"Detective Fisher?" They both turned to me. "Did you fold it?"

He held up the piece of paper. "Yes. To put into my pocket."

"It wasn't folded when we found it."

"What does that have to do with anything?"

"It means it was never in someone's pocket. Or reticule, for that matter."

Pearl tipped her head. "But you said it was a suicide note. Mrs. Olsen wrote it."

"Regardless of who wrote it," I said, "it was either penned in this room or carried here wholesale. Not far. Easily from a room or two over. But one wouldn't carry an obvious item like this by hand through the corridor or in an elevator. Would the staff have noticed?"

"If they'd been near," she said.

"My thought is that anyone who'd forged a suicide note with the idea of murder would not have put it on display."

"Does that rule out Madame Fabbri?" Detective Fisher asked.

"I think so. Do you think she came here herself? She would have been noticed." I asked. "I'm only guessing it didn't arrive in a case of some kind." I pointed at the briefcase on the table.

"Why couldn't the killer have been in this room and written the note on the spot?" he asked. "After she died?"

"We can prove that," I said. "Or disprove it." I slid the narrow desk drawer open. "Pearl, how many sheets of stationery does the hotel provide its guests?"

"Two, Mrs. Kelly. And two envelopes. More if requested."

I held up both sheets. "The paper did not come from this desk. But it did come from this hotel."

Detective Fisher sat abruptly on the sofa and smoothed both items out next to each other on the table in front of him. Pearl and I came to look over his shoulder. Mrs. Olsen's suicide note was brief. Her letter to Madame Fabbri filled two sheets of paper before she signed off.

They were a match. I could not argue it. Although a spot or two on the note appeared smudged and it had been written in obvious haste or angst, the curves of certain letters and loops on others matched the hand of a single owner.

"All right," he said, gathering them back up. "Next, we compare these to what's in the registry."

I gripped the back of the sofa as a sudden idea came to mind. "What if…"

This time, he stood and turned on me. "One idea at a time, if you please, Mrs. Kelly. I can hardly keep up."

"When I was in Minnesota," I said, "I corresponded with

my fiancé. Only he was illiterate. Someone else wrote his letters for him."

Detective Fisher and Pearl looked at each other.

"I am only suggesting that Mrs. Olsen may not have been involved in the contract or chatty with Madame Fabbri in the first place if she had no education. Which could explain why she was unsure about the contract details." I thought hard. "And how Mr. Olsen remains, despite his apparent grief, unflappable through all of this. The earrings, too. What if he impersonated Mrs. Olsen in the letters? Including this one? What if he's been behind this entire thing?"

"You think he set them all up?" Detective Fisher pocketed his notes and ran a hand through his hair.

"He's sophisticated." I shook my head. "As much as I want to believe him innocent, I still don't know enough about him." The idea that he had lured his father to San Francisco to murder him and his young wife was too horrible to dwell on. But the notes in his diary nagged in the back of my mind. Why did he leave no trace of his handwriting?

Detective Fisher sighed. "If there's a way to complicate things, you find it."

"I am only considering all possibilities."

"I'm going downstairs to find out. The signatures in the registry will tell us what we want to know. If Mr. Olsen's handwriting looks like the one in her letters, he's our top suspect. If one of the names matches the handwriting in this suicide note, we have our killer."

Pearl wrapped her arms around herself.

"Aren't I coming, too?" I asked, picking up the veil.

"You'll be recognized, even with that." He held up a hand. "No. If you would please stay and go through this paperwork, it will speed things up. We need anything that will help us build a case for one person or another."

"Are you going with him?" I was surprised at the sudden pang of jealousy that came with the petulant question I fired at Pearl.

"She can get me in and out of the lobby fast." Detective Fisher was already walking away.

"Can't you take all of them to the jailhouse?" Pearl asked, following him. "I have staff waiting on them. I won't have my maids in danger."

He paused with his hand on the doorknob. "These murders were personal. I can't see that any of the staff were ever in danger." His eyes moved to me. "Except for Mrs. Kelly." After a beat, he came back to where I stood and held out his hand.

The key was in it.

"Lock the door behind us," he said. "I don't know how long it might take, and I want to go through the other rooms and count paper." When I took it, he said, "Stay here until I come for you. Please. I don't need to remind you what might happen if you're seen."

I mustered a stoic face. He was right. But I didn't have to like it.

When they left, I turned the key in the lock, dropped it into my own pocket, and settled in on the sofa. Aunt Mary wasn't the only smart woman on our family tree. If there was a clue in the paperwork, I was going to find it.

What felt like an eternity later, I had to admit defeat. Stretching my shoulders, I stood and went to the window.

The view was as dismal as my thoughts. Where were they? Was Pearl being twice as useful as I'd been?

Had they already found and arrested the murderer and forgotten me entirely?

I wandered back and picked up the contract. The cause of all the trouble. There had been no receipts for any purchases in San Francisco. The ledgers held several years of tiny numbers and columns, and I only gave them a scan before moving back to the contract.

Wondering if I'd actually memorized it by now, I glanced over the final page of the contract.

And froze.

A click came from the door. A jiggle in the lock.

And the doorknob began to turn.

Leaping to my feet, I looked around frantically for anything that might be used as a weapon. I put the sofa between myself and the door as a scream filled the room.

It wasn't mine.

Chapter Twenty-One

MY HEART POUNDED in my chest as another scream reverberated from the other side of the hotel room door.

I rushed across the room and flung the door open. The hall was empty and the door across from me—Mrs. Berg's door—stood gaping wide. Men called loudly, both within her suite and out in the main corridor, and it sounded as though all the fourth-floor guests had come out to join them.

A man and woman passed by, calling out to someone, and I flinched. The corridor promised instant exposure.

Mrs. Berg's suite was a buzz of activity, and I pressed myself behind the doorway, trying to see what was happening in the lamplit room.

Wails, sobs, and hiccups accompanied Mrs. Berg as she was placed firmly on her own sofa by tall, stalwart Mr. Nilsen. She waved a handkerchief frantically in the air, nearly keening with fright.

"It's all too much, Matthew!" she cried. "I can't stay one more day!"

She was suddenly a frail, elderly woman, far from friends and home. Something in me softened at the idea.

Detective Fisher went striding past them and I ducked behind my own door, closing it until only a few inches were left to spy through.

"Stay here with them," he commanded. "I'm searching the next room over."

"Yes, sir."

It must have been one of his sentries. Why had my hall been unguarded? Another sentry moved quickly through the room, ignoring its occupants.

Who had nearly let themselves into this room? Who had screamed? While I was fairly certain it had been a woman, there was no way to find out now.

"Please, Mrs. Berg, calm yourself." Mr. Nilsen stood aside with a ferocious frown.

He was as emotional as a brick wall, whether you sobbed at his feet or accused him of murder.

"How can you say that?" she retorted. "He attacked me! I tell you the madness was passed from mother to son. I've been afraid of him this whole time."

"Can you give us a description of the man?" the guard asked.

"Indulged," she said scathingly. "He was indulged from the moment he was born, but could I warn him? No! The sun rose and set on Josiah Olsen until the day it turned on him and burned down their house!"

Mr. Olsen? He'd attacked Mrs. Berg? He was glaringly absent from the little party.

"After everything I did for him!" she continued. "I scrubbed floors and polished pews for years in loving gratitude. You know this, Mr. Nilsen. How often did I join you in your errands and support you around the churchyard? We planted those roses that tumble over the arched entry today." Further words were caught in the handkerchief she applied to her face.

Detective Fisher reappeared, and I closed my door another two inches.

"Mrs. Berg," he said, "there's no sign of him. You must try to tell me exactly what just happened. Are you certain you are unharmed? He managed to grab your arm, you said. Does it hurt?"

Even from where I stood, I felt the heat of her glare at him.

"I told you." Her shaking voice rose. "He that troubleth his own house shall inherit the wind! I told you both times you questioned me that Josiah Olsen was trouble. He was not invited on this trip, but he thrust his unwelcome presence on us anyway and his father refused to send him away. He's a degenerate! His father sent him away years ago and told him to never return."

"Mr. Nilsen already confirmed that," Detective Fisher said. "What I want to know is how you ended up in his room."

"Oh!" Her handkerchief waved in the air. "The scoundrel forced his way through the door between our suites! One minute, I was sitting by the window grieving, and the next, he was standing beside me, ranting!"

"The door between your suites is still open," he said patiently, "but he isn't there."

She straightened. "I should say he's not! I leapt from my chair and attempted to flee out my door, but I'd no sooner opened it than he took me by the arm and hauled me all the way into his room!"

"To what purpose, Mrs. Berg?"

"As if I knew or cared! He was ranting! How dare he lay a hand on me! I screamed and screamed again, then he ran out through his own door." She wiped her face. "And that is where you found me, detective!"

"Jumping Jehoshaphat!" Pearl's exclamation caused me to slam my door closed and I caught half my skirt in it.

I bit back a curse as Pearl said, "I'm trying to calm our guests, Detective Fisher, but it's no use. Mr. Sedgwick is on his way!"

"Tell him I've got it under control."

This time, I made an unladylike snort from my side of the door.

"We can't have guests dying and screaming and running amok!" she cried.

"They're leaving first thing in the morning," he said, and his voice was much closer to the door. "All of them."

"They'd better."

There was a pause, and I became acutely aware of my skirts. A small tug did nothing for the situation.

"Mrs. Kelly, did you manage to see or hear anything?" He did not try to open the door.

"No. I heard the screams and looked out, but saw no one. Where was our guard?"

"I'd just dismissed them. I was counting Mr. Nilsen's

stationery when we were disturbed with slamming doors and screams." He made a grunt of disgust.

"Someone tried to come into this room right before it happened," I said. My words were met with silence, and I hoped they were still in the hall. As anyone else could be standing there by now, I kept the door firmly shut.

"Did they knock?" he asked.

"They had a key. To this room."

"Are you certain?"

"The lock and the knob both turned."

More silence.

When I heard his muffled voice in the other suite, I slowly eased open my door and snatched my skirt free.

"In the hall?" Mrs. Berg asked.

She glanced through her doorway at the worst possible time.

I closed my door with a swift click and leaned against it, frustrated beyond words. One single moment, and our eyes had met. In any other circumstance, it wouldn't have been an issue. Who would believe her? But if Mr. Sedgwick was on his way, the clock was ticking. How was I going to get out of here without being seen?

Mrs. Berg's animated voice rose, but it was impossible to hear what was being said. I went to the window and forced it open. Frigid night air flooded the room and slapped at my face as I stuck it outside.

A carriage lumbered down the dark alley of Jessie Street below and the building standing on the other side of it had a window here and there lit from within. There wasn't so much as a trellis near my window to climb down on.

Not, I told myself as I shoved the window closed, that I would have done so.

I faced the table. Littered with paper and a small brown bottle. Whoever had a key to this room could not have known I was inside. They were after whatever was in the briefcase. It was not, by process of elimination, anyone in the next rooms over. But who else knew it was in here? And where, for the love of all holy things, did they get a key?

The thought unsettled me further and I snatched up my veil.

A deep, sinking feeling nearly dropped me to the floor, and I put a hand on the wall to steady myself.

I trusted Pearl. If it was anyone on the staff, after all … well. She would know.

Did she think my position as scapegoat well worth the price of her hotel and everyone in it? She had been in a hurry to solve the murders. Until my arrest. And she seemed in an awful rush now to simply get rid of the mess, especially with Mr. Sedgwick on his way.

Worse, our time was up. Without a different suspect, Detective Fisher had no hold on anyone. Slumping against the wall, I thought of the jail cell. My skirts had already been dragged through it. Been slammed in a door. I already carried the look and scent of prison.

It wasn't Detective Fisher's fault. And it was unreasonable to think he could continue on with the farce.

"Sink or swim," Aunt Mary said.

I couldn't just stay here and wait for my fate to fetch me.

I'd have to run for it.

At the moment, everyone was otherwise occupied. I gathered all the paperwork back into the briefcase, as jumbled as they'd been in the first place, and tossed the bottle in on top. Then, I wrapped the veil around my hat and took one last look around the room.

The door between the suites.

Of course.

Holding my breath, I took the key from my pocket and locked the suite door first. Even if Pearl had access to a second key, it would still bide me a little time. Then I approached the narrow central door that connected this suite to that adjoining it. Cleverly disguised by wallpaper and molding, the knob was designed to coordinate with the fireplace trim. When not needed, guests could ignore its existence. But large parties who wished to mingle could open it with their room key.

The lock turned easily, but there was another, only accessible from the other side of the door. There was no time to hesitate. After a good look at which way it hinged, I took a deep breath before throwing my weight behind a solid push. The door gave way suddenly and if not for my grip on it, I'd have fallen on my face into the next room.

No one there. Scrambling, I retrieved the heavy briefcase and dashed into the next suite, closing the door behind me.

"Leave it on the table, please," a voice drawled from the bedroom.

Aghast, I rushed to the front door and took myself out. The hall here emptied into a corner of the fourth floor. It was only a few yards to the elevator and a staircase. Judging by the noise still rolling down the corridor, things had not yet settled among the disturbed guests. I straightened my veil and my posture and strolled deliberately away.

I counted my steps. Ten, with my back to the fourth-floor disaster. A sedate left turn. Five steps toward the elevator.

With such force that my arm was nearly wrenched from my shoulder, a hand reached out from the stairwell and yanked the briefcase. I reeled with it and crashed into the rest of the person, and we both staggered three steps down before I braced myself against the handrail. The man wrestled silently, but he hadn't counted on my own desperation.

Whatever was in this briefcase was my only hope of freedom. Of justice.

"Mrs. Kelly?" He was incredulous and stopped, panting, to look at my face.

The veil had slipped.

Mr. Olsen, wide-eyed and rumpled, kept one hand on the briefcase and said, "I have to run. Let go. Please."

"I won't!" I hissed. "They're coming for you! Run!"

He'd attacked Mrs. Berg, lied, stolen, and, for all I knew, committed murder.

"Mrs. Kelly, please. You don't understand. Any of this. I'm trying to help."

"I understand enough." I glanced over my shoulder. Any minute, someone was going to come around that corner and see me. "I can't help you, Mr. Olsen. And I'm taking the briefcase." I gave it another tug.

His counter-tug pulled me closer to him. He tipped his face into mine and said, "I did not seduce Mrs. Olsen."

"I know."

He blinked. "Mrs. Berg is a lying old hag."

I couldn't really argue with that one.

He tugged again. "I did not kill my father."

Voices in the corridor grew louder.

"Then why are you running, Mr. Olsen?"

"It's over. I'm through with them all!"

"That's not what they say." Another glance over my shoulder. "Come with me."

"And why should I? You're with the police."

"Not anymore." I gave the case an almighty heave and loosened his grip. Instead of going down the stairs, I headed up. If he had a weapon, he hadn't threatened me with it. I did not look back.

His steps fell heavily behind mine and I saved what little breath I had left for climbing. Another two floors put a stitch in my side. I wiped the damp from beneath the veil with a finger. The elevator was faster, but we hadn't passed anyone on the stairs.

"Where are we going?" he asked.

The stairwell ended on the seventh floor. I hurried toward the southwest corner of the building. The one overlooking both Market and Montgomery Streets. To the penthouse, where one of the most expensive whores in San Francisco lived.

The atrium was silent and full of shadows. Rain fell softly on the dark glass ceiling.

I stopped in front of the ornate door. I'd seen Lina at

social functions. She'd very likely been escorting the mayor or Chief Crowley to the New Year's Eve party. I'd been introduced to her once in extenuating circumstances. And I'd even been in this suite when it was occupied by someone else. Lina had been here long enough to know all the hotel staff. But I didn't know her last name. Or even if Lina was her real name.

It didn't matter. What I needed was information. And somewhere safe to hide until I got it.

Lina liked to toy with the police. She didn't let them toy with her. She was our only hope.

"What are you doing?" Mr. Olsen ran a finger around his collar. "We need to get out of the hotel."

"And go where, Mr. Olsen? It's late and cold and we're on foot." I quirked an eyebrow at him. "Unless you have a fortune tucked away and a home on Nob Hill?"

He closed his eyes and rubbed hard between them. "How?" he asked. "How did I get here?"

"You followed me."

"Not what I meant." He sagged. "None of this makes sense." He eyed the door.

It was a gamble that she would be in. And a bigger gamble that she would be alone tonight.

"Who lives here?"

"Why Mr. Olsen, I thought you knew."

I wanted to go home, but it was the first place they'd look for me.

Instead, I knocked on Lina's door.

Six floors above my apartment where Becky and Spoon would be, once again, frantic with worry.

Chapter Twenty-Two

A BEAUTIFUL WOMAN opened the door. A clear complexion with rosy cheeks and full lips, dark hair piled high and decked with glittering hairpins, and a figure squeezed inside a violet dress with more ruffles and flounces than anyone required outside of the opera stood framed in the doorway like a painting.

"Good evening, Lina," I said, both hands gripping the briefcase. "I hope this is an opportune time to pay a call?"

Her dark eyes took us in, then glanced down the empty hall. "Perhaps."

"It's a personal call," I said. "We need your help."

She sized Mr. Olsen up, and he frowned at her. With a sudden smile, she opened the door wider and said, "Please come in, Mrs. Kelly."

The fact that she'd known me immediately was disconcerting. I wasn't safe in the Palace. My thoughts were corroborated when I saw the newspaper open on her suite table. What must she think of me?

As the beneficiary of one of the largest and most opulent suites we had, Lina enjoyed a drawing room full of windows on two sides with sweeping views of the city and the twinkling water beyond it. Spacious, with attached bedroom and washroom, it was an extravagance paid for by her *paramours*.

Lina held out a delicate smooth hand with a perfect manicure to Mr. Olsen. "Lina. How do you do?"

He bent graciously over her hand and said, "Charmed. Mr. Josiah Olsen."

"You two haven't met?" I could detect nothing in either face that said so.

"We have now," Lina said, gliding to a curved, embroidered camelback sofa. "And I want to hear all about whatever lovely adventure brings you to the seventh floor." She sat amidst a rustling swirl of silk and patted the seat next to her.

It wasn't meant for me.

While Mr. Olsen tried to decide where exactly to perch on the sofa, I closed the door firmly, set the briefcase on the carpet on my side of the table, and took an overstuffed chintz armchair.

"Oh, my," Lina said. "Have you gone into mourning again, Mrs. Kelly?"

I tore the veil and hat from my tousled head. "No."

Tossing the mess to the floor beside the briefcase, I fastened a baleful eye on Mr. Olsen. He'd settled on a spacious twelve inches away from the violet froth.

"It seems I was mistaken about you, Mr. Olsen," I said. "I hope I can say the same for the rest of the charges laid at your feet."

"Charges?" Lina's eyes grew animated.

"Assault, not an hour ago," I said. "Murder. Theft. Slander. Take your pick." I shook out my black, bedraggled skirts.

"Oh, my," she purred. "It's been a busy evening."

Mr. Olsen seemed fascinated by her and kept his hands clasped firmly in his lap. "Indeed," he choked out.

"I've sent for a supper tray," she said. "My breakfast, of course. I'm used to all-night adventures." She gave Mr. Olsen a wicked smile. "May I order you something?"

Mr. Olsen was absolutely tongue-tied.

"I'll take a strong pot of coffee," I said. "And if you don't mind, no one can know we are here. Especially the staff."

She arched a fine eyebrow. "Oh. I see. It's like that."

"Lina," I said, taking the initiative, "do you recognize my earrings?" I turned my face so she could clearly see them. "Sapphire. Small diamonds. There's another pair exactly like these ... somewhere."

"They're lovely. No."

"And you have no history with Mr. Olsen here?"

"Not yet." Her smile was calculating, and Mr. Olsen blinked.

"Detective Fisher came up and asked you much the same questions earlier." It wasn't a question so much as I needed to get all the facts straight.

"He did. Same answers, I'm afraid. Is that why you're here?"

"In part. Josiah?" He dragged his eyes away from her. "Where were you when your father died?"

"Asleep." His words were terse. "In my room. Liquor never sits well with me. I woke with a start when midnight erupted."

"Why did you allow your party to think you were..." I

glanced at Lina. "Elsewhere?"

Sudden understanding lit Lina's face.

Mr. Olsen stood and walked to a window, as if the answers to our problem might be there. He locked his hands behind his back.

After a deep breath, he said, "It was the easiest excuse I could come up with. There's a billiard room downstairs next to the gentlemen's bar. I should have gone with a drunkard or a gambler. But damned if the good people of Minnesota aren't ravenous for a sex scandal!"

I bit my lip, and Lina laughed.

"She's my age," he said, turning to us. "Did you know that? Edith was kind and lost and desperate, although she wouldn't admit it. She married that ... that ... ancient old man with the withered view of life. She was a pawn her whole life."

He paused to collect himself. "No. I didn't seduce her or love her in the way Mrs. Berg is salivating over. But I felt sorry for her once I understood some things."

I shook my head. "Perhaps we should go further back, Mr. Olsen. To the beginning. I was there when you left home. You were gone for years and, personally, I think it was for the better. But where did you go, if not to school? Who are you, and why did you return?"

"Yes. A small school in New York, living with a distant cousin of my father's and their family. Nothing that would cost money, you see. I was not worth investing in and my father and I were clear when we parted that we'd never see each other again."

Lina slumped with boredom. Perhaps she'd heard this tale before.

"I excelled at school," he continued, "mostly to avoid the house. I got a job selling newspapers on the street corner, then worked my way inside the office where at least I wasn't rained on. Eventually, I became a reporter. A writer." He rubbed a hand over his neck. "Investigating fraud."

Now he had my attention, but Lina was distracted by a rap on the door. Mr. Olsen and I pounced on the briefcase at the same time and, after a quick tug-of-war, I offered my grudging trust and picked up my hat instead. We both stood still in the next room as Lina opened her suite door.

We waited, holding our breath, while Lina took her supper tray and ordered coffee. When the door closed, we swapped positions. Mr. Olsen dropped the case near the table and collapsed into the armchair. I strolled to a window and waited impatiently for a strong cup of courage.

"A reporter," Lina said cheerfully, setting her tray on top of the newspaper on her table. "I've never had the pleasure. But it does seem strange, doesn't it? I know secrets that a newspaper would dearly love to print."

It seemed to please her that her little speech caused Mr. Olsen to stare at her afresh as she fussed over the sauteed mushrooms and rice on her dish.

"Secrets seem to be my specialty," he muttered.

"You told me earlier," I said, "that you expected to find fraud when you came home."

"Yes." He blinked up at me. "There had been a string of insurance frauds that no one could solve. Department stores, mostly. But when I heard Tiffany's had made a claim, I jumped in. It would make my career if I could find the person or people behind the fraud."

"Tiffany's?" Lina said. "The jeweler?"

"The same. A very high-end problem that they wanted solved quickly and quietly. I suspected an inside job. They always are, you know. But I wasn't the only person on the hunt. Police, of course. Employees." He shrugged. "I was combing through a mountain of receipts, comparing them to the ledgers, long after midnight, when I came across something that stopped me. Indefinitely, it seems. An address. My address. The Reverend Olsen's address, to be specific. A set of sapphire earrings ordered through the Tiffany Blue Book and shipped to Waterford Township."

Involuntarily, my hand crept up to the blue baubles hanging from my ear.

"And that's not all," he continued. "Deeper into the pile of receipts, I found a duplicate. The exact set of earrings sent to the exact same address. Two months apart."

"Ah." The idea that we had two sets did not seem so wild now.

"I admit, I jumped before thinking it through. But what were the chances? Either the fraudster used a random address to steal earrings, or someone in Waterford Township had four ears. And what possible need is there in the running of a Lutheran church that required fine jewels?"

Lina smiled and nibbled on a slice of pear. "There is always a need for fine jewels, Mr. Josiah Olsen."

"I decided to come home and sniff this one out. And

find the woman with impeccable taste and marry her, of course." His voice dripped irony. "Or send her to prison. I had no preference. A story is a story. The problems I walked into weren't anything like I was expecting. Father had remarried. I was anathema on all counts. And no one within miles of the church wore blue earrings."

"I'd already left," I said. "With mine."

He threw his hands into the air. "No one even has pierced ears. Did you know that?"

I did.

"I circled in on the new wife. She had a vague past and a flair for the stage. Singing, that is. A presence when she turned it on." He hesitated. "Not that she turned it on often. Seems Waterford Township requires all its talents to be handed directly to God. At any rate, if anyone had an interest in jewels, I figured it would be her."

"She had one of them." I walked forward and met his startled eyes. "I found it hidden on a picture frame in her room the morning we discovered her."

It was a moment before he cried, "So, she did take it! I told you I found her handkerchief in my room!"

"No." If we were going to get to the bottom of this pie, we needed to pool all of our information. "That was my handkerchief. I snuck into your room looking for clues to your father's death and accidentally dropped it."

"You what?"

"Detective Fisher has them both now. He pulled the first one out of your vest pocket the night of your father's murder."

Lina followed the story with wide, delighted eyes.

"Then Edith lied to me." His bitter words surprised me. "She claimed not to have seen an earring since she handed the first one to me."

"She what?"

He rubbed hard at the back of his neck. "At least they are all accounted for. I can't condemn you for doing exactly what I did. I snuck into my father's house more than once, looking for earrings. But I was caught. Edith demanded the truth, and I gave it to her. You've met her." He turned his face away. "I could deny her nothing."

Lina all but purred.

"She gave me the single earring. She'd found it among my father's things and thought the worst but had no way of proving it. If it belonged to another woman her new husband was seeing, well, she didn't want to know, and she wasn't going to ask him. She was happy to get rid of it but had no idea where it had come from."

He sniffed. "I've kept it in my pocket. It's the only proof I have that I'm not mad."

"You didn't confront him with it?" I asked.

He shook his head at me like I was a simpleton. "She didn't want to know. Besides, it's my father. The reverend! Was I going to confront him with a breath of scandal and walk away unscathed?"

I chuckled grimly. "Never."

"I tried the only thing I could. I offered to reconcile and step into his hypocritical shoes. Spouted scripture and attended every gathering, trying to get him to talk to me."

"You did, at least, give him an idea for that ridiculous will."

His face fell. "Do you know how it was? Before? You knew us. My father made it abundantly clear that I was to succeed him in the ministry. Everyone expected it. I had to tell him to his face that I renounced our Lord and Savior before he'd send me away." He paused and gave me a pointed look.

I'd clutched my throat at his statement.

Aunt Mary had fainted dead away.

He smirked. "What that means, in actual fact, is that I renounced him. You mustn't fret over my soul, Mrs. Kelly. It's tucked safely into a pew in an Albany, New York Lutheran Church."

Aunt Mary stayed on the floor, waiting for the other shoe to drop.

"I had to give him a reason for my sudden appearance, so I told him I'd seen the light and wanted us to be a family again."

Lina shook her head. "You have a face that can never tell a lie. However have you muddled through so long?"

He glared at her.

"Why not simply leave?" I asked.

The thought of trying to butter up the reverend was more repulsive than the outright war I'd waged against him.

"There were too many oddities. I couldn't place my finger on it at first. Mr. Nilsen was keeping all of father's business records. The man was fixing the roof when I left. You can't imagine a more ignorant person. Left school in the fourth grade, as I discovered. What was my father thinking? Mr. Nilsen never let me anywhere near the paperwork and I assumed it was because he could not have explained it to himself, let alone anyone else."

I eyed the briefcase.

"And the rumors. The congregational gossip centered around a woman who had stalked their reverend and then mysteriously vanished. That my father had narrowly avoided having his name dragged through the mud. Fervent protests to his purity and character."

"Not the new bride?" If anything, that should have set them agog.

"Nothing but congratulations and delight over Edith. I assumed Edith was what the mystery woman had been contentious over. The best woman won and all that. Women do, I've heard."

I gave him a crooked smile. "Hardly. I'm the one they were talking about. I'm the one who dogged Reverend Olsen's heels from Christmas to June. I gave him no peace whatsoever. But he still wouldn't give me the information I needed to bring Aunt Mary's killer to justice."

He stood and joined me at the window. "And how would my father know anything about a murder?"

"People confess to ministers. Confide in them."

"And the police?"

"Useless. They said she was an elderly, confused, and foolish woman who got turned around in a blizzard."

The words came out in a rush and, when the coffeepot arrived at the door, I was happy to take a minute and recover my dignity.

Chapter Twenty-Three

THE SCENT OF coffee filled the room as I sipped.

Lina placed a hand on Mr. Olsen's arm. "You poor thing," she said, looking up at him through her long, dark lashes. "To have lost a father so suddenly."

He shook her off and addressed me. "You asked why I stayed? Why I'd play such a false charade? Because in some deep, inadmissible truth, I wanted him to love me." His scowl was frightening. "But I knew. I've always known. It wasn't possible unless I relinquished everything that mattered. My voice. My dignity. My freedom. With him, it was all or nothing."

Lina moved quietly back to the table and her supper.

He struggled with his emotions. "Father told me he'd rewrite his will once he decided I was serious about my sudden reform." His abrupt laugh was bitter. "Which told me I'd already been written out of it. Now that we know what he amended it with, I'm inclined to think the wizened old man was trying to get his way, even from the grave. His last attempt to manipulate and own me."

Everything in me reached out to him in sympathy. At least I'd been loved, thoroughly, by my family.

I blinked as a sudden wave of guilt flowed through me.

Mr. Olsen would not get another chance at reconciliation.

I shook it off and reminded myself that he still had a lot of confessing to do.

Possibly to murder.

"You are still looking for your story," I said. "You didn't find it there. How about San Francisco?" I peered at him over my coffee cup. "I know you are the one who introduced the Olsens to the theater and Madam Fabbri."

He squinted back at me. "You would make a decent reporter, Mrs. Kelly."

"I'd rather catch a killer, Mr. Olsen."

"In an effort to prove myself harmless, I gave Edith the gift of a correspondence with a woman she idolized. I had no idea it went further than that. Even I was shocked when he announced they were leaving. The idea that my father would bring her here is simply impossible."

True. "Did you write her letters for her?"

"Do what?"

"Was Mrs. Olsen literate? Did she write her own correspondence with Madame Fabbri?"

"She did indeed."

"Ah, me." Assuming he was telling the truth, at least we had one honest signature from her letter. And that meant her suicide note had been written in her hand.

"But the Tiffany earrings seemed to have never existed," he said. "If it weren't for the one she gave me, I would have given up sooner, I think."

"Mr. Olsen…"

He kept going as if he hadn't heard me. "I could see their marriage wasn't ideal—who couldn't—and Edith was often in tears. I didn't realize until later that she was trying to win her husband over. Desperate for his affections and he treated her as coldly as myself. Now that I know about the contract," he spat, "it makes more sense."

That, the earring, and knowing they'd never consummated the marriage.

"Mr. Olsen?"

"Did you not notice our room placement?" He didn't leave me an opening. "I never saw a fraction of the trust my father bestowed on Mrs. Berg all these years. Edith tolerated her as best she could, but Mrs. Berg wouldn't let me anywhere near either of them if she had anything to do with it. When I saw that she and Mr. Nilsen were leaving as well … I couldn't not follow. Uninvited or not!"

I reached for the coffeepot to refill my cup. "When did you know Mrs. Olsen had consumption?"

He slumped in his chair. "I should have guessed sooner. She was always coughing. Not until we arrived here, I think."

"Madame Fabbri knew." I waited for this information to sink in. "She and Reverend Olsen made a deal. Her copy of the contract is not the same as the one in this briefcase. Hers says the theater will accommodate Mrs. Olsen until her death, which was expected soon. And they will keep every penny of the patronage, whether she is dead or alive. The terms are signed for by all parties."

"Except hers." His hand formed a fist in his lap.

"So you see, Mr. Olsen, her murder did not further your inheritance."

"I beg your pardon?" The other hand fisted.

"I think you loved her." I set down my cup in case I had to bolt to the door and keep him from running. "I think your intentions were honorable until you realized their marriage was as good as dead. Until she realized it and the two of you came up with a plan to kill your father so you could be together. But she had a sudden turn of heart. Could not handle the guilt. Considered turning herself in, if not you both, and you had to give her a quick and romantic exit."

He shot out of his chair and I rose, prepared for his next move.

Lina bit her lip, and her face glowed with excitement. I couldn't tell whose side she was on.

"I think she kept the other earring the whole time in order to tease you along until she could discover how far her new husband would go to give her what she wanted. For all you know, your father really did order her a set of sapphire earrings."

He looked stricken, and his face paled. "She would never…"

"You gave her flowers." I nodded slowly. "A huge bouquet. When she broke down later that night with you in her room, there was no other choice. You had to do it."

"And you think me capable of this?" he snarled.

"You bought the flowers and the poisons. Both signed for by you."

Suddenly, he laughed. It was a sad, howling sort of laugh, and it wiped the smile from Lina's face.

"Oh, Mrs. Kelly. I thought you believed me. This was all a ruse to trap me." He looked at Lina as though she were party to the dastardly plot. "Though sorely tempted, I've never killed anyone in my life."

"I believe you," she said, and gave him a hopeful wink. "More's the pity."

"There were receipts," I said sternly. "Mrs. Olsen told me the flowers were from the hotel. She covered for you. Lied to protect your relationship from prying eyes."

"Why?" His fists rested on his hips, and mine copied them. "Why must people from small backwoods places insist their story contain big city sins? You're no different from Mrs. Berg."

The jab struck home. "Why did you attack Mrs. Berg down there?" I spat back. "She says you forced your way into her room and grabbed her!"

"I jiggled the door, sure," he said, "but when it opened, she came charging at me with fire in her eyes! She attacked me! Had me pushed all the way back into my suite, screaming her head off."

"If you're innocent, why were you running away? What are you doing here? You grabbed the briefcase from me!"

He took a step back but did not give up the floor.

I threw the evidence in his face. "Why did you order red roses if you didn't love her? And all those purchases at the pharmacy are quite damning!"

"What flowers? Which pharmacy?" He shook his head.

"You'll have to be more specific if you're going to write headliners. You are too scattershot. So far, your audience isn't buying it."

I blinked. "They are both in Chinatown."

"And they will recognize me if we go down there?"

"I would think so. Are you offering?"

"Absolutely, if that will make you believe me."

I swallowed. "If it wasn't you, it was someone using your name."

He nodded. "Which doesn't help us, because all the people involved know my name. Someone tried to frame me."

"Why?"

He looked at Lina. "You may have noticed that I am desperately unpopular. Everyone is ready to turn me in for a murder I didn't commit. Maybe I'll go back to New York tonight and pretend the last six months never happened."

I'd also been framed, it seemed, but I had nowhere to go but prison.

"Are you truly a reporter?" I asked. "You have a job waiting for you?"

Plopping down next to Lina, he bent to untie his shoe. "And you aren't to tell anyone." Casting the shoe aside, he slid a finger into his sock and fished out a press card. "Here."

Lina peered over his shoulder. "Press card. New York."

"The case of fraud at Tiffany's was solved three weeks ago. That's when the Olsens announced their immediate exit and when I decided to go back by way of San Francisco."

He replaced his card and retrieved the shoe. "Instead of settling in and producing a proper heir, my father chose to run. Something big was driving him, and it very much appeared that he was running from something rather than running toward something. I don't buy his interest in opera."

"He was going to dump his new wife here," I said. "I'm not certain what he was going to do after that."

Mr. Olsen tied his shoe with a deep sigh, and I bent to retrieve my coffee. It was cold.

"This is murder. Twice. And it's personal." He looked me in the eye. "I'm going to find out who killed the good reverend and his wife." Reaching for the briefcase, he said, "There has to be something in here or Mr. Nilsen wouldn't have guarded it so well."

"Detective Fisher and I went through it earlier," I said. "The only thing of note was the altered contract."

"Why would they have two?" He frowned into the interior of the case and poked at the papers on top.

"I assume they did not want her to see the actual terms."

He gingerly held up the empty bottle. "And this is…"

"The poison that killed your father. It was found at the bottom of the vase on the table."

He dropped it back in the case. "We have to find out who purchased it."

"We can go to Chinatown," I said, glancing at the dark window, "but there might be a faster way. Through the flowers."

"You said it all came from Chinatown."

I set my cup down. "Yes. Delivered. But someone had to order and pay for it using your name. And my guess is that they did it from the hotel lobby, since it was the hotel vendor. Mrs. Olsen herself said they were from the hotel. They might have that record." And several others that only Detective Fisher had access to, I thought with frustration. "We have to hurry. Mrs. Berg and Mr. Nilsen might leave in the morning."

He shook his head. "They don't dare go home without..." He swallowed his sadness. "Them. But I can't go down there," he said. "I'm a wanted man. The entire hotel heard Mrs. Berg's screams."

"I can't show myself anywhere in the city," I said. "I'm supposed to be rotting in a jail cell."

We both turned to Lina.

With a smile meant for Mr. Olsen and Mr. Olsen alone, she said, "Just when I'd resigned myself to a dull week. I had no idea you two were such desperate criminals. Although I'm delighted, of course." She rose and folded her hands before her. "Make yourselves at home. I have no objection to a stroll, although I insist you both remain until I return."

Mr. Olsen rose and offered his hand over the table between them. "We are at your mercy, Miss Lina."

She laid a hand in his. "Lina. And yes. You are."

He brought her hand to his lips and murmured, "Delighted."

Lina's smile of victory carried her on her way, and I stopped myself from asking her how she was going to go about collecting the information we needed. After she left, Mr. Olsen stared at the closed door for several more moments.

And I stared at Mr. Olsen, going back over all of our conversations, searching for the lie.

"Your notes."

He turned to me. "Notes?"

"The diary. I saw it in your room. When I lost my handkerchief. Why do you keep your handwriting secret?"

"A reporter keeps everything private. It's shorthand." He moved Lina's tray and the newspaper off the table and hefted the briefcase onto it. "Couldn't take a chance someone might snoop through my room, could I?"

His irony wasn't lost on me. With a long-suffering sigh, he paused to glance over the front page of the paper. I looked much older in black and white. Shooting me a grin, he dumped the briefcase out over the table, letting papers spill onto the floor.

Shuffling through the mess, he said, "You've gravely misrepresented Mrs. Olsen with your theories, Mrs. Kelly. She wanted to sing, perhaps at any price, since she convinced my father to bring her here. If she understood the terms or her condition, she never once hinted at it. But she would have gone through with it. So why?" He ran a hand over his face. "Why did either of them have to die?"

"They had the other earring," I reminded him. "If you didn't do it, someone is very eager to make it look that way."

He threw his hands into the air at me and said, "Turn me in, then! Claim your freedom and relinquish your bid for truth. For justice!" He dropped his hands back into the paperwork. "Or let me do my job as fast as humanly possible."

Sulking, I went to the window and stared at the moon.

He was sifting through the paperwork when an animated Lina returned.

"There's a manhunt going on down there." She smiled at me and went to the sofa. "Actually, more of a woman hunt. Your name and likeness are on everyone's lips."

"I suppose Detective Fisher is furious with me," I muttered.

"That could be an understatement. I wouldn't venture far if I were you." She seated herself, eyes on Mr. Olsen.

"He knows I'm innocent," I said with irritation. "But he has to make it look good."

"It never looks good to be shot," she pointed out, "while making a daring escape. Ruins the gown every time."

"He wouldn't." I mustered some confidence for the two little words.

"Someone else might." Her quick look over my black wreck of a dress made her add, "Although that one is already a complete loss."

She could afford to be flippant. Until someone discovered us in her suite.

Lina ignored me and said primly, "There is no one registered in this hotel by the name of Mr. Josiah Olsen."

He looked up at her.

"There is no Reverend Olsen," she said. "There's a Dr. Olsen and a Mrs. Olsen. And no other Olsen. Your name is not in the register. Anywhere. Who are you?"

His smirk offered my first real hint of the man he'd become. It had the air of slick city men who knew their way about the streets.

"I used an alias. It's a prudent way to cover one's trail."

"You wouldn't have gotten away with that in Minnesota," I said.

"It's clever." Lina reached up to pat her hair into place. "You've heard of Mark Twain? Mr. Samuel Clemens, that is?" she asked. "I could arrange an introduction. Once this little matter is settled."

"Why would your father use doctor instead of reverend?" I asked. "He isn't a doctor of anything."

"Another alias?" He squinted in thought.

"We are surrounded by them." Lina fluffed her violet skirts. "The man who ordered your flowers and signed your name was hard to understand, according to the bellhop. A heavy accent. Balding."

"Mr. Nilsen!" Mr. Olsen and I cried at the same time.

She sighed, thoroughly enjoying our reactions. "He had a ferocious set of side whiskers. No beard."

"Madame Fabbri's husband?" I asked.

"And he smelled strongly of cigar smoke," Lina finished.

"Has to be Muller," Mr. Olsen said. "He was aloof at the dinner party. Never said more than two words together."

"Sims claimed it. I heard him." The discrepancy leapt forward in my memory. "But ... red roses?"

Lina shook her head. "There's where you miss the subtlety of color, Mrs. Kelly. The order was for crimson."

There was a difference?

"Red is for love," she said, with a pointed look at Mr. Olsen. "Crimson is for mourning. Death."

Mr. Olsen stood and made an elaborate bow. "My darling, Lina? Would you do me the honor of attending the opera with me?"

"The burlesque," I said drily.

His smile was all city. "The burlesque," he amended.

Lina's smile was all business. "Yes, indeed."

Chapter Twenty-Four

I T WAS HUMILIATING. Once again relegated to the role of second fiddle to a high society couple, I stood in the vestibule of the California Theater in Lina's least attractive dress. The brown skirt was topped with a russet and green plaid overskirt, forming an ill-fitting costume both too snug in the bust and too short in the hem. Last year's shabby fashion included a hat that we'd plucked the feathers from and attached a drab veil that wrapped beneath my chin.

The idea was that all eyes would follow Lina.

And they did, with the ensemble she'd hastily donned. With her plunging peacock blue gown and matching gloves, she made certain her entrance into the lobby was as grand as any on stage by removing her black velvet cape with a languid shrug and a dazzling smile.

Lina didn't miss a trick, and the doorman nearly bumped his backside into me as he gave her a pretentious bow.

Thunderous applause from the theater seemed to be just for her, although we could see the backs of the audience through the open doorways. The gentleman behind the ticket window gestured to Mr. Olsen over the din.

"The performance is nearly over," he said, voice raised to

be heard. "No more tickets."

"We are not here for the show," Mr. Olsen said, looking around for any familiar faces.

"The party," Lina said, flashing a dimple at the concierge, "is upstairs, is it not?"

Mr. Olsen looked at her over his shoulder as the concierge nodded. "Yes, madame. But we are not seating yet. Perhaps you care to wait? Or if madame prefers, there is a salon next door."

She moved to Mr. Olsen, who gave her his complete attention. "There is always an after party," she crooned up at him. "Upstairs in the banquet room."

"Will Madame Fabbri be there?" I asked. "With her husband?"

"We will find out," she said with a shrug. "The staff and performers must eat sometime."

There were too many people here. The odds that someone would recognize my face made me tug at the veil.

"We can't stay here," I said. "We have to go somewhere we can speak to him without drawing a crowd."

"Then the banquet is out of the question," Mr. Olsen said.

Lina pouted.

"The office?" I hated to suggest it, but I could think of nowhere else that might be safe. "Madame Fabbri is seldom in it unless called for."

"And if she is?" Mr. Olsen leaned forward and lowered his voice. "Her gun is real."

"We're looking for Mr. Muller," Lina said. "Why not

simply ask for him?"

Mr. Olsen rubbed the back of his neck. "We need a reason to summon him. Why would he stop everything on a busy night to talk to us?"

"Especially as we're going to accuse him of forging your name." I bit my lip and watched the audience.

"May I be of service, madame?" The doorman stopped at a discreet distance, his head tipped down. His question was for Lina, but his eyes were on me. With a bland face, he waited for her answer.

"Yes." Lina took a step forward and commanded his attention. "I inadvertently left my little bag in my seat after last night's performance. It's my understanding that Madame Fabbri has set it aside for me in the safety of her office to retrieve at my convenience. It's convenient now, since we are early for the party upstairs."

He straightened. "I see."

"It is of sentimental value," she added. "I must have it at once."

The doorman bowed again and led us to a very familiar staircase.

"It's this way, madame. Allow me to send for Madame Fabbri for you."

She fluttered her lashes and laid a finger on his padded jacket shoulder. "Oh, don't disturb her! She's working right now! But you might send for her husband, Mr. Muller. He's the one who found my bag, and I'm determined to thank him personally."

"As you wish, madame."

I caught his second scrutinizing look as he left. My heart began to race. "He's going to call for the police. We have to leave."

"But we've just arrived," Lina said. "Don't give up that quickly."

Mr. Olsen looked around the foyer and gave a decisive nod. "Right. Up we go, then." He took Lina's elbow and led her up the staircase. I gathered my short skirts and followed.

"This place is tighter than a herd of Holsteins," I said. "If he tells anyone else we're here, Mr. Sims is going to show up."

"His gun isn't real." Mr. Olsen tried the doorknob and cursed under his breath.

"Locked, darling?" Lina reached up to smooth her hair and came away with a hairpin. "Give me a moment, will you?"

Mr. Olsen's surprised eyes met mine over her somewhat seductively bent back. While I freely admitted to knowing nothing about the woman's profession outside of the obvious, picking locks did not strike me as a required skill.

It made me wonder how secure any locked room could be. We'd left the briefcase in her seventh-floor suite, but whether a maid or anyone with a hairpin could open the door, its safety was in the fact that no one would look for it there in the first place.

It bought us more time, I thought nervously, as we waited for Lina. While the Olsens' bodies could be shipped separately, if necessary, Mr. Nilsen would not return to Minnesota without his prized paperwork. And Mrs. Berg would never travel without an escort.

If we couldn't get a confession out of Mr. Muller to-night, we could at least return to Lina's apartment and try once again to find a clue among the ledgers.

"There you are." Lina slid her hairpin back into place as Mr. Olsen opened the door.

"At least we know we're alone," he muttered, and she gave him a wink of approval.

The woman was tenacious. What Mr. Olsen made of it, I couldn't tell, but he played along well enough.

Immediately moving behind Madame Fabbri's desk, I slid open the drawer where I'd seen her withdraw the contract. It wasn't there.

"What are you doing?" Mr. Olsen looked back at the door.

I pulled open another drawer. A revolver lay handy inside and I snapped it shut again.

"The contract. It was in here somewhere. I want proof."

"You're going to get caught."

"I'm already going to jail for murder, remember?" The bottom drawer had a plate full of crumbs and a bottle of whiskey in it.

When the doorknob turned, Mr. Olsen leapt to Lina's side, much to her delight. I moved away from the desk and positioned myself in the shadows behind them.

It was not Mr. Muller.

"What on earth?" Mr. Sims's words rained down like fire and brimstone. He recognized Mr. Olsen right away and took deliberate time looking Lina over as he reached into his jacket pocket. "I will throw you out myself. How dare you enter this office uninvited?"

"We are waiting for Mr. Muller," Lina said, flashing her charm. "You are welcome to wait with us, sir."

But Mr. Sims had seen me, evaluated the situation, and decided otherwise.

"You're wanted by the police." It wasn't a question.

"I am." I moved swiftly, coming between my companions and his building wrath. "But if you would allow me a moment only. To explain?"

He pulled the gun from his jacket. Lina gasped.

Knowing it was a prop, and that he likely recalled that he'd already told us as much, I continued calmly. "We need Mr. Muller. You were at the dining table on New Year's Eve. You saw what happened."

"I believe Mr. Olsen here was also present." He scowled.

"Mr. Muller remained in the background the entire time of the tragedy," I said. "He didn't have much to say."

"Neither did you." He waved the gun in my face and I rolled my eyes. "Although, I recall you ranting as the evening progressed. Had to be dragged off by the police. How did you escape?"

"I didn't do it."

"You fed the man poison. It's murder, plain and simple."

I wasn't going to get far with this obstinate man and skipped directly to the point. "We want to know why Mr. Muller sent flowers to Mrs. Olsen before she died."

His face turned a ghastly gray, and he leaned back in the doorway.

"You know she died." I asked. "She was murdered. We told Madame Fabbri when we were here earlier. But there's a question about a floral delivery to her room. After the reverend died and before she did. Ordered in the hotel lobby and signed for by Mr. Olsen."

Mr. Sims turned the gun on Mr. Olsen and said, "Is it not obvious? That means the police are after you as well, good sir."

"He didn't do it, either." I stepped in front of the gun and pushed it aside. "And I think you know it. The hotel staff said it was a man, certainly, who ordered the flowers. But he was hard to understand and smelled strongly of cigar smoke."

The room was silent, tense with accusations, and the crowd downstairs roared.

"Mr. Olsen does not smoke," I pointed out. "Furthermore, there was a cigar stub on the dining room table when the New Year's Eve party concluded. I believe you claimed it, Mr. Sims."

Mr. Sims pushed his spectacles higher on his nose with his free hand. "What are you implying?"

"That you lied. You don't smoke. You don't smell of it and your fingers and teeth are clean. Mr. Muller does. Why did you cover for him that night?"

"Whatever else happened, Mr. Muller is innocent."

"Not if you need to lie for him."

"It was expected. Is." A small bead of sweat appeared at his temple. "The man is a baritone." He shrugged as if that explained everything. "A supporting role. He stays in the background where Madame Fabbri keeps him."

"Singers don't smoke. It ruins their voice."

"Smoking is his way of defying her."

Hands on hips, I waited.

"Part of my job is to keep him in her shadow. I readily accepted the question, in case smoking at the dining room table was a problem for the police."

"She pays you to take the blame for him?" Was there no end to the madness in this city?

For the first time, it occurred to me that I could have, with the right coins, bribed my way out of jail. Except for the picture in the papers, of course. Reporters were rather damning, now I thought about it.

"Mrs. Olsen was our new protégé," he said. "When her husband died, Madame Fabbri asked him to send up flowers. In sympathy."

"Why would he sign it in Mr. Olsen's name?"

Mr. Sims's shrug involved his whole body. "He could not have! Why would he?"

"Send for him so we can ask him ourselves."

"Mr. Muller defers to his wife in all matters," he stuttered. "I cannot see him doing anything without her sanction."

"As well he should not."

The new voice came from behind Mr. Sims, and a pair of slender arms circled his waist. Other than a sharp inhale, he did not react.

"Every man should defer to his wife," Miss Everleigh said, pushing him into the room. "Women are the cleverer of the species." She had closed the door with an impish smile before turning to see the room full of people. Her eyes narrowed. "George? Did you bring an audience?"

"Kate..." Mr. Sims waved his gun helplessly in the air. "Miss Everleigh. They were already here."

Miss Everleigh's gaze rested on Lina's and the two shared a knowing smile.

"It isn't what you think!" Mr. Sims cried.

Lina nodded with a knowing wink. "Oh, yes, it very much is."

Miss Everleigh was still in costume. Mr. Olsen openly admired it. I had to admit, her ankles were irrefutably attractive.

She leaned into Mr. Sims and asked, "Are you going to shoot them? The good Madame Fabbri is giving her speech. She will be a solid twenty minutes yet."

"I don't suppose the good madame also pays you to ... dally ... with the actresses?" I asked.

"Don't be absurd." His words for both of us and another bead of sweat dropped to his bushy brow.

"Here now, man," Mr. Olsen said with a step forward. "It's time to come clean. What do you know, and how can you help us? If you are innocent, prove it. If you are guilty, well, you will be here when the police arrive either way!"

Miss Everleigh turned wide eyes to Mr. Sims. "George. What have you done? If you've played me for a fool, I'll make certain you sing soprano for the rest of your life."

Lina snickered behind her glove.

"Kate, my love," he said, taking her hand, "you know I

do not sing. Please do not upset a hair of your head. I am yours, body and soul. These people mean nothing. They are leaving."

I fought down bile as he kissed her hand.

"Like hell we are." Mr. Olsen crossed his arms.

A small clock on the mantle chimed, and the passing of time felt acute. "Where is the contract, Mr. Sims?" I asked. And as the thought popped into my head, I added, "And where are the police?"

We all looked at each other, bewildered.

"Did you send for them?" Mr. Sims asked in a low voice.

"Did you?" Mr. Olsen retorted.

"I assumed the doorman did," I said in bewilderment, "but here we are."

"Hurry!" Mr. Sims said. "There's still time!"

"For what?" I asked as he flung the door open.

"To explain," he said, beckoning for us to follow as he tucked the gun back into his jacket with one hand and slid his other around Miss Everleigh's trim waist. He didn't look back.

With an oath, Mr. Olsen took Lina by the arm and steered her out of the room and down the stairwell. People surged into the lobby and the volume in the building grew. Slamming the door behind me, I followed Mr. Olsen's hat and the deep blue of Lina's gown into the melee.

Lights blazed in every corner of the theater as the audience flowed from their seats. Participation in the final act of securing coats and waiting impatiently for each coach would keep theatergoers underfoot for another hour. Those invited to the upstairs banquet created a second wave of foot traffic in the opposite direction.

Lina's gown merged with others down a long passage-way, and I struggled to follow. Many people simply lingered in the middle of the carpet to talk to each other and I wondered whether Miss Everleigh was being stopped every other foot to sign autographs and receive bouquets.

But I couldn't catch up to her.

I'd circled another crowd and edged past a doorway when a rough hand grabbed my arm.

"You there!" The surly usher in an ill-fitting uniform squinted hard into my face.

With a yank, I was free and pressed through the crush, searching in vain for a familiar face.

Chapter Twenty-Five

G ONE. THEY WERE gone. I pushed through the crowds, moving as fast as they parted, and struggled between looking frantically in all directions and avoiding anyone recognizing my face. Mr. Olsen and Lina must have made a turn down another hall or through a closed door, which meant there was no hope at all of discovering where Mr. Sims had been leading us.

The passage I found myself in was soon deserted, and I reached deep into my memory for guidance. When Detective Fisher and I had been shepherded through an eerily empty theater, the hall had felt very similar. Head down, I tried to recall the door that would drop me at the rear exit into the alley.

I'd wait for Mr. Olsen and Lina in the coach. With any luck, they would return with information.

A heavyset usher rumbling toward me made my decision. I ducked through the nearest door and rushed headlong into a maze of stage props and setting rigs. The passing people didn't spare me a glance. A woman brushed by with an armload of costumes. A boy jogged past, balancing an elaborate candelabra. Overhead, curtains, flags, and a huge golden disk fluttered in the shadows as ropes and pulleys shifted them into place. Footsteps echoed over wooden floorboards and barked words came from every direction.

The thick scent of cigar smoke stopped me in my tracks. Leaning against a wall, I faced a large partition painted with a forest scene that blocked my view of whoever stood on the other side. The person's shadow floated and flickered in a distant lamplight and smoke curled above it. The shadows that joined, mingled, and parted with it by turn were easier to decipher once the conversation started.

"We lost them." Miss Everleigh was out of breath. The wide mutton sleeves of her costume lowered as she placed both hands on her knees and laughed.

"Lost?" Mr. Muller's guttural voice rumbled through the room.

"Unexpected visitors," Mr. Sims said, and he brushed his hands over his jacket.

"Our ten-minute tryst was canceled." Miss Everleigh's shadow merged with Mr. Sims's. If a shadow could pout, I was certain it would have.

"They were looking for you," Mr. Sims said, his chin extended by the wiry beard.

"I was told as much," Mr. Muller replied. "I nearly went up. Thought the doorman must be mistaken. No one ever requests an audience with me. But it was time for our appointment. I came here to wait instead."

There was a pause, but the shadows didn't move, so I didn't, either.

"I got rid of them," Mr. Sims said. "But they asked an

unusual question. Perhaps you have an answer."

Mr. Muller's mutton-chops dipped forward.

"You sent flowers to Mrs. Olsen?" Mr. Sims asked.

"Flowers?" Mr. Muller paused. "You were there when I did it. We stopped at the desk on our way out of the building the night her husband died."

"Did you sign for them with Mr. Olsen's name?"

The shadow grunted. "My good man, I was distracted, as you might imagine. But not to the point I can't recall my own name."

"You signed for them yourself?"

"Should have used madame's name. It was her idea, after all. Melodramatic waste of funds. Thought it might speed up the process. Flighty Americans."

"Do hurry," Miss Everleigh said with a tug on Mr. Sims's arm. "I'll be late for her speech."

"Trying to rally more funds, is she?" Mr. Sims tapped a finger beneath Miss Everleigh's chin. "You see to it she fails."

"Why would anyone be interested?" Mr. Muller asked.

"Because I told them I smoked." Mr. Sims sounded exasperated. "I'll be glad to leave the continent behind me once and for all."

"You don't smoke."

"No. For all my orders to maintain your anonymity, they've reached that conclusion, anyway. It seems the killer has yet to be found, but I made it clear you and I have nothing to do with it."

"Madame and I were not in the room," Mr. Muller said with finality.

"A ghastly way to die," Mr. Sims said. "I wonder who poisoned the ugly toad?"

Miss Everleigh smothered a laugh. "Oh, was he?"

"One of his own," Mr. Muller said with a puff. "The woman with the cake. Isn't that always how the story plays? Our task was only to ease the girl's life while it lasted."

"It lasted not two days."

"What, man?"

"Mrs. Olsen is dead too."

There was something between a growl and a sputter before Mr. Muller said, "Madame keeps a great many things close to her heart."

"Does she not tell her husband everything?" Miss Everleigh's teasing words caused Mr. Sims to put his arm around her. "Terrible run of bad luck in that family. Not that she would have ever replaced me."

"Run along without me, darling," Mr. Sims said. "All is cared for, and you can pack your trunks tonight."

"I am also required upstairs," Mr. Muller growled.

"You go without me, as well. I am done bowing before your wife," Mr. Sims said. "You do realize once the theater is gone, she will have no one but yourself to order about?"

"We move to Germany." Mr. Muller cleared his throat. "Home. How I miss the European manners. This country is a disgrace. A mockery."

"Why do you think we're going?" Miss Everleigh asked. "I'm tired of being ogled like some toy instead of a serious actress. These fools act like I'm one of the whores that dance on Pacific Street."

"You're a great deal beyond the Barbary Coast, my darling."

Miss Everleigh's shadow disappeared into Mr. Sims's and the distinct sound of kissing had me turn my head away until it was replaced with her fading footsteps.

"A tryst, eh?" Mr. Muller asked. "In madame's office?"

"Even her dressing room is not private."

"You've learned well. Keep the talent happy and we all get what we want."

"Mr. Hayman will arrive at any minute."

"Then I will go. Do not let him change his mind. Here is the paperwork. All there was. Once madame realizes it's missing, she will call on all the demons of hell to search for them."

"This I know. *Danke*, Herr Muller."

"*Auf Wiedersehen*."

My mind raced as the lone shadow remained hovering on the partition. I didn't doubt for a moment that Mr. Sims had just acquired the Olsen contract. And it wasn't a stretch to imagine myself, Mr. Olsen, and Lina accused of taking it from her office. We'd inadvertently provided Mr. Sims the perfect suspects.

I focused on pressing against the wall behind me to keep from barging headfirst through the partition and tackling him.

I recalled his comment about Miss Everleigh leaving for London, but he hadn't suggested he was accompanying her. Why would he and Mr. Muller be in cahoots to remove Madame Fabbri from the theater as well?

Who was Mr. Hayman? What had we stumbled upon?

The rustle of paper sliding into Mr. Sim's jacket was drowned by approaching steps. They boomed across the floor, and another shadow, shorter but wider by half, joined Mr. Sims's. A tall top hat and a cane created an imposing silhouette. It was easy to follow the well-projected, if slick as a snake-oil salesman, voice.

"Sims," it said, "your girl is a real head-turner. I may have to visit London in the summer."

"I'll extend an invitation, Mr. Hayman." Mr. Sims's voice cooled by several degrees.

"Is all in order? My lawyers are standing by, waiting for the word."

"Yes. You'll have it next week. Monday, if at all possible."

The shadow leaned forward. "Tomorrow, Sims. I like to sleep in on Mondays."

"Impossible. The banks will not have the records you need. Give it a day or two."

"But the benefit was New Year's Eve."

"And the banks were closed the following day. You see how it is. Never fear, the record will show that the check written out to Miss Roseau is false. She's already left for the East Coast. Somewhere along the way, she will discover it worthless. What will she do? Nothing. It was a gift, after all. Not wages."

"A worthy move on madame's part. Not enough. But a worthy move."

"The funds will be in the Fabbri account under some

false label. Miscellany for all I know." He chuckled, but Mr. Hayman did not join him. "The benefit was sold out. Madame Fabbri offered the proceeds—all of it—to Miss Everleigh. And my Kate accepted."

After a pregnant pause, Mr. Hayman said, "I see the student has become the master."

"Quite. We will withdraw the monies the day we board the steamer for London."

"She will not catch on?"

"I am not unfamiliar with the stage. Madame is desperate to keep the troupe on, of course. She has nothing to replace it with. She's already ordered playbills for their next ten performances."

"That will never be performed. Well done. And the unexpected patronage? You've dealt with that?"

"It's come to nothing. We don't even have to work with the original patrons. They are both dead."

"Also unexpected, Mr. Sims. Or have you gone too far this time?"

"And what do you mean by that, sir?" Mr. Sims's indignant question surprised me. "I may have an agenda for my career, and I may be a man in love..." Here, Mr. Hayman snorted. "But never have I stooped to murder!"

Mr. Hayman tipped his hat. "I beg your pardon. It was only idle curiosity."

"Perhaps I'll keep my curiosity, idle or otherwise, to myself on questions of your acquisition of the Baldwin Theater?"

The hat went firmly back on his head, and Mr. Hayman

raised his cane. "Careful, Sims."

"Since the Olsens were removed from the situation through no intentions of mine, I've reconsidered our arrangement."

"Oh?"

"I want more money."

"I thought your Miss Kate is taking care of that."

"I won't be tying my future to her apron strings. That's hers, free and clear."

"Destroy that contract, Sims. I paid you handsomely to bankrupt the California Theater by the end of this week."

"So you did. But unless you want to double my fee, the contract must go through."

Mr. Hayman leapt forward and yanked Mr. Sims forward by the cravat. I stopped breathing.

"Don't toy with me, Sims. We've come too far. Fabbri will squeeze me for every penny when she sells."

Mr. Sims was perfectly calm. "Don't make an offer, then. Wait for the foreclosure. Buy it at auction."

"That takes too much time. I don't want it in three months. I want it now. It needs to be swift, before the staff has a chance to leave. Before she has a chance to let it fall into ruin. I want to upgrade the place. Electricity. Fresh carpets. Not replace every tapestry and velvet seat cushion. You'll have to persuade her to sell now. Show her the numbers. Make it bleak!"

"It will be. Very."

Mr. Hayman released him. "If you skip town before she approaches me with a proposition, there is nowhere you can go I won't find you."

"Would you like to hold on to my steamer tickets?"

"Cocksure, are you? I want proof that the patronage contract is destroyed."

"I'm going to collect on it before they leave, destitute, for Minnesota. In madame's name. I am her business manager, after all."

"And if she finds out?"

Mr. Sims raised his hands. "Madame Fabbri will have no money, no act, and no manager. What more do you want? I need that money to set myself up in London. You think that's cheap?"

In the long silence that followed, I cowered, waiting for a blow to fall.

"Collect on it, then," Mr. Hayman said at last. "But don't let it anywhere near her bank accounts. I don't want any trace of it when my lawyers come through. And make certain it's destroyed after. So long as madame cannot prove she had the offer, she will have to capitulate."

"Smart man."

"Do not patronize me, Mr. Sims. I'm late for a party. You will send word by the end of the day tomorrow."

"All will be done by then. And I will be gone before the demons of hell are unleashed."

"What?"

He held out his hand. "An honor doing business with you, sir."

Mr. Hayman ignored it. Turning, he left, and Mr. Sims's shadow was alone.

I had a single moment in which to decide where my loyalties were. I didn't care if Mr. Olsen's inheritance vanished in a London fog. I didn't care whether Madame Fabbri kept her theater or went to Germany to tend her husband. But I very much cared whether I hung for murder.

As surprising as it was that it was neither law enforcement nor clergy were involved in my rescue, I had to thank the good God for throwing me in league with a criminal.

Mr. Sims, I understood.

Clearing my throat, I tapped lightly on the partition and said, "I beg your pardon, Mr. Sims, for arriving late to your explanation."

The shadow straightened into a solid line.

"I wonder if you would kindly hand over the contract in your pocket? The letters from Mrs. Olsen as well. I imagine Mr. Olsen might like those in memory of her."

He paused, then asked, "Why should I cooperate with a wanted criminal, Mrs. Kelly?"

"Because I heard everything. I know who and how Madame Fabbri will be ruined. It's a story I can tell from a prison cell if necessary. A close friend of mine is with the press, you see."

He didn't immediately bolt, which was hopeful, so I continued.

"Did they know there were two contracts? The reverend and his secretary?"

"Yes, indeed. Theirs was a decoy, drawn up at their insistence. Ours is binding. Mr. Nilsen should already have a check prepared for me. We were going to claim it, anyway," he finished with the snarl of a cornered stray dog.

"By we, you mean you."

"Exactly. I won't let you destroy it. I want the money."

"Now here is where we make some mutually beneficial decisions. Listen carefully, Mr. Sims. I want something as well. I don't care who killed the Olsens. I'm searching for a killer who murdered someone a year ago. If I can dangle this contract in front of Mr. Nilsen and get information that will find that killer once and for all, I will be at peace."

"You will be in prison."

"I think the killer is one and the same. I only need a name."

"You think to trade the contract for information?"

"I think they want the money. Badly. Someone may have already killed for it."

He gave a dry laugh and said, "If they will do anything to see it destroyed, what makes you think the killer won't simply shoot you and burn it?"

"I'm counting on it. That will give them away. I don't believe for a minute they will tell me what I want to know. But if it's worth killing for, then the killer must present himself."

"And I won't be paid a red cent. No deal, Mrs. Kelly."

"It can be done together. I want you to go forward with your meeting with Mr. Nilsen to collect the money. The contract has a blank page for both signatures once the amount changes hands. Get it signed and take your money. But before you arrive for that appointment, I am going to give Mr. Nilsen an out. I'll offer to destroy the contract if he will tell me what happened to my aunt."

"I can't take that chance."

"You can't afford not to. I can march into Madame Fabbri's party right now. While her bribery money is still in her bank account."

"And if the killer presents before I collect?"

"Then I will be out of the way and you can conclude your business in peace." I smiled in victory. "*Bon voyage*, Mr. Sims."

Chapter Twenty-Six

LINA STARED AT me the entire ride back to the hotel. "You never backed down! Not an inch! In the face of a gun!"

She would have been impressed further yet, had she known I carried the gun in the cylindrical leather case in my hands. The music case was a stage prop, but conveniently close to hand when I needed something to carry the contract in.

Mr. Sims's face had twisted in physical pain when he'd handed me the ticket to his wealth.

Asking for his gun was an afterthought, but he agreed when I told him we had Mr. Nilsen's patronage check. The guaranteed payment gave Mr. Sims some little comfort, and his gun did the same for me.

When we arrived, Lina tossed her dark curls and smiled at Mr. Olsen. "I, at least, earned a kiss for my well-performed part."

He didn't meet my amused eyes.

Mr. Olsen and I continued our grim conversation all the way up through the slumbering hotel to Lina's rooms. He acknowledged that our killer intended to frame him for one, if not both, murders, if I myself did not swing for them. Giving him most of the details, I proved that no one in the theater was interested in the Olsens' demise. If we still believed Mrs. Olsen did not commit suicide, our killer was either Mrs. Berg or Mr. Nilsen.

Neither had anything against the Olsens or Aunt Mary.

And neither had any use for a fortune.

"It has to be in the ledgers," I mumbled as Lina opened the door. "In my aunt's handwriting."

We stumbled, weary to the bone, into the suite. When the lights came on, a voice said, "Glory be. About time."

Sitting on the sofa, arms crossed and her small shoes up on the table, and the briefcase on the cushion next to her, Pearl bestowed one of her sternest scowls on our ragtag group.

"Good morning, Pearl," Lina said. "I think we will sleep in today." With a wink over her shoulder at Mr. Olsen, she walked into her boudoir and closed the door behind her.

"Pearl." I approached with no energy left to do anything but collapse into the armchair. "How did you know where we were?" It was useless now. If Pearl found us so quickly, it was only a matter of time before Detective Fisher arrived.

All that work for nothing. I curled my arms around the music case and hugged it to me.

Mr. Olsen went to the dark window and leaned against the sill. "The stableman told, didn't he?"

Pearl put her feet down and sat upright. "When Miss Lina leaves her rooms to make a quick snack out of one of our bellhops, I take note. But she went back upstairs without him." She stood. "And he wouldn't tell me anything except she wanted a look behind the lobby counter. The kitchen, though? Miss Lina ordered coffee. She doesn't drink coffee. And she requested two cups."

"So, you just let yourself into Lina's suite and had a look around?" I asked. "I suppose you have keys to every suite in the hotel." Setting the case at my feet, I took off Lina's ugly hat and rubbed my temples. "The door locks around here are pointless."

Mr. Olsen picked lint from his jacket sleeve, looking very much like a petulant boy, but I saw him glancing at the case in my hands with speculation. "How else can the maids go in to clean things?"

"Mr. Olsen," I said. "Do you know you never lock your door? It's a bad habit left over from your Minnesota upbringing. How did you survive in a big city?"

His face reddened. "I do. When I remember to."

"Furthermore, you had no problem getting the central door between the suites to open for you. Perhaps neither of you had locked those, either. And Lina!" I turned to Pearl. "She can pick a door lock with a hairpin! Did you know that?"

"I'd think less of her if she couldn't," Pearl said.

"When it truly mattered," I said with frustration, "we couldn't get the door open. Mrs. Olsen died in her bed and no one..." My words trailed off.

"The maid let us in," Mr. Olsen said.

"Missy lost her job because of it," Pearl said. "She's much too timid with our guests. There are rules to uphold."

"But where was Mrs. Olsen's room key?" The question brought me to my feet. "You said you gave Detective Fisher your only key to the suite. The maid's key. Where is the other?" I tossed Lina's hat on the table.

"It wasn't in her room." Pearl's face grew thoughtful.

"Pearl, I was in that room when the screaming started. When Mr. Olsen and Mrs. Berg had a tussle."

"We did not!" Mr. Olsen said.

I ignored him. "I had the door locked. And Detective Fisher gave me the only key."

"We broke that door," Pearl snapped. "It's ruined now."

"But someone tried to get into the room while I stood there, watching. The lock turned and the knob turned. Someone has that other key. It's the only explanation!" My voice jumped along with my conclusion. "It's been bothering me. How it could be murder instead of suicide if Mrs. Olsen was alone and locked herself in? Whoever killed her took her room key and locked the door behind them."

"No key in the room proves it's murder," Mr. Olsen said. "But, of course, we assumed that from the beginning."

"That's why I ran with the briefcase." My knees shook, probably in weariness. There was nothing to be afraid of. But I resumed my seat with a sigh. "How soon will Detective Fisher arrive?"

Pearl tapped the briefcase next to her. "Do you have any idea how much that Mr. Nilsen raised Cain over his case gone missing? Threatened to sue the hotel. Threatened to get Detective Fisher fired. Threatened you with ... well, a body can't hardly keep up with it."

"Mrs. Berg," I whispered. "She saw me."

"You, Mrs. Kelly, are the city's most wanted woman. A dangerous, escaped criminal. Discovered, not in jail, mind you, but at the very scene of the crime." Her eyes narrowed. "Mr. Sedgwick nearly dropped with a heart seizure on the spot."

"I'm sorry," I said. "I didn't want anyone to be hurt by something that followed me to San Francisco."

Pearl's gaze went back and forth between Mr. Olsen and me. "Well. You both look too tired to cause much trouble right now. I don't think we need to bother the detective just yet."

My mouth hung open but that was the extent of my speech.

"We owe you, Mrs. Kelly." Pearl sighed deeply. "You took the blame on yourself even though you didn't do it."

"Thank you, Pearl." My dry eyes stung.

"It might be the biggest mistake of my life, but I'm putting the entire hotel at your disposal." She sat down again and folded her hands in her lap. "Please try, Mrs. Kelly. Even Detective Fisher, while sworn to haul you to the gallows, knows you're the key to this here mess. We need every clue we can use."

It might have been my imagination, but her eyes grew damp, and her lips thinned. For one moment, I felt like Pearl remembered we were family.

"I have a plan," I said once my throat stopped swelling with tears. "The theater gave me something that will force Mr. Nilsen to tell me the truth. All of it."

Mr. Olsen stood at attention and Pearl looked hopeful.

Opening the music case, I slid the papers from the leather cylinder. "The real contract. And Mrs. Olsen's correspondence with Madame Fabbri."

"How did you get that?" Mr. Olsen asked in reverent awe. He stepped close. "We couldn't even find Mr. Sims."

"I found him to be a cooperative fellow once we understood one another." I reached for the briefcase. "Would you help me, Mr. Olsen?"

He sat next to Pearl with alacrity. "If it brings this killer to justice, I'll do anything you wish, Mrs. Kelly."

"Thank you." The two words were heavy and I let them rest between the three of us as he helped drag the case up next to the table. "Look through this and find the check Mr. Nilsen has prepared for the California Theater."

He removed paperwork in handfuls. "I can arrange it by size, I suppose," he said.

"Mr. Sims is going to demand a meeting today with Mr. Nilsen. They will arrange to meet in the small gentlemen's parlor downstairs at two o'clock to complete the contract agreement. Mr. Nilsen is bound to the contract terms, even with the Olsens removed. He must present this check and sign for it."

"They's supposed to leave," Pearl said. "All traces of the dead are gone from room 412. We've cleaned it out completely." She glanced at Mr. Olsen. "But Detective Fisher didn't tell us what to do with your room yet."

Mr. Olsen never paused in his task, but he rolled his eyes. "It's paid for through the week, you know."

"I expect criminals don't get a refund when they leave early for jail."

"Criminals?" Here he paused and turned to her. "I've got the cleanest hands of the bunch!"

She nodded sagely. "Only Mrs. Berg's all but put the evil eye on you. Claims you've done the unthinkable."

From the look on his face, Mr. Olsen had no idea where to begin with her comment. Even I couldn't decide what she meant, and I had no interest in finding out. Anything to do with Mrs. Berg was automatically unthinkable.

"I don't suppose you can have all of my things sent up here?" he asked.

"That's on Miss Lina."

"She won't mind." He caught my look and added, "I'll work it out with her later."

"I expect it'll save us the trouble of shipping it. We already got a box full of Olsen things ready for the train." Pearl turned to me. "What can I do to help, Mrs. Kelly?"

The contract remained in my lap, far from the table that grew messier by the minute. "When Mr. Nilsen arrives, it will be me, not Mr. Sims, waiting for him at the table."

"But you'll be seen."

"Not if you help me." I looked down at Lina's ill-fitting gown. "I need clothes. My clothes are spread out between the apartment and the jailhouse, but I can't wear anything recognizable. Pearl, can you get me a uniform?"

She looked doubtful. "I s'pose. Not your usual one, though? Maybe a black one, like the room maids wear."

"Anything that will blend in." I nodded. "Most people

ignore the staff."

"Keep your hair all bundled up in the cap," she agreed. "We can't cover your face, but maybe you can carry something. A tray or feather duster. Something you can look down at."

"Thank you."

"What do you plan to do with Mr. Nilsen once he arrives?" Mr. Olsen lifted the small brown bottle and dropped it back into the case, repulsed.

"Have a little chat. I want him to tell me what he knows about my aunt's death."

"Why would he suddenly do that after all this time? None of us have gotten more than three words out of the man."

Pearl nodded. "Detective Fisher said the same thing exactly."

"Mr. Nilsen fixes things." I sorted Mrs. Olsen's letters in my lap by their postmark date. "I will persuade him to fix this. He won't do it for compassion. For all I know, he killed them all. And I know him to be a bold man. I can't intimidate him. But the man likes tuxedos. He had no problem enjoying the hotel's finest drinks at the party. The man's quiet, but he's greedy. And he's held the reverend's purse strings for a year, now."

Mr. Olsen pounced on an oblong ticket among the slippery paperwork. "Found it." He held it up and whistled in appreciation. "Nice chunk of change."

"I'm going to use it as bait to gain his attention. If he thinks I will release the money back to him and destroy this contract, he might tell me anything I want to know."

Mr. Olsen handed it to me and said, "I knew it. If we hadn't gotten our hands on this briefcase, he would have slunk out of town already. He needs to see this check destroyed."

"Among other things." I reached for the music case at my feet, nestled the contract and check within, and smoothly replaced its lid before anyone could notice the gun.

Adding the correspondence to the general mess, I gathered the ledgers into a tidy pile at the corner of the table. "I think the evidence of something much bigger is in here. Something was wrong during the two years Aunt Mary wrote in them, and she did up to the day she died."

"She was killed because she figured it out?"

"I think so, yes."

Pearl squinted at him. "Ain't that your money? You just handed your own money to Mrs. Kelly."

He made a sour face and took the ledgers into his lap, sorting them. "This patronage money came from Minnesota. Mr. Nilsen wants to take it back home with him. Despite his declarations of staying with my father in San Francisco. It's my opinion that a man who dumps a large amount of money someplace not one of his acquaintances would ever look, is hiding ill-gotten gain. I'm not touching untraceable fraud money."

I couldn't decide if that was noble or foolish. "Reverend Olsen was guilty as sin," I said, running a hand over my tired eyes. "But of what? And why did he die because of it?"

"Mr. Nilsen changed his mind," Mr. Olsen said, his face

growing hard. "He saw the foolishness for what it was and couldn't talk my father out of it."

Pearl rose. "I'm going to set aside a uniform for you before the morning staff come in. I'd stay up here and not make a peep if I was the two of you. Lina's awful nice to put up with it."

Mr. Olsen gave the ledgers a wry grin. "I may have offered her a bribe."

She raised an eyebrow at this as I said, "Thank you, Pearl." Though I was dog-tired, I rose and went to her.

The hug was stiff, then melted into one that sisters shared.

As quickly, she straightened away from me and said, "I'll come back after noon so's you can get ready." She made a fuss about tidying her apron and bonnet.

"Pearl, if you meant it," I said, "about the entire hotel, please bring back the maid."

"Missy?"

"Yes. It wasn't her fault. We were rather ... belligerent about it." Mr. Olsen had the grace to look abashed.

Pearl gave her apron strings a final tug and said, "That's putting lipstick on a pig. Good night, Mrs. Kelly. Mr. Olsen."

The door clicked closed behind her.

"When this is over, Mrs. Kelly, I'm getting you a job on the paper in New York. I don't know how you do it."

He meant well, but I swayed with fatigue and closed my eyes. "Desperation is incredibly motivating, Mr. Olsen."

He rose immediately and took my elbow. "Trade seats

with me. Lie on the sofa. I'll sit there and read the ledgers for a while."

I had no energy left to argue. What he suggested was the height of impropriety. A man and a lady alone together overnight in a whore's house, no less.

I slept like the dead until someone knocked on the door.

Chapter Twenty-Seven

M R. OLSEN HAD the audacity to appear clean-shaven and freshly pressed when I awoke. Light streamed in through all the windows and set the coffee service into an unholy glow on the table beside me. A uniform lay folded in the chintz armchair with a perky, frilly white bonnet on top.

I groaned as Mr. Olsen hummed to himself, smoothing a last hair into place using the glass in the mantle clock as a mirror. It chimed half past the noon hour in his face.

"Good morning, Mrs. Kelly," he said. "You just missed Pearl. She brought your things."

I sat up groggily and placed my shoes back on the carpet. "Was that her, knocking just now?"

He chuckled. "Half hour ago. You must have dozed off again."

"How can you be so chipper?" My hair had come loose and drooped over an eye.

"My things arrived. I spent an hour this morning updating my notes on this saga. It's one hell of a tale so far."

"We are going to have one hell of a discussion before you share it with anyone. Including that newspaper of yours."

Either Aunt Mary was finally beyond offense or she'd

decided a swear now and again was warranted.

Especially when one was about to receive justice.

His gaze moved to the window and he settled in to watch whatever was playing on the corner of Market and Montgomery Streets. "Lina's gone. She's off to see her sister, whatever that might mean. She left her boudoir at your disposal and said to tell you that the bathwater will benefit from the salts she left next to it."

I was already pouring coffee into a cup with a shaky hand. "Bath?" No gentleman would have let such a word escape his lips in front of a lady.

"I am here as your protector. None shall pass the door unless I say so," he said with a wink. "And I won't say so."

"Mr. Olsen, more than ever you have proved your abdication from all things polite society."

He grinned and gave me a bow.

The coffee was heavenly and I drank deeply. Swallowing, I said, "I hope Pearl doesn't get caught."

"It isn't Pearl I'm concerned about." He cleared his throat. "I've spent some time pondering our situation and come to the conclusion that I must be the sacrificial man my father was looking for. Mrs. Kelly, I'm ashamed for not speaking up sooner, but you must allow me to confront Mr. Nilsen downstairs."

The cup thumped to the tray without spilling, and I searched frantically for the music case. Snatching it from beneath the armchair, I looked inside.

Startled, Mr. Olsen said, "Nothing's missing! I touched only what you asked me to. If we cannot trust each other, we are done for! I suggest it only to protect you, not beat you to the prize."

Willing my heartbeat to slow down, I closed the case. The gun was there. Everything else was in place, and the ledgers and correspondence remained on the table where I'd last seen them.

"I apologize, Mr. Olsen. I am not myself just yet."

He leaned against the windowsill. "Please. Take the coffee with you. Take the case if you like. You said the appointment is not until two."

I squinted puffy eyes at him. "You're staying here?"

"Nowhere else to go." He held his hands out, palms up. "And if it's a gesture of goodwill you need, let me tell you that I did indeed discover something in your aunt's ledgers."

I was torn. As excited as I was to hear what he'd found, I was equally excited about a bath in the next room. Horrified to think a man was anywhere nearby and horrified to think he might wander out while I was indecent and ruin the only chance I had to find Aunt Mary's killer.

He laughed outright. "Mrs. Kelly. Would you prefer I keep my head out the window for the next hour or would you rather I sat on the other side of a securely locked door and told you what you need to know while you…" He circled the room in general with a finger. "I can't very well leave."

"I no longer believe in locked doors," I muttered, slinging the music case under an arm and gathering up the uniform.

"Then you would be from Minnesota," he agreed. "I'll sit

out here and keep an eye on both doors, shall I?"

"When is Lina returning?"

"She isn't. We have the place until it's no longer need-ed."

"Generous of her." *And worrisome.*

I opened the door to her bedroom and slammed it shut in Mr. Olsen's curious face.

"Don't be a stranger," he called after me.

Perhaps he'd see her room sometime in the future if he kept out of prison and remained in Lina's good graces, but I wasn't going to divulge its contents today. Even standing in an ugly dress, no one could be in this space without feeling charmed, romanced, and altogether lured into another world.

And I had to remain solidly in this one. I forced a scowl to my face, but couldn't maintain it.

Rosewood furniture, pale silk wallpaper, pink and gold drapes, and brocade bedding edged with green and gold tassels made a lavish display over plush, cream-colored carpet. The four-poster bed had a canopy at the head and posts carved into pineapples at the foot and could have slept a family of six.

A fainting couch, long bureaus, a full-length footed mir-ror, chests, tall wardrobes, and a tufted ottoman filled the room, and her bay windows looked down onto Market Street. I scanned the room for any adjoining doors, pitifully grateful there was only one door to worry about after all.

The private bathing room was small and ready for me. A claw tub sat to one side, half-full of steaming water. I nearly collapsed into it, dress and all. My working hours had become reversed and it was starting to show. A generous helping of bath salts created a rose-scented haven and I eventually sank into the tub with a sigh.

My body went to pieces as I commanded my mind to attention.

"Mr. Olsen?" I called. "Can you hear me from out there?"

"Ahoy, Mrs. Kelly!" he called back. "Thin doors, but firmly closed, I can assure you."

I closed my eyes. "What did you discover?"

"The expenses and donations align," he said, "and they total out beautifully at the bottom from year to year. But the special collections—taken for various causes and over separate events—are irregular."

"They would be." I sat up to make myself heard. "They are single contributions and anyone can make them."

"A list of donors and amounts line up with each event, but those totals don't add up to the numbers in the regular ledgers. What I'm saying is that the funds were skimmed before going into the main account."

"Ah, me. It must have gone on for years to build up such a large amount of money."

"But that's not the kicker! Here's the order for the bell you told me about. It was cancelled. Don't know about the belfry, but the bell wasn't paid for, yet the expense is posted in the ledger along with lumber, paint, and supplies. The bell, at least, makes up a large portion of the amount on that check for the theater."

"But not all of it?"

"No. I'm still looking. There must be more. But we can, at least, prove there was a thief in the fold."

"Was it done in my aunt's hand? Did she take the money?" I kept my eyes closed.

"Now that is an interesting question, Mrs. Kelly. Your aunt must have done the regular ledgers, right? But the special event lists are done in a different hand. And both the order for the bell and its cancellation is in a third. And none of this is in the same place. Give me a minute."

I gave him several. There was too much paperwork to expect he could sort it all by the style of everyone's script. Reverend Olsen had taken more than one volunteer over the years to serve as his secretary. The contract and the check would have Mr. Nilsen's signatures, but I wasn't handing them over to Mr. Olsen.

"The hard part," he said, "is that everything, no matter what it is, is signed with my father's name. Although it's impossible, if everything is done by others, isn't it? His signatures don't all match."

"Start with something we can prove," I said.

"Right. Mr. Nilsen's hand must be this one," he said. "If he's done the ledgers for the last six months?"

"Yes," I agreed.

"And immediately preceding him would be your aunt. Once I have those assigned, I can tell you that your aunt must have discovered the errors, but did not make them. And Mr. Nilsen's hand…" There was a pause. "It's hard to tell simply with tiny letters and numbers, but I'd say it's very likely he's the one who ordered and cancelled the bell."

"And he would have been the one to build the belfry," I said. "It was his project."

"Mr. Nilsen is our man." Mr. Olsen boomed.

"He will know what happened with the bell," I said. "That means he knows what happened when Aunt Mary uncovered the theft. Surely, she asked him about the missing bell."

"And maybe he killed her."

Mr. Olsen's words drifted into the room, and the rosy steam evaporated along with my moment of peace. I reached for the soap and went over my plan.

Thankfully, the parlor near the grand hotel entrance had those large windows facing Montgomery Street. More importantly, it presented us with a public area where Mr. Nilsen would at least hesitate to create a scene.

Mr. Nilsen was the kind of man who needed tangible objects to work with. A hammer. A pencil. If I didn't have the contract—the real contract—that he'd already reviewed and signed with Reverend Olsen in hand, he wouldn't work with me. With both the contract and the check in front of him, I could force him to talk.

Once I had the information I wanted, Mr. Sims would enter from the Montgomery Street walkway at my signal through the window and join us to collect his items. No matter how furious, Mr. Nilsen would have to watch as I handed his nefarious proceeds to the theater.

And served him right.

If Mr. Nilsen did not talk, or outright confess, or if the

killer suddenly appeared, a different signal through the window would alert Mr. Sims to enter with a policeman in tow.

Knowing my luck, the police would come for me anyway, the minute I was recognized.

I would have to be fast.

I had Mr. Sims's gun. It was a shame, but if the carrot didn't work, I wouldn't hesitate to use the stick.

One of us was going to jail and it wasn't me. My heart pounded.

"Mrs. Kelly?"

"On my way." I stepped from the tub and reached thoughtfully for a thick, pink towel.

There was no reason to trust Lina.

Heaven only knew if she were regaling a sister somewhere over tea with her evening escapades or standing in the jailhouse making explanations to Mr. Merrill in exchange for expunging her name from any manner of petty crimes.

It wasn't possible to reach out to Detective Fisher and tell him what we knew. I couldn't risk him or anyone else knowing where I was. I couldn't even make myself send Pearl to him with a message.

I forced myself to breathe slowly.

On the one hand, could I trust Pearl? Could I trust Pearl not to tell him, anyway? I mentally berated myself. *No.* With familiar pain, I knew it was almost guaranteed she would. Her hotel came before her friendships, and I could not blame her for it.

I dressed quickly. The odds were good that Detective

Fisher was already stationing his men around the rendezvous room, creating the perfect trap. He'd be forced to capture me before spending another minute on capturing the real killer. Hopefully, I could give him both at once.

On the other hand, could I trust Mr. Olsen? It was his money, after all. Was he noble or was I foolish? Which did he want more, a story, a fortune, justice, or his old home? Did he have to make a choice? After all, land could be sold for a small fortune. And he was a reporter. A bigger snoop than I, and perhaps even more invested in getting to the truth at the decaying roots of his family tree.

Would he simply stay up here and wait while I went through with my plan or would he come crashing down and scare Mr. Nilsen back into silence, defeating us both?

It was laughable that I could not trust the ones I needed to because of their trustworthy predictability.

And frightening that I had to trust the word of strangers.

Not that I had any choice in the matter.

Working my hair up into the frilly bonnet, I reminded myself that I hadn't actually seen any of the paperwork anomalies Mr. Olsen had revealed. The clock struck quarter to two as I stepped into the parlor room.

Mr. Olsen held a paper in his hands. Slowly, he turned to me. "This is from Tiffany's. It's the receipt that started it all. It had my father's signature, remember? But it matches the events list. It matches the thief."

"The thief took the skimmed funds and bought earrings? Two pairs?"

He scratched his jaw. "Yes. It's still an odd thing to purchase. By anyone in the backwoods of Minnesota."

"And they aren't mentioned anywhere in all of Reverend Olsen's paperwork?"

"Not that I can find."

Defeated, I said, "How are we ever going to figure this out?"

"You are, Mrs. Kelly." He added the receipts to the tidy stacks of paperwork. "You are going down there and figuring it all out. Once and for all."

He hadn't repeated his offer to do it for me. And he hadn't shown me the paperwork that put the suspicion squarely on Mr. Nilsen. And nowhere near himself.

A glance at the clock told me there was no time for questions. No time for a better plan.

"You look the part," he said with an encouraging smile. "Pearl left these for you."

A giant vase of flowers sat on the table. "How thoughtful. I believe I never want to see another bouquet again. Ever."

He nodded soberly as I tucked the music case under an arm and picked up the heavy vase. "It will hide your face, though."

"I'll be back when Mr. Sims is gone and Mr. Nilsen is arrested. Thank you, Mr. Olsen."

"I'm going to rant and pace the entire time." His grim face held no promises.

"Then I'd best be quick about it."

He opened the door for me, and I squared my shoulders and left the sanctuary.

Chapter Twenty-Eight

I KEPT A tight grip on the smooth, heavy vase. Outrageously pink zinnias, carnations, and fuchsia clogged my nose with a sharp, peppery scent. With measured steps, I moved through the conservatory as solemnly as I had moved through the cemetery for Aunt Mary's funeral. Like gravestones, large white urns and impassive angelic statutes bore stony witness to my passing. The glass above whirled with gray clouds. Intensely aware of my black skirts brushing along the tile floor and the deafening silence of the cavernous Grand Court, I came to an uncertain stop halfway to the staircase.

The only sound was my heartbeat.

Where was everyone?

The Palace Hotel carried the cold, stifled air of a mausoleum.

I nearly turned and ran back to safety. At least Mr. Olsen was alive. Focusing on the case beneath my arm, I reminded myself that he was also eager to pounce. Could pounce at any moment.

With stiff steps, I moved to the balustrade and peered over. Two guests wandered out of sight and into the lobby.

No buggies. The bottom of the porte cochère touched the drive. At two in the afternoon. There was no way to get a closer look at the doormen, tucked out of view, but a man stepped around the corner and took position behind a huge potted palm.

Detective Fisher.

I considered dropping the vase on his head.

Did he truly think I would walk by and not see him there? The vase wobbled and I stepped back before disgust got the better of me. There was no meeting in the parlor. He would have other men in place, likely with orders to arrest me before I ever made it inside. Mr. Nilsen would sit alone and wonder what was taking Mr. Sims so long.

A shiver ran down my back like ice water and I looked over my shoulder.

If Detective Fisher knew I'd taken refuge up here, it was logical he'd have someone watching me this very moment. *Damn.* A slow, focused turn revealed nothing, but I hurried toward the stairs. If someone had been watching the door to Lina's, then that person was already between me and safety.

There was no going back. So be it. The vase could buy me time or create a distraction. I'd use what I could improvise.

Keeping the flowers in front of my face made for slow navigating down the spacious and carpeted stairwell. A door overhead slammed as I reached the fifth floor. I ignored the heavy tread on the stairs above me until the muttering began. Exiting the stairwell as silently as possible, I waited for Mr. Olsen to pass, uttering oaths and epitaphs to himself as he dashed by. I leaned against the wall, muttering a few of my own as a second set of feet followed him down.

Why couldn't men do as they were told?

A movement caught my eye and I straightened quickly, lifting the vase. Mr. Nilsen, striding toward the elevator, clasped his long hands behind his impeccable suit and frowned beneath his top hat.

I set the vase on the carpet. Calling out was folly. I took up my skirts in one hand and the case in my other and dashed headlong to intercept him. He'd nearly turned the corner out of sight before he noticed me and stopped.

"Mr. Nilsen!" I whispered frantically. "I must speak with you!"

He'd never been one to wear his heart on his sleeve. Mr. Nilsen's posture did not improve and his face remained in a frown, but a thinning of the lips acknowledged my presence as at least distasteful. They became nearly invisible within the confines of his beard.

"Miss Langland" he said in his deep, sonorous tones, "we meet again. I'm afraid I cannot linger. Business. But I shall inform the concierge of your presence. Best of luck in prison."

He tried to step around me, but I moved in counterpoint and blocked him.

"Mr. Sims cannot meet you."

He raised a bushy eyebrow, and I wondered it didn't knock his hat off.

"The police are downstairs," I said. "Mr. Olsen is about to rush headlong into them."

As if on cue, the lobby erupted with voices. Detective Fisher called out and Mr. Olsen hollered back and several others joined the scuffling sound of many shoes in the Grand Courtyard.

Mr. Nilsen's hands dropped to his side. "What do you know of Mr. Sims?"

"That he isn't waiting for you in the parlor." I glanced up and down the empty corridor. "And that you don't have what he wants. We took your briefcase. I have your check."

His long fingers flexed, but remained in place.

"I also have the contract," I said. "The real one from Mr. Sims. Neither of you can complete the deal."

Tossing his head back and staring through his spectacles and down his nose at me, he said, "You are a thief, Miss Langland."

"No more than you are." The commotion in the lobby grew louder. "We need somewhere to speak privately. Detective Fisher has just discovered that none of us are falling into his trap. If he listens to Mr. Olsen for five more minutes, we're done for."

"We? Why should I not cry out and let him do his duty?" Mr. Nilsen's eyes grew cold.

"Because I will hand it all over to Mr. Sims if you do. I go to the highest bidder, Mr. Nilsen."

"And you demand payment for what is rightfully mine?"

"Information, clear and simple." I tightened my grip on the music case. "You tell me what I want to know, and I'll give you both documents. Mr. Sims and the theater will never see a penny."

He stood stiff as a poker for a minute, and I itched with the need to run.

"I never helped you before," he muttered. "You've done nothing but try to destroy the reverend."

I nodded. "We can't go on like this. I'm willing to help now. Take his money back home to church where it belongs. But I must know the truth."

It was his turn to look both ways down the corridor, as if noticing for the first time how desolate the hotel was. The lobby continued to reverberate with clipped words.

Pressing for a crack in his armor, I said, "My aunt should rest in peace. You can't go home without giving her that. The truth can set you both free."

Blinking, he said, "My suite, then." Without waiting for a reply, he turned on his heel and marched ahead.

After hesitating, I followed. He was right. Not even Lina's rooms were safe now. My only hope was that Detective Fisher would go there first, so I had enough time to get my information and leave Mr. Nilsen.

We were at Mr. Nilsen's hall when Detective Fisher charged around the corner. Mr. Nilsen froze, Detective Fisher recognized me, and I wrestled the lid from the music case.

"Stop!" Detective Fisher was nearly on us. "Stop right there!"

I pulled the gun from the case in time to rest the business end against his chest.

"I won't," I said evenly, meeting his confused eyes. "I have business of my own just now."

Pearl had come running up behind him, nearly breathless, and panted, "Detective, where're you going so fast?" Her eyes went round as saucers when she saw the gun.

"Mr. Nilsen," I said, "please open your door." I stepped back and waved the gun, encouraging Detective Fisher and Pearl to raise their hands in surrender and move into the hall.

"Mrs. Kelly," Pearl said, but that was as far as she got.

Mr. Nilsen unlocked his door.

"Go inside, colleague. Hurry up." I aimed the gun at Detective Fisher's face and watched his shock turn into fury.

It was his own fault. He'd ruined everything.

"Mrs. Kelly, they don't know where you are..." Pearl's words cut off as the door slammed shut again. It was only a matter of time. I prayed there was enough.

"Lock them in," I told Mr. Nilsen. The bolt slid home with a sharp click. "Let's go."

He complied without a word.

At this point, there was only one option left. "The staircase over there. Faster." I used the gun to direct Mr. Nilsen to the staff stairs and followed him up. The Palace Hotel was no longer mine. It offered neither home nor family nor any kind of refuge from the past. A hollow shell, an empty promise. I'd burned my bridges.

The stairs emptied onto the seventh floor and I directed him to the far corner where a hall turned abruptly and stopped at an unmarked door. It creaked opened at his touch and I left it ajar, using the last of the hotel light to navigate the dim and narrow staircase leading up.

Mr. Nilson put his shoulder to the door at the top and it

gave way.

"Onward," I said as a sharp draft sliced through us.

We stepped out onto the hotel rooftop into a world of frigid cold and swirling mist.

Gulping, I hugged the case with an elbow and put both hands on the shaking gun. It wasn't a public place. I had no witnesses or alibi. For all I knew, Mr. Sims was still standing on Montgomery Street, staring into the parlor window, waiting for us.

But at least he'd have a coat on.

Mr. Nilsen went several paces ahead and turned abruptly to face me. I stood my ground, blocking any notion he might have of bolting back inside.

To my right, ladder rungs protruded from the sides of tall metal boxes secured with thick bolts to the roof. Machinery hummed inside. Chimneys rose throughout the vast expanse, belching trails of smoke that dissolved instantly into the mist. The acrid scent of tar mingled with soot and rain.

Wind gusted over the rooftop, swirled around the prominent curved glass ceiling that glowed warmly from within, whistled through the machinery, and passed us to be instantly absorbed in the fog on our other side.

We'd come out onto one of the widow's walks that encircled the building—architectural features that appeared elegant from street level but proved disappointing up close. The elegant promenades had once been advertised as the Palace Hotel's crowning glory. In reality, the narrow catwalks, designated by decorative three-foot wrought iron railing and a flagpole at each end, had been quietly closed after discovering San Francisco's infamous fog rendered them useless most days of the year.

It obscured everything beyond our immediate surroundings, leaving no trace of neighboring buildings or the street far below. We were adrift. Invisible. Alone.

"I believe we've arrived," Mr. Nilsen said.

His dry words nettled. After a year of turmoil, I finally had him cornered.

Holding the gun steady, I asked, "Did you kill my aunt?"

"No." Condensation grew on the glass of his spectacles and he removed them to wipe across his vest. "I always regretted her ... passing." He replaced the spectacles and they were promptly opaque again. He took them back off.

"Then who did?"

"I don't know, and that's the truth." He squinted at me. Not the gun. "You were kind to me over the years, Miss Langland. I regretted your leaving as well."

"You took her job," I sputtered. "You refused to speak to me. Guarded the books and watched everyone turn against me." I sniffled, but it was the weather.

Nothing like Minnesota. But enough to sniff at.

My clothes were growing damp. "All of that money was stolen from the church. And Reverend Olsen killed Aunt Mary when she found out."

"Hand me the check, Miss Langland. I told you what you wanted to know. I'm not your man."

My mind raced with ideas for how to get a confession from him. He had to know more.

"Did you visit Chinatown when you got here?" I asked.

"Did you buy those things at the pharmacy?"

He folded the spectacles and put them carefully into his inner vest pocket. "Yes."

"I knew it!"

"I bought several things for the entire party," he said, blinking like an owl. "Not for me."

"You killed Reverend Olsen! Admit it! Was it to avenge my aunt? Was it over the contract?"

"Neither, but those are compelling arguments I shall consider."

The voice came from behind me, and in the moment I was distracted, Mr. Nilsen lunged for the gun. With a desperate cry, I wrestled him for it. His fingers dug into my arm, his long body bent over mine, and shoved me against a metal wall. I stepped on his foot with all of my weight and he howled.

It was a stage prop. But it was all I had against the lies and death that haunted me.

Our hands locked over the gun in a test of will and I gasped as his grip over mine crushed my palm. His beard smothered my face and I kicked out, but wet skirts tangled and softened the blow. Twisting, I pulled back and slipped. My hands were empty as they scrabbled to catch my fall, but the momentum sent me reeling. I took the full blow to my head and sank to the ground in blinding pain.

"Why didn't you strike her? You flopped about like a fish, Nilsen."

"I don't hit ladies. How dare you suggest it?"

"It's a good thing for you I saw you head up these stairs.

She nearly shot you."

"She wouldn't."

"Don't underestimate her." Steps came closer. "Did you do what I told you to do?"

"I didn't have to. She brought it all to me."

"How is that possible? What happened to Sims?"

"Never saw him."

"What?"

"She knew everything. She had the contract and the check, both."

"Everything?" A shoe poked me in the leg.

"No. I guess not."

"Do we have the papers?"

I groaned as he said, "Yes. Here."

"Then shoot her."

"There's blood on her bonnet. Maybe she's already going to die."

"No more of this, Matthew. Enough."

"Can't we just leave her here?"

A soft grunt as someone dropped next to me. "Not yet."

"What are you doing?"

"I spent a king's ransom on these." I winced at the sharp tug on my ear. "I'm not leaving them behind."

The damp was all the way through my clothes. It was into my bones. My teeth ached with it.

"We need to hurry." Mr. Nilsen said. "I can't see up here."

"And who bought those useless spectacles for you?" Another vicious yank on my other ear. "Who bought you those fine clothes and that ridiculous hat? Where is it? She knocked it off your head! I won't buy you another."

"Are you done? All she wanted was to know about her aunt."

"That old saw?"

"We have the money. Let's go."

I groaned. Every part of me had shattered like ice.

The voice leaned down to my ear and said, "Your aunt died in the cold, too. Why are you up here without a coat? The blow to your head was not quite enough, I see, but then again, I am not driven to desperation this time, what with Mr. Nilsen holding a gun."

My mind spun with grief, and I opened my eyes.

"I wanted more for you, Miss Langland. Much more. I have the bottle in my pocket. Would you like a sip? Or would you rather jump?"

She laughed in my face.

"No sense in shooting you. As it turns out, suicide is a lovely way to go. Guilt would not suffer you to live. You killed the Reverend Olsen. Your own shepherd." Was she crying? "But you can ask forgiveness today. When you meet Gott."

Mrs. Berg stood and yanked her skirts into place.

"Toss her over, Mr. Nilsen, and let's go back inside."

Chapter Twenty-Nine

G INGERLY PUTTING A hand to my head, I felt for the growing bump beneath my bonnet. I'd done my hair in traditional braids, wrapping the crown up to be well-hidden. They had absorbed most of the blow, but there was still blood on my fingers when I pulled them away.

Mrs. Berg stood before me, wearing a heavy black coat and fondling my earrings in one hand while clutching the music case with the other. Gray hair, plastered tightly to her thin scalp, parted with a thin pink stripe down the middle. And while her mouth was a grim slash, her watery eyes burned into mine.

Mr. Nilsen, taller than her by a foot, kept the gun aimed at me. He appeared comfortable in his victory. Breathing hard, he alternately wiped at his eyes and tugged at his damp, wrinkled suit jacket with his free hand.

I couldn't run. Sitting up made the mist swim and swirl in disturbing patterns. I couldn't wait. Not long. Everyone in Minnesota was familiar with firearms. Even if the entire police force had freed Pearl and Detective Fisher, even if they figured out where we'd gone, Mr. Nilsen would discover the gun was fake before then and toss me over the rail.

"You killed Reverend Olsen," I said. "Did you kill his wife too? Aunt Mary? Everyone?" My head pounded as I tried to form cohesive words.

"You never could let things go," Mrs. Berg said. "Your precious aunt was just like you. Never met a nosier person in all my days. Got right up in my business." Her smile grew into something hideous. "She went down with a tussle too. I expect you can discuss it with her momentarily."

"Mr. Nilsen, you lied to me." With a huge effort, I sat up straight. "You said you didn't know who killed her."

Whether my uniform blended in with the wall behind me or he was actually blind without his spectacles, the gun didn't move. It was some small comfort.

"I did not know." His words were clipped, and he darted a squint at Mrs. Berg. "Not definitely."

"No one knows," Mrs. Berg said. "I was visiting Elias when she arrived, ranting over the ledgers and that foolish bell, and she didn't know I was in the kitchen. She ruined the reverend's Christmas supper."

"Why didn't you kill him then?" My words came in short, irrational bursts and I rubbed my aching neck.

It wasn't surprise I felt. It was a coming home. To an empty house. It was like losing Aunt Mary all over again.

Mrs. Berg clutched her things to her heart. "She killed him. She killed him! She was supposed to take the poison!"

My mouth hung open and I gasped, "Aunt Mary?"

Her face was abruptly in front of mine as she leaned down and screeched, "Edith! Edith of course! That Jezebel appeared out of nowhere and turned a fine man away from his duties. If it weren't for her, Elias and I would be married. If she hadn't had insisted he eat that stupid *krumkake* you brought him, instead of eating it herself, that greedy pig, it would have fixed everything!"

She stood abruptly, and her thin shoulders shook. "All of this is her fault! I'd planned to comfort him. After. Again!" Her words grew wild. "I set that money aside for us! With Edith dead, he would have to keep it after all. I told him over and over again; there was no shame in keeping money people wanted him to have! Why did he insist on giving it away?" Her words ended on a sob. "We could have gone anywhere. Done anything."

My mind reeled with it. I cut off the laugh of disbelief that bubbled up out of nowhere. It hurt.

"You and Reverend Olsen?"

"He loved me." Her chin came up. "We were intended. After his first wife died."

"Never. I was there. He never looked at you twice in all those years."

The mist had lifted enough to see the color that suffused her wrinkled, gray cheeks. "He gave me a token."

"The earrings?"

Her color deepened. "He would have, had he known about my plans for us. I spent years waiting for him, but the congregation took all his time. I knew he'd have nothing if I didn't take care of him."

"Oh, you took care of him." Sarcasm dripped from my tongue.

"I cleaned his house! I served him suppers! I scrubbed his

windows and organized his fundraisers!" She held out her tightly closed fist. "I earned these!"

Exhausted, I said, "No. You stole them. Twice. Three times, actually."

She shoved the earrings deep into her coat pocket. "You must have gotten them from Mr. Olsen the day we arrived. Who else? How did he find them?" She turned on Mr. Nilsen. "If you'd been paying better attention, that wouldn't have happened!"

"I've apologized many times, Mrs. Berg."

"All you had to do was keep everything locked up. Even an illiterate simpleton like you can do that!"

"I'm sorry, Mrs. Berg."

"I gave you the job, and you're in my debt, Mr. Nilsen. Never forget it. You are a tool in my right hand. You understand tools. You got rusty."

"I did everything you asked me to. I never asked questions."

A hand to my head, I winced at our foolish assumptions. Mr. Nilsen could neither read nor write, let alone do sums.

"See that you don't." She patted her pocket.

"Those are mine." My cheeks were wet. I blamed the damp. "Aunt Mary gave them to me."

The wind gusted past us, but she went very still. "Then she did take that first set. I thought so. Refused to confess. I want to kill her all over again. Where are the others?"

"Somewhere safe."

Bursting into action, she yanked the gun from Mr. Nilsen and pointed it in my face.

"Wait!" Mr. Nilsen threw up a hand. "Not yet!"

With an incredulous look, she said, "I believe I've waited long enough. I'm going home."

"We still need the briefcase," he stammered. "They probably hid your earbobs with all the papers."

She leaned forward. "Where is it?"

"Lina's room. Right below us. I can take you there." Below the folds of my skirt, I flexed my feet and hands. If I could distract her, I'd find a way to run for the staircase. All she had to do was chase me to fall directly into the hands of the police.

"Do you think I'm a fool?"

"Be careful," Mr. Nilsen said, pointing at the gun. "You don't know how to use that!"

"Mr. Nilsen," she said, "you are one of the most worthless men I know. Between you and Elias wringing your hands over Mary and the money, I don't know how I've managed to come this far. I truly don't."

"Edith was the way out." Mr. Nilsen stared in her general direction. "It was Reverend Olsen's last wish."

"That simpering tramp."

One inch at a time, I'd gathered my legs under me. I'd have to beat Mr. Nilsen to the door. He had the considerable advantage.

Holding a gun had given Mrs. Berg a renewed interest in her own story. She used it to punctuate her words.

"I was delighted when she confided in me. Did you know the marriage was never consummated? She told me herself. Dear Elias only had eyes for me. She was his first and only mistake. He was going to find absolution by dumping all of the money I'd saved for him into the lap of the dying virgin daughter of a pious stranger."

She nodded to herself. "So, we came here. And I had to stop his foolish plans. I was prepared to lend him my hankie and my bed." Her eyes widened. "But the idiot had a moment of guilty sentimentality. Over a cookie."

"Is that what you did?" Mr. Nilsen looked away.

"If he thought he was going to get rid of two wrongs to make a right," she said in disgust, "he had another think coming. I had it all figured out if he'd only listened to me."

Mr. Nilsen's head dropped. "That's why he wouldn't let me call him reverend anymore."

"No more of this, Mr. Nilsen, I beg you." She ran a finger below her eyes.

"You didn't tell me what those bottles were for." Mr. Nilsen took a small step away from her. "That you ... how could you, Mrs. Berg? How could you kill Mrs. Halvorsdatter? She was very kind to me."

"She told him about the money. Before I could explain. It was the only time in all my life he ... he ... raised his voice with me."

"I never asked." He thrust his hands into his trouser pockets. "But I found the shovel in the barn. With blood on it." He shrugged his bony shoulders. "I cleaned it."

She nodded and turned back to me. "As well you should have. And now you must help me clean up another mess, Mr. Nilsen. Well done bringing her up here out of the way. Miss Langland will satisfy those police downstairs so we can all go home. Put her over. You're strong enough. She can't even stand up."

He straightened and put his hands to his side. "Do your worst, Mrs. Berg. I may be a simple man. I may not know how to be a valet, or a bookkeeper, or a secretary. But I won't harm a lady."

"Throw her off the roof, Matthew."

"I won't. I'm done."

She turned and said, "I'm old and I'm tired and my beloved is ... oh, Matthew, don't you want to go home? I miss him so much! Don't you love having nice things and not working yourself to the bone for others? Hurry!"

"Did he know? What you did?" Mr. Nilsen's question hung in the frigid air.

"Do I look like a fool? Reverend Olsen never knew what happened to Mary. He was kneeling at the altar all night in penitence over the money! Nobody does, I tell you. We're safe." She waggled the gun. "If it weren't for Miss Snoop here, he'd have left it in the past where it belongs. We'd still be happily at home."

"We?" Mr. Nilsen reached into his vest pocket. "I don't believe I will be returning to Minnesota after all, Mrs. Berg."

He pulled his spectacles out at the same time the gun went off. I came to my feet in a panic as Mr. Nilsen doubled over and went to his knees. It was my moment. I took three uneven steps toward the door.

"Not so fast, Miss Langland!"

Staggering, I leaned against the wall with my back to her and waited for the pounding behind my eyes to stop.

"You shot him!" The shocked words ripped from me. Mr. Sims had given me a proper loaded gun, not a prop.

"He was a lost cause the day we arrived." She stepped around in front of me. "He liked to dress a dandy and, once I saw the way he was drinking, I knew he'd thrown his lot in with the devil. You know, I came this close to accusing him for Mary's death. Just to shut you up. But he's been useful." She shrugged. "And you left."

"Please. Just leave us. Go back to Minnesota. You'll never see me again."

The door we'd come through slammed against its frame with every gust of wind. Mocking me.

I'd come so close.

"How did you know where we went?" The quiver in my voice repulsed me.

"I was waiting for him." She was so pleased with herself. "Mr. Nilsen was supposed to get the contract from Mr. Sims and bring it back to me. How exciting it was to watch you appear out of thin air with everything we wanted."

I shoved myself away from the wall and she pushed the gun against my corset.

"Why is everything so difficult? Why can't everyone mind their own business? Running was the smartest thing you ever did. You just didn't run far enough. Your death was inevitable, Miss Langland."

"There's something else," I said, desperation creeping into my words. "Please, Mrs. Berg. Tell me. Did my aunt take any of the money you set aside?"

"Mary? Steal? Cover your mouth! Your aunt was as pure

as the snow she died in. She wouldn't have dared. Why would you ask such a thing? For shame."

Although I'd needed to hear it from her own mouth, the knowledge didn't comfort. It was shame I felt. Shame that I hadn't found any of this out before today. Shame that I'd let myself get trapped by a woman twice my age. Shame that I'd locked up two of my favorite people in my arrogance.

Shame that I'd run from the snow. From my family. From my home.

Smiling, she set the music case at her feet and slid a hand into her coat pocket. She withdrew a small brown bottle. "Edith's death was a mercy. The cyanide was meant for her. I made certain she knew that. She thanked me before she went, as well she should have."

"You told her." My stomach fell like a stone.

"I was so upset. I tried to kill her again the very next morning. Took the card from her flowers and tried to pour this into her coffee. But that scoundrel of a shameless excuse of a son showed up too soon." She held the bottle up between us. "I even went downstairs and changed the name on the flower order so he'd go to prison for it. It's still too good for him."

I stared at it. Stalling the inevitable. Picturing Reverend Olsen's agonized face twisted in death. Picturing his son's. Imagining mine.

"You can't kill everyone you don't like, Mrs. Berg."

She grimaced. "I'll do what's needed to cleanse the land and restore balance. Drink."

My body was numb. My hands hung limp at my side.

"You can jump if you'd rather," she offered. "Frankly, I'd prefer it."

Only steps away, the rail stood no more than three feet tall. It would take no effort at all to step over it. If I closed my eyes and embraced the swirling fog … it would be fast.

The door flew open and slammed against the wall behind Mrs. Berg.

"Mrs. Kelly!" Detective Fisher charged through the doorway, gun raised.

Mrs. Berg spun partially around and fired, dropping the bottle. His panicked eyes found mine as, without firing a shot, momentum carried him forward. Mrs. Berg snatched up the music case and turned to flee.

With both hands full and a single glance over her shoulder, she tripped headlong over Mr. Nilsen's body. The gun went flying over the rail, and she followed it. Detective Fisher narrowly missed crashing into me and came down hard next to Mr. Nilsen.

I found myself at the edge of the hotel roof, on both knees, praying the rail would hold firm, clinging to the back of Mrs. Berg's wet coat on the other side of it. She dangled in space, spitting unintelligible words and clawing desperately at the music case. Its strap was caught tightly in the railing. Fog threatened to consume us both.

A strong pair of arms appeared over the rail next to mine.

"Mrs. Kelly," Detective Fisher said. "You can let go now."

Chapter Thirty

I N A SEA of red velvet cushions with gilt edges, my blue-violet gown showed to extremely good advantage. I fanned myself with a playbill and spent a moment admiring my opera gloves. Delicate embroidery and pearl buttons tempted me to fan everyone in the row, simply to show them off.

Becky grinned at me from her front-row seat. A private grin between friends. The gloves were a gift and a promise. It was not always going to be winter, she'd said. She turned her attention back to Mr. Merrill and dipped her head to speak into his attentive ear, a brown velvet sparrow next to a near-sighted heron.

Winter raged outside of the California Theater. The stage, hot with anticipation and erupting with limelight, proclaimed it high summer. Intermission was in full swing and I savored a fruity punch redolent with sunshine.

The Magic Slipper's exciting conclusion was about to begin. Miss Kate Everleigh's understudy played the prince. No one had seen Miss Everleigh or her troupe leave town, although the papers gave a glowing account of her steamer, her next destination, and her fond regards to San Francisco.

Directly beneath the front-page article full of facts and fiction that relegated the tale of yesterday's exciting capture of the "Minnesota Murderess".

Of Mr. Sims, there was no word. From the ticket master to the doorman, the California Theater unanimously announced him as vanished into thin air. What bumbling machinations occurred without the steady hand of a stage manager merely added to the evening's entertainment.

The honorable J. T. Maguire had opened, per usual, with a manly, hearty speech, elevating it with dramatic flair and pompous devotions to the arts. But Madame Fabbri and Mr. Muller were glaringly absent.

And we had no wish to seek them out.

Tonight was for me alone.

Detective Fisher cleared his throat. "I understand there's a violin concert next week. A matinee." His strong, clean-shaven jaw worked it into something like a suggestion, but I couldn't be certain.

My return smile was a great many things. Agreement. Gratitude. Hope.

The man wore that same dark suit whether he was hunting down criminals in alleys or attending New Year's Eve parties. I supposed he had several identically pressed suits hanging in his wardrobe. But they looked good on him. Defined him as the polished authority that he was. A presence I was learning to lean on. To trust.

"Don't believe everything you read on a playbill," I said, giving his knee a tap with the one in my hand.

"Perhaps not here," he agreed amiably. "You should see

the real opera, though. Try a ballet."

I lowered my chin along with my voice. "Will you bring me tickets to every show in town? I promise not to tell Mr. Sedgwick where his money is being spent."

At this, he leaned abruptly away. "We're here tonight to put your reputation back in place. This is business. Every reporter in town is here, watching you."

It was true. Beyond a doubt, Mrs. Kelly was above all suspicion. She was sitting right next to the detective who captured the famous killer. Celebrating. I felt every eye on the back of my coiffed and hatted head. A head that still ached beneath the hairpins.

I hoped the message was clear and final. I never wanted to relive the past again.

Detective Fisher scanned the room as if to confirm his words. "And the Palace Hotel is paying handsomely for the overhaul on my jailhouse."

Startled by a flash of irritation, I quipped, "Mrs. Berg will appreciate it," and turned to study the stage curtains.

After a pause, he said, "We both know she doesn't know the definition of the word."

When I didn't respond, he said, "I couldn't shut the woman up, but she never told me anything useful. First, she blamed the wife, then she blamed the son, then she blamed you. She even had Mr. Sims in the lineup for a brief and snapping accusation."

"Mr. Sims?"

"She recalled his lie at the table. That he'd been smoking."

"Ah, that was Herr Muller."

"You knew that? I am no longer surprised that you are a constant surprise."

"It seems Mr. Sims's job was to keep Mr. Muller out of all spotlights of any kind." I settled into my seat. "You have my sympathy. She has no one left to gossip with. You stood in for at least ten of our neighbors back home."

I wanted to chuckle, but it choked out as a sigh.

Detective Fisher misunderstood. "He's safe." He tipped his head around to get my attention. "Mr. Nilsen is recovering nicely. He'll be able to testify."

Yes. Between Mr. Nilsen and Mrs. Berg, justice would run its due course. They were someone else's problem now. My own problems sat beside me.

I nodded and examined the playbill cover. "Put some of Mr. Sedgwick's money into central heat."

"I will add it to the list."

"And a real kitchen."

"You can't domesticate the police. It's against the law. We live on whiskey and chop suey."

I cut him a look. "That explains a few things." After a beat, I faced him and asked, "So. How did you manage to get those first two tickets to the theater?"

"I already had them. They were my personal tickets."

I digested the statement, taking a breath to set the playbill carefully in my lap. "Who were you going with? I owe her an apology."

His eyes were gray. Slate. "She managed to go without me. Did you enjoy it?"

No, they were dove gray. They held a peace offering.

"Except for the angry gentlemen in the second act, yes."

We both glanced two rows over at Mr. Olsen. His resplendent tuxedo was a perfect counterpoint to Lina's golden yellow gown. Lina would perhaps forgive me for stealing her audience, however briefly tonight, as she only had eyes for him. He hadn't divulged the nature of his agreement with her, but neither had he removed his things from her room.

"Do you think he will regret his decision?" Detective Fisher asked.

"He got his story. I assume the man knows what he wants." I shrugged a bare shoulder, trying to decide how I felt seeing a duplicate of my own earrings sparkling in her ears. They were the only thing Mr. Olsen had requested.

"I meant Sims." He straightened his tie. "He complimented you. Said you were smarter than the entire police force put together."

"Then I'm glad he took the check." The flattery pleased me more than it should have, coming from a criminal.

"The California Theater's days are numbered."

"I suppose so."

"And you?"

How did his eyes change colors like that? "What do you mean?"

His momentary confusion told me I should have known.

"It's a new year," I amended quickly, "with new things in it. I've already learned how to pick a lock with a hairpin."

He gave a relieved little puff of a laugh. "Well. Perhaps I'd better ask for a lesson. It'll come in handy for the next time my colleagues lock me into hotel rooms."

"It must happen often."

Again, he was nettled. "Not once."

How many times were we going to discuss it? "I thought it was a stage prop."

"I'm with the police. Do you truly think I was fooled? Would I have obeyed you if you hadn't waved that thing around and tried to kill me?"

A gentleman in the seat in front of us turned and gave us a scathing look.

"Nothing was hurt but your pride," I whispered.

He had an entire list for that category, and at the top was the fact that Pearl had backed me instead of him.

She hadn't told him a thing. Not where we'd hidden. Not a breath of our plan.

Pearl had told me afterward, however, the rest of what she'd discovered.

"It was Missy," she'd said over a late-night tray of cheese and fruit. "I took her back and she told me that woman complained from the minute she stepped foot in our hotel. Ol' Mrs. Berg had her hopping from dawn to dusk, bringing fresh pillows and coffee trays and finding fault as fast as her tongue could wag. She told Missy she'd lost her key and demanded another. Only it was the key for the Olsens' room. And Missy deserved firing for giving it to her." Pearl had smiled. "But guess she'll never do it again. She's beholden to you, Mrs. Kelly."

Detective Fisher, his dignity regained, interrupted my thoughts with a fresh subject.

"Do you know you hum? I don't always know the tunes, but I always figured you liked music."

"My brothers used to tease without mercy over it. You don't plan to, do you?" I sipped my punch.

"I wouldn't dare."

"Then I'm glad she missed."

He still had his dander up. "It's part of my job to not get shot."

"Merely shot at, I suppose."

"Her shot went wild."

We left the rest unsaid, but his face was transparent enough. Perhaps he would have returned fire with Mrs. Berg. If I hadn't been in the way.

"But colleagues don't shoot colleagues," I said.

"No." His smile returned. "They only lock each other up."

"Right you are."

Detective Fisher held out a hand and I placed my empty cup in it. "Thank you."

He stared at it as chimes sounded, and the last of the audience straggled in, looking for their seats.

His knee bounced up and down.

"Mr. Sedgwick," he said quickly, "offered you any job in the hotel you want. You earned that."

I smiled and fanned myself again. "He didn't offer me free rent, though."

"But." He frowned. "Your inheritance is clear. Your aunt is exonerated."

Sobering, I dropped my hands to my lap. "She is. I cannot thank you enough, Detective Fisher. I…"

There truly weren't words for how I felt.

"You won't…" His eyes wandered. "Run off again?"

"Whatever do you mean?"

"Go home. To Minnesota. Now that your troubles are over."

The lights dropped and the rest of his words were lost in an avalanche of clapping, cheering, and whistles as the curtains lifted. The scents of body odor, cigars, coal fire smoke, and thick dust assaulted my nose.

I pondered his abrupt question as the act began.

"I have been a stranger in a foreign land," Aunt Mary said.

I closed my eyes, and thick fog swirled around stone urns. Gunshots. Blood. I shivered.

"Is this the land of promise?" she asked.

Several minutes passed.

"Yes." It was a hiss that ran beneath the burst of laughter from the audience.

"You were always full of promise, Karine my love. You don't need me anymore."

"Never."

Eyes flying open, I devoured the bright scenery, colorful costumes, and the actors creating magic right in front of us. My blood hammered along with their firm tread over the stage. Every inhale was rich with the layers that made San Francisco. Each sound the music of its people. It was never the same city two days in a row.

I belonged here.

Aunt Mary made herself comfortable and watched the

rest of the show with me.

When the curtain dropped on the final bows, Detective Fisher still had my cup in his hands. It made for awkward clapping, and I laughed. Words were impossible until we were reunited with our party in the foyer.

Mr. Olsen was holding court with Lina's pretty hand held securely in the crook of his arm.

"The lines are handsome," he said, "but even in its finest hour, it would never compete with the modern theaters back East. New York prides itself on the latest architecture, and rightly so."

"I'll show you the Baldwin Theater," Lina said. "*The Hunchback* is playing and the salons are quite elegant."

"Afraid there's no time. I'm leaving tomorrow. I have a paper to run."

She did have a lovely, if practiced, pout. "But Annette Ince is playing Julia. She's toured all over America! She's a star!"

"No offense to the current party," he said, glancing around at us, "but the west leans a great deal into the gauche." He raised a challenging eyebrow at her. "I'll prove it to you. Why not come see for yourself?"

Her stunned silence lasted through the mass exodus swirling around us. Within five minutes, the bulk of the crowd had thinned enough for her to ask coyly, "Shall we discuss it upstairs?"

Detective Fisher hastened to say, "Let's. The banquet is to begin immediately." Somehow, he had followed me stiffly into the circle with my cup still in his hands.

Mr. Merrill, blinking solemnly behind his spectacles, helped Becky into her coat. He nodded briskly to the group. "I shall bid you all goodnight."

Becky tucked her hand decisively into his arm and, beaming, said nothing at all.

"Detective Fisher?" Heyes pushed his way into the foyer against the outgoing crowd, arching his neck to peer over their heads. "Detective Fisher! Sorry, sir. You're needed."

Detective Fisher slid the cup into the ticket master's vacant window. "Heyes, I'm otherwise engaged."

Heyes bobbed his head to the group in general and said, "Yes, sir. But Ross says it's urgent." He dropped his voice. "A fire on Long Bridge. The restaurant."

Detective Fisher looked at me. "He can handle it."

"Sir. They fished a couple bodies out of the Bay. Not good. You'd best come on the double."

There was a question for me on Detective Fisher's face. But which one was it?

"Mrs. Kelly is welcome to ride back with us," Mr. Merrill said. "Or if she prefers to stay and dine, I will return myself and collect her."

A quick glance at Becky showed she had no argument with the idea.

"Do dine with us," Lina said. "It's the best caterer in town, Maison-Doree. You can sample and critique."

"Indeed." Mr. Olsen was less effusive. "We cannot let Madame Fabbri down. This is the final act in a very long saga. Although, in the end, it's a tragedy." He shrugged at Detective Fisher. "Madame was generous with our tickets and invitations. We must play out our parts."

I waited. For a word. A look. Some sign that told me what Detective Fisher wanted.

In the gap, Lina met my eyes with a conspiratorial smile and tugged Mr. Olsen away.

Sam escorted Becky toward the front doors, beckoning with his hand. "Give me the details, Heyes."

"Mrs. Kelly?" Detective Fisher was trying to out-wait me. He won.

"I'm going with Becky to change," I said. "I can be ready in an hour."

A smile played at the corner of his mouth.

"This city is the devil's own playground," I added. "But the show must go on."

"You're staying?"

"You know too much. You've got every one of my secrets in that blasted notebook."

"Don't you trust me?" He seemed very pleased with himself.

"Once I have yours." My eyes narrowed. "And I'm very good at investigating."

"I'm counting on it."

Heyes brought my coat and helped me into it. I fussed with it, waiting for my face to cool. The theater was much too warm.

Detective Fisher quickly offered his arm. "It will be an honor to work with you, Mrs. Kelly."

I took his arm with a nod and let him escort me out to the waiting carriage.

"With your approval," he said, "I'd prefer to call on you in the morning, instead. After I have Ross calmed down and we collect some initial information." He paused and lowered his voice. "Rest."

The impulse to push back flashed and died. Colleagues had to be sensible, didn't they?

"Agreed. Good evening, Detective Fisher."

He handed me into the carriage and we drove away.

My companions seemed lost in their own thoughts, and the night felt full of possibilities.

Already, I was composing words that might explain the inconceivable to Peter.

My proper farewells to Waterford Township.

"Weeping may endure for a night," Aunt Mary said. *"But joy comes in the morning."*

The End

If you enjoyed *Murder at the Palace,*
you'll love the other books in the…

A Mrs. Kelly Mystery series

Book 1: *Shadows in Chinatown*

Book 2: *Death at the Wharf*

Book 3: *Murder at the Palace*

Available now at your favorite online retailer!

About the Author

Award-winning author Jolie Tunnell brings the past to life in suspenseful historical mysteries with a hint of romance, bringing the flavor of the turn-of-the-century Wild West to the isolated mountains of Idyllwild and the writhing underbelly of San Francisco.

Her books gallop to the last page.

A Southern California native, she loves on her sprawling family, forces her freeloading tomcat to cuddle, and can drink her weight in Yorkshire Gold tea.

Thank you for reading

Murder at the Palace

If you enjoyed this book, you can find more from all our great authors at TulePublishing.com, or from your favorite online retailer.

TULE
PUBLISHING